HIS LORDSHIP'S BLOOD

*Book Four of His
Lordship's Mysteries*

Samantha SoRelle

Balcarres Books LLC

*For Elliot,
when you're old enough*

CONTENTS

CHAPTER 1

Bath, England
May 1819

If Alfie never saw the inside of another carriage, it would be too soon.

He bit back a groan as he stepped down onto the marble slab at the entrance of Bannerman's Hotel. He desperately wanted to stretch his arms back until he could hear his spine crack, but unfortunately, neither social etiquette nor his tight-fitting coat would allow it. As soon as he was behind closed doors though, it was the first thing he would do.

Well, possibly the second thing. Dominick did deserve some sort of reward first for putting up with Alfie's pained grumblings the entire ride from London to Bath. He'd even made the trip less unpleasant by massaging Alfie's leg for most of the journey, which was likely the only thing keeping him from collapsing face first and cracking his skull on the hotel's gleaming white steps. They said time healed all wounds, but apparently getting shot in the leg took more time to heal than most.

Looking up at the elegant facade, Alfie couldn't help but wonder if he'd ever spring nimbly from a carriage again after a long journey, or if he'd be stuck hobbling around until he blended in with all the other old men. At least his leg gave him an excuse to carry his sword cane with him. That had proved beneficial more than once.

"Are you just going to stand there or can I get out too? Christ, I feel like I've been folded in half."

Alfie stepped aside so Dominick could exit the carriage. He tried not to be too jealous as Dominick stretched his hands over his head with an overly pleased sigh. Normally, he was annoyed when Dominick intentionally ignored a social rule such as "no obscene sounds in public", but now all he felt was envy. A good stretch and some obscene sounds seemed like the perfect antidote to their miserable journey.

Dominick hummed. "That's better. Although I could still could use a hot bath and a soft pillow."

"You're going to tear that coat. You'd never speak to me again if I told you how much it cost," Alfie said under his breath, making sure the footmen unloading their luggage couldn't hear. "And you're far too pampered. I remember a time you'd only bathe when the nits got too bad and slept perfectly well on old sacking."

"That's because I didn't see a reason to bother with the pests when you'd just pick them up again. And if you thought I ever slept well with you warming those ice blocks you call feet on me, you'd be wrong." Dominick grumbled. "Not that that's changed any. You do bring a lot fewer pests to bed now though. Not counting yourself."

Perhaps Dominick didn't deserve a reward after all.

Rather than reply, Alfie made his way up the stairs to the hotel, leaning heavily on his cane with each step. He could feel Dominick's presence behind him, ready to catch him if he should fall, and let that feeling warm him in the brisk evening air.

Spring was slow to come this year, the chill of a damp English winter refusing to give way to the slightly lesser chill of a damp English summer. He and Dominick had spent the last several weeks shivering in Spitalfields with no warm baths in sight, only long hours of work that made his leg scream in agony. All while trying to hunt a murderer before he could strike again. Given the choice, Alfie would take the mild discomfort of a several-day ride in a well-sprung carriage any day, especially one that ended at such a fine establishment as Bannerman's.

If they'd gone straight back home to Balcarres House from London, they'd still likely have at least a week left in their journey, a thoroughly unpleasant prospect. Not that it had ever been a choice. The moment they'd realised the old French maid at their London hotel had known something about Dominick's ring and directed them to Bath, nothing would have stopped Dominick from coming here. And nothing could have stopped Alfie from coming with him. That ring was Dominick's only link to his family. If there was even the slightest chance that there was someone in Bath who could tell them more, they had to take it.

How they would find that person in a city of thousands, Alfie had no idea, but that was a problem for tomorrow, after they were clean, fed, and rested.

He approached the front desk of the hotel and was gratified to see the manager behind the counter stand a little straighter at his approach.

"Hello," Alfie said, leaning his cane against the

gleaming mahogany of the counter. "I'm Lord Crawford. I wrote ahead about having a suite reserved for myself and my companion."

"Yes, my lord, we did indeed receive your letter," the man in the neat black suit replied. "However, it unfortunately seems that our return missive must have arrived after you were already en route."

There was a heavy thud as Dominick rested his elbows on the counter next to Alfie. Not threatening the manager precisely, but not *not* threatening him either.

"What's that mean?" Dominick asked, voice deeper and darker than usual. Both Alfie and the manager shivered, but likely for different reasons.

"I'm afraid, sir, my lord," the manager replied, nodding to them both in turn, "that it means the hotel is fully booked. There are currently no suites available."

Alfie sighed. "A pair of rooms will be fine then. At least until a suite becomes available."

"My lord, I'm afraid that won't be possible. The hotel is fully booked."

"What about a single room?"

The look on the manager's face was answer enough.

In London, it wouldn't have been a problem. There were plenty of hotels perfectly suitable for a lord and his "cousin" to stay in. But in Bath, Bannerman's Hotel was really the only option for those of his social status unless they had friends they could stay with, which Alfie did not. He hesitated to use his aristocratic privilege to get some other poor soul kicked out of his room, but it had been a long day.

"You do know who he is, don't you?" Dominick cut

in before Alfie could say anything. "This is the Right Honourable Alfred Pennington the Earl of Crawford you're talking to. How's that going to look, you pushing an earl out onto the street?"

Clearly, Dominick was as tired as Alfie was and didn't give a damn about other poor souls.

"I'm afraid, sir," said the hotel manager with the even tones of a diplomat, "that if I were to give Lord Crawford a room, I'd have to eject a different earl to do so. Or someone else of an even higher standing."

Alfie raised his eyebrows at this. It was rare that untitled people didn't throw themselves into helping him in whatever way possible when they heard the word "earl", usually accompanied by a lot of scraping and bowing. Except for Mrs. Hirkins, of course. And her granddaughter, Agnes. And Jarrett. And… But that was beside the point. He was tired, sore, and frustrated. Was a little scraping and bowing too much to ask?

"What are my options then?" he sighed.

The manager brightened. "Not to worry, my lord. We here at the Bannerman's Hotel pride ourselves on anticipating our guests' every need. Foreseeing that you might not have received our message, I went to the trouble of securing you lodgings at The Primrose Inn. It's only two blocks away and I'm sure, quite suitable to your needs. I believe a number of baronets are currently in residence. I'm certain you'll feel right at home."

Alfie caught Dominick's confused look out of the corner of his eye. He wasn't mistaken; the manager's words were most definitely intended as a subtle insult. But in fairness, Alfie could admit his exhaustion was turning him into a bit of a spoiled brat. If he had to spend every day catering to the whims of lords and ladies who expected everything immediately, no matter how impossible, he'd probably end up saying much worse.

"I'll direct the footmen to take your luggage to The Primrose immediately and ensure everything there is prepared for your stay. For the inconvenience, your carriage and driver are welcome to use our stables free of charge. Shall I give him directions to take you to The Primrose or would you prefer to walk? It's a pleasant evening."

"Pleasant" was a bit of an overstatement, but Alfie couldn't bear the thought of getting back into the carriage. His leg was stiff, but given the alternative, he could handle a short walk.

"The carriage and driver are both London hires. See that he and the horses are well cared for. I imagine they'll be headed back to London tomorrow. Now, how do we get to this hotel?"

"Very simple, my lord. As the footmen are going that way with your belongings, they can lead you. Apologies again for the inconvenience. Is there anything else I can do for you?"

"Why's it so busy?" Dominick cut in again before Alfie could say what the manager could go do. With the horses in the stables if he wanted.

"I believe most of the clients here are fortifying themselves for the London season. Many choose to take in our healing waters in preparation, as I'm told the rigours of the nobility's social calendar are quite exhausting."

"Not half as exhausting as dealing with them, eh?"

"As you say. Sir."

Looking over, Alfie saw that Dominick was grinning broadly now. Give him another few minutes and he and the manager would be gossiping over the ridiculousness of the aristocracy like a pair of washerwomen.

"Thank you, I believe that will be all," Alfie said. "Let's just get to the hotel. What did you say it was called again?"

* * *

The Primrose Inn hardly lived up to the name. From a quick glance around, the clientele was less than prim and it hardly smelled like a rose, but Alfie knew he was being picky. God knew he'd stayed in far worse places, even within the last few weeks.

If he was honest, The Primrose wasn't really that bad, but after their experiences at The Rose in Spitalfields, he was leery of any place named after a flower. And after the grandeur of Grillion's Hotel in London and Bannerman's Hotel here, it just couldn't compare.

The walls of their room were whitewashed wood rather than marble. The rugs on the floor were plain and thin rather than imported opulence. Just looking at the beds, Alfie could tell the pillows weren't as plump as they would be at Bannerman's and the linens not nearly as soft.

Their "suite" itself hardly lived up to the name either, consisting of merely one oversized room with a bed at either end and a small table and reading chair between them that was likely meant to be the sitting room. A wash stand stood behind a folding screen with a wooden tub on the floor beside it that Alfie wasn't sure he'd be able to sit in, never mind how Dominick would fare. The only upside was that the tub was already half-filled with steaming water, with several more bucketfuls sitting beside it for rinsing.

For all it lacked, the room still had what he wanted: a bed, a bath, and a door that locked.

"Get over here," he growled.

Dominick eagerly complied, his hands coming up to frame Alfie's face the moment he was in reach. The kiss was fierce, their noses colliding painfully until Dominick turned his head just the smallest fraction, and then it was perfect. Alfie would never grow tired of the feeling of Dominick in his arms, of how large and strong he was, his thick muscles giving Alfie's hands something to dig into, assuming they weren't being used to pin Alfie to a wall or other convenient surface.

But for all that, Dominick was almost exactly of a height with Alfie, so neither of them had to crook their necks uncomfortably at times like this. Well, not unless they wanted to get their lips on other parts of each other's bodies, which as the kiss deepened, started to seem like a wonderful idea.

"Stop, stop, stop," he gasped as they pulled apart for air. He turned around and thrust his shoulders back towards Dominick. "Get this blasted coat off me."

Dominick chuckled. "And what a hardship it is, helping you undress."

Alfie shook his shoulders impatiently. The second the coat was off, he stretched his arms as far out to the side as he could, revelling in the wet cracks as his joints popped.

"Christ, I can hear that," said Dominick. "You're

revolting."

"So, you don't want to help me with my trousers too?"

Apparently, Alfie was no longer quite so revolting, as Dominick wasted no time in unbuttoning the fall of Alfie's trousers and getting a hand around him.

"God, Nick." Alfie hissed, dropping his head onto Dominick's shoulder. "That feels amazing. I want—ah!—I want to get my mouth on you, but if I kneel, I'm not sure I'm going to be able to get back up again."

"Then we should move this to the bed." Dominick nuzzled behind Alfie's ear before taking his earlobe gently in his mouth and sucking.

Shivers raced down Alfie's spine and he almost missed what Dominick whispered next. "Your lodgings or mine?"

Alfie huffed out a laugh. Of all the men he could have fallen in love with, he had to pick the most ridiculous. Even though he had no doubt both beds would be thoroughly used before the night was over, neither was really his or Dominick's as they'd be sharing the same one to sleep.

"You choose." Alfie laughed.

Ever the pragmatist, Dominick dragged him over to the nearest one. Alfie fell back against the blanket, which was indeed not nearly as soft as the ones at Bannerman's would have been. He was about to make a truly obscene suggestion for what Dominick should do next when he heard a noise.

Dominick paused in yanking off his hated cravat and tilted his head to the side to listen.

"Is that... singing?"

It was. At first it was only a dull humming, a tune that Alfie recognised as "Spanish Ladies" but then the singer found his confidence and transitioned into a version of "The Lusty Young Smith". He had a good voice and in other circumstances, Alfie might have enjoyed the performance. As it was however, the man's voice coming from directly behind his head was distinctly souring the mood.

"The walls are thin," Dominick whispered. He stepped back from the bed, letting his cravat drop sadly to the floor.

"I can be quiet," Alfie whispered back.

Dominick shook his head, but a smile was tugging at the corners of his mouth. "Love, the fact you still say that despite the many, many times we've proved you wrong worries me."

Alfie gritted his teeth and forced himself to keep his voice low. "Well, perhaps I'll be quiet if there's something in my mouth keeping me quiet."

Dominick's eyes flashed and he crawled back up the bed. He leaned over Alfie until their lips were just brushing. Alfie strained up to take more, but Dominick pulled back just a little each time he did, the incorrigible tease.

"Ah," Dominick said, his breath washing over Alfie, scented with the aniseed sweets he'd been eating in the carriage. "But the only way I know to keep you quiet will make me very loud."

Alfie collapsed back onto the bed with a huff. He hated when Dominick was right. "I suppose it would be a waste to let the bathwater grow cold anyway."

Dominick bent down to finally give him that kiss before sitting up. He perched on the side of the bed next to Alfie's hip and began working off his shoes. That accomplished, he stood and continued undressing, walking around their room as he did so, taking stock and humming along with their neighbour. Alfie propped himself up on his elbows. Just because he couldn't touch didn't mean he wasn't going to watch.

"I'm sure a room will free up at that fancy hotel soon," Dominick said. "A room with nice thick, stone walls where you couldn't hear if your neighbour was being murdered, never mind… anything else."

"I'd say we've both had enough of murder for a lifetime, but I agree with the rest of it. I suppose I can wait a day or two."

A now shirtless Dominick leaned over Alfie once more and pressed another, gentler kiss to his lips. "It'll be worth the wait."

Alfie felt the tap of Dominick's ring against his chest as it swung from its chain around his lover's neck, but before he could grab the damn thing to hold him in place, Dominick slipped free. Then he let his trousers drop to the floor, and padded naked over towards the tub.

"I'll be quick so there's plenty of hot water left for you," Dominick said, raising his voice to be heard over the lyrics of "The Good Ship Venus". "If your leg's still hurting after, I'll see where those blasted footmen stored Mrs. Hirkins' salve and give it a rub down."

Alfie collapsed back against the sheets in happiness at just the thought. "Dominick, as that condescending manager was so keen to point out, I am only a lowly earl, but you, sir, are a king amongst men."

Dominick looked back over his bare shoulder and winked. "As soon as we have a bit of privacy, I'll show you how right you are."

CHAPTER 2

Over a late breakfast in the hotel's dining room the next morning, Dominick and Alfie began their plan of attack. The room was relatively full, but they'd secured themselves a table in a corner where they'd be free to talk without anyone listening in.

Honestly, Dominick wasn't even sure where to begin. It was one thing to have a crazy old French woman leaving cryptic notes lying around suggesting his family was in Bath, but it was another thing entirely to find them once he got here.

He pulled the scrap of paper out of his pocket and carefully smoothed it out on the table.

Ils sont à Bath.

Written in the French's maid's blocky handwriting, the words made no sense to him, but according to Alfie they meant, "They are in Bath," meaning the city and not a tub.

Below the words was a rough sketch of a bird, its wings outstretched. He placed his hand against his chest, reassured by the feel of his ring beneath his palm. A lifetime ago, someone had left that ring with a squalling infant on the steps of a workhouse in Spitalfields, London.

It was a common story, children left with a small token that only those with a right to claim them would know about. If the parents ever wanted their child back, all they had to do was describe the object left behind and their child could be returned.

That had never happened for him. When he'd finally aged out of the workhouse, they'd given him the pewter ring but no money or skills that might lead to a job. At least, no job on the right side of the law. He should've pawned it that first night, but he'd been too sentimental. He and the ring had gone into the workhouse together and they'd left the same way.

In the years since, he'd worn the engraving on the ring down, but it was still there. A bird, with wings outstretched. Just like the one the maid had drawn on her note.

It was that note which had sent them to Bath, following some glimmer of hope that it might lead him to his family. But now they were here, it felt like a fool's errand. Even if by some miracle they stumbled across a likely couple, what could he do? Knock on their door and say, "Beg pardon sir, but you didn't happen to abandon a child almost thirty years ago? No? Well, I suppose your wife might have without your knowledge. Would you mind asking her?"

At best, he'd be challenged to several duels before the day was out. More likely he'd just be shot on the doorstep.

All because of an old ring and a scrawled note. They'd been unable to find the maid later when they'd gone to ask her more questions. She'd absconded with their far-too-generous tips and left the hotel for good. It was just as well for her sake. Even if she was right about the ring, an eccentric old maid who went around revealing guests' secrets was one likely to find herself out of a job. Still, that didn't give them much to work with. And it did raise troubling questions, one Dominick had tried to push from his mind the entire ride to Bath.

What if they were on a wild-goose chase? What if the maid was nothing more than she'd seemed—a doddering old woman who was queer in the attic? What if they were chasing nothing more than a madwoman's fancy?

He pushed the note aside and tried to focus on his breakfast. It was a passable meal for a passable hotel. The toast was cold and the sausages were bland, hardly the sort of breakfast they'd be serving at Bannerman's Hotel. Still, once they had finished in Bath, they'd be headed back to Balcarres and Janie's cooking. With that thought in mind, he added another slice of toast to his plate. It was better to enjoy a breakfast he could actually stomach while he had the chance.

"Would you like my eggs?" Alfie asked. "They're a bit overdone for me."

Dominick nodded and gratefully accepted the plate Alfie slid across the table to him. He'd learned enough about etiquette to know that if they were at Bannerman's Hotel, Alfie never would have done that. But apparently because he was slumming it in only the second-nicest hotel in the city, such things were allowed.

At times like this, it was hard to remember that Alfie had come from the same workhouse mud that he had. The foul-mouthed urchin he'd known had grown into a perfectly prim and proper lord as naturally as if he'd actually been born to it. Of course, Alfie wasn't quite so proper when he was holding a sword to the necks of Dominick's enemies or in bed with another sort of sword to hand.

Dominick snickered to himself as he slid the now egg-free plate back, but Alfie had had a lifetime of knowing when it was best to ignore him and did just that. Instead, he began cutting his sausages into neat little slices. Apparently not all manners were out the window then. Dominick speared a whole sausage with his fork just to see his lover wince.

"Any idea where to start with this?" Alfie asked, tapping the note with the tip of his knife.

"Not really. You?"

Alfie dabbed the corners of his mouth with his napkin. "A few ideas. It occurs to me that we have two avenues to pursue. The first is your ring and the second is the French maid. She knew someone here. If we can find that someone, even if they're not your family, they might be able to point us in the right direction."

"Sounds fair."

"Good," Alfie said. "Then I suggest we start by asking around, see if any jewellers recognise the ring."

"Pawnbrokers too," Dominick interrupted. "They're more likely to see pewter rings than a proper jeweller."

Alfie nodded. "Good thinking. Then if that leads nowhere, we can see if there are French restaurants in town or even just any pubs with continental proprietors. A French woman who barely spoke English is more likely to have kept company with her own countrymen."

"Shame we don't even know her name." Dominick speared another sausage with more force than was necessary. "'Do you know a crazy old French woman? She drew me this bird.' It isn't exactly specific."

"True." Alfie scrunched his nose in thought. "And that's

all assuming whoever she knew here is still alive and not a figment of her imagination."

So, Alfie had been wondering about that too. Despair began to gather strength in Dominick's mind. He forced it back. "What about churches?"

"What about them?"

"I saw that big one as we drove in, and I imagine there's a good few more. They keep track of that sort of thing, don't they? Births and marriages and all? If we can't find anything about the old woman, we still might find something about me."

Alfie nodded. "That's a good idea. Assuming you were born here and then brought to London, there might be a record of your birth, or at the very least your baptising. When were you born?"

Dominick closed his eyes, trying to remember. "My release papers from the workhouse guessed late 1789 or early 1790, I think."

"And since we all received new names when we arrived, I imagine 'Dominick' wasn't the name you were given at birth either. Did the paperwork give your real name?"

Dominick's toast suddenly required all of his attention. He didn't respond, but after a moment, a foot brushed against his under the table.

"I'm sorry," Alfie said softly. "I didn't mean that the way it sounded. Let's call it your *original* name. No matter what, you'll always be my Nick."

Dominick trapped Alfie's foot between his, although even that was more affection that it was really safe to show in public. Good thing everyone else was more focused on their own breakfasts than on the two of them. "Even if my original name is something truly repugnant? Eustace perhaps. Or something even more dreadful, like Alfred?"

Alfie laughed. "Especially then. I'm hoping for something unspeakably Gallic. All vowels with an 'x' or two on the end. Perhaps six or seven names all strung together. After all, if that old woman knew your family, there's a chance you might be French."

Dominick shuddered. "Don't even jest. But, no. No other name on the paperwork. Looks like you're stuck with just 'Dominick'."

"And nothing could make me happier." Alfie went back to his sausages. "That said, without a name and with only a rough year to go by, we're looking at hundreds of births, at least. And that's assuming all the churches have records dating back that long *and* are willing to let us look at them."

Something of how Dominick felt must have been clear on his face, because Alfie's foot tapped his again.

"We've got time," Alfie said. "You've waited this long to find out about your family and this is the first lead you've ever had on where they might be. I'm not going to give up just because it might take a while. If I have to read through every crumbling old record book in the county, I will. After working at The Rose, I think I can handle a little dust."

"Better dust than blood and teeth," Dominick agreed.

Alfie shuddered and dropped his knife and fork onto his plate. Apparently, he was done with breakfast.

"In all seriousness," Alfie said. "I mean it. It'll take however long it takes, Nick. I won't give up until we find them or you tell me to stop. I promise."

Dominick didn't have the words to describe how Alfie's

promise made him feel. He pressed his foot back against Alfie's and that must have conveyed enough because Alfie gave him a soft smile in return. Then he downed the last of his tea and set his napkin on the table.

"All right, we've got enough to get started on. I say we begin with the jewellers and pawnbrokers then go from there. Once we've been to all of those, we can consider churches. And perhaps we'll have more ideas along the way."

Dominick squinted. "That sounds like an awful lot of walking."

Alfie shrugged far too nonchalantly for Dominick's liking. "Well, I imagine there are quite a few jewellers along Milsom Street. It would be ridiculous to have a carriage drive us half a block at a time."

Dominick hummed. "Ridiculous, is it? How's your leg?"

Before Alfie could let out the tirade Dominick saw building, he raised a hand to cut him off. "I'm not being a mother hen. I'm just asking. We both fell asleep before doing your stretches last night and I know how long carriage rides bother you."

Alfie huffed, but seemed placated. The damn man was like an alley cat; the more Dominick tried to care for him, the more he hissed. Dominick could all but see his fur settling down.

"It's still a bit stiff," Alfie admitted. "A little exercise would be good for it, but I probably shouldn't overtax it."

"Fair enough. Like you said, it's only the first day. Tell me when you need to stop, otherwise I might have to carry you back to the hotel like a fainting maiden in one of those fantastical novels you love so much."

Alfie rolled his eyes. "Perhaps we could begin with a visit to a few hotels, then see if I'm able to do more. That will kill two birds: allowing us to inquire as to any French staff they may have and see if there are any better accommodations to be had. Not that this is bad—"

"It's just not up to your lordly standards." Dominick grinned. "That sounds like an excellent idea. Who knows, perhaps one of the hotel managers will recognise me as his long-lost son and fall into my arms weeping. We should ask the one over at Bannerman's if he's misplaced any children."

"Now who's fantastical?" Alfie muttered. "It would be very convenient though. I'd much prefer that than hunting down every church in Bath."

Dominick took a last few bites of toast. "Then let's be off. The sooner we go, the sooner we'll find a nice quiet hotel with no blasted singing."

"One with nice thick stone walls?" Alfie grinned wickedly.

Dominick grinned back. "Exactly. Promises were made last night and I intend to see them through!"

❋ ❋ ❋

A few hours later, Alfie and Dominick had discovered a nice walking path along the river, an excellent pub to rest their feet, and absolutely nothing in the way of either accommodations or French persons.

"I'm not complaining," Alfie complained. "Our current hotel is perfectly acceptable. It's just that it would be nice to be able to conduct our investigations from a place of quiet and elegant seclusion."

Dominick snorted. If he didn't know Alfie as well as he did, he'd think him nothing more than a spoiled fop, the sort who'd faint if they smelled a whiff of anything stronger than lavender water. Fortunately, he knew better. Alfie was like the sword cane he carried—elegant, expensive, a bit overdone on the outside, but sharpened steel within.

"You could just buy one of these townhouses if you wanted," he offered. "Pay enough and they'd probably leave every last silver spoon in the drawers too."

Alfie shook his head. "I may be a member of the dissipated aristocracy, but I'd like to believe I'm not quite that bad."

"It would be nice to have a bit more privacy," Dominick conceded as they turned the corner. There was a sign ahead for a jewellery store and they both headed towards it without a word. "But a few days of… separation won't kill us."

"Speak for yourself," Alfie muttered.

"I better be quick about finding my long-lost family then," said Dominick as he opened the door of the jeweller's and gave Alfie a mock bow as he waved him through. "For the sake of your health."

Alfie laughed. "See that you do."

CHAPTER 3

"Bonjour, messieurs! Bonjour! How may I be of service?" The man behind the counter gave a deep bow as Alfie and Dominick entered the jewellery store.

Alfie couldn't believe their luck. The first day of their search and they'd found a proprietor who both knew jewellery and spoke French? Surely, that meant there was double the chance of him knowing something useful. They could be having supper with Dominick's parents tonight and be on their way home to Scotland before breakfast tomorrow. If they had good weather, they might even beat Mrs. Hirkins back to Balcarres.

Well, perhaps they wouldn't leave quite that quickly, doubtless Dominick would want to take some time to actually get to know his family. Although if they were incredibly lucky, this Frenchman who knew jewellery might actually *be* one of Dominick's parents and he could get started on that now. Alfie couldn't see many similarities between Dominick and the small, slightly stooped man behind the counter, but maybe he took after his mother.

"Good day," Alfie said cheerfully. "We're trying to track down the origins of a ring and were hoping you could help us."

"Ah, *certainement!* All of the finest jewellery that comes

to Bath passes through my hands."

"It's not so fine," said Dominick. He pulled the chain from around his neck, but hesitated before giving it to the jeweller. The ring had only been out of Dominick's possession twice in his entire life. The first was during all the long years at the workhouse, and the second was barely over a year ago when it had been stolen for blackmail. Alfie could understand why he was reluctant to hand it over now.

The jeweller pulled a loupe from his pocket and made a great show of examining the pewter ring as if it was one of the crown jewels. It was farcical, but Alfie supposed their obvious wealth made them deserving of a show. Doubtless they weren't the first aristocrats to come to him with worthless jewellery, but at least they'd all be spared the embarrassment of him decrying any gems as made of glass instead of diamonds.

"It is an interesting piece, sir," the jeweller said diplomatically. "I'm afraid, however, that I have not seen its like before. Perhaps I could recommend you some of my competitors who deal in items with origins that are—how you say—more humble?"

Alfie didn't remember much French, but he was pretty sure the word "humble" was the same in both languages.

"You still might be able to help us," Dominick said. He didn't quite snatch the ring out of the jeweller's hands, but it was close. "It's one of your countrymen we're after."

The moment of confusion on the jeweller's face was all the confirmation that Alfie needed. His tailor in London was *Bonheur et fils*, but neither Mr. Bonheur nor his *fils* were any more French than Wellington was. Alfie had caught their accents slipping more than once, flat Yorkshire vowels replacing the pinched French imitations.

He supposed Mr. Bonheur and this jeweller were in similar lines, catering to wealthy patrons who wanted to be treated as if they were acquiring the latest Parisian finery, but weren't willing to take the boat trip required for the real experience.

He decided to spare them all further confusion. "The previous owner of this ring may have been French, or at least, associated with persons who were. Or had French servants? Does that sound like anyone you know?"

It was hard to tell how much of the story to share. He didn't want to leave something out that might spark the man's memory, but Dominick didn't need his life story laid bare for some stranger either.

The man gave him a wink. "Afraid I don't know too many real frogs," he said, slipping his accent off like a coat. Dominick started but Alfie just nodded for the jeweller to continue.

"You missed your chance on Frenchmen in Bath by a good few years. That fellow who's king there now came through here bringing all sorts with him then, but I don't personally know any who stayed. There's one fancy sort and his family who's been in Bath longer than I have, but they never come in here. I don't know if his servants are French, but he certainly is."

The jeweller snapped his fingers. "There's a great house by one of the nearby villages I think has a French cook. Near Bathhampton."

Alfie let out a huff of pleased laughter. "Thank you, that's actually most helpful."

"Or was it Batheaston? It may actually have been Bathford, now that I think on it. Something like that at least." The jeweller tapped the counter. "Although it might have been Swainswick. And didn't that cook die? Or no, that was some years back, some other frenchie."

"Quite a few of them have died in recent years," Dominick muttered. "I can see how it'd be hard to keep track."

"Mostly by English cannon fire and *not* in the English countryside," added Alfie, trying to rescue the conversation. "I'm sure these French servants were memorable enough that you can tell us precisely who they worked for?"

The jeweller clicked his tongue. "Sorry, sir. I get quite a few gentry in here, it can be hard to keep track. She was a housekeeper though, the one that died. But the cook is still alive. Unless I'm thinking of the wrong person. And come to think of it, he may be Italian."

Wonderful. They had a lead to follow of one possibly French, possibly Italian cook who may or may not be dead and working for a great house in Bathhamptoneastonfordwick.

A quick glance over at Dominick showed he looked about as hopeful on tracking down this cook as Alfie was.

"It's still only the first day," Alfie said softly.

The jeweller clearly thought Alfie's concern had been meant for him instead of Dominick.

"Well, I do appreciate you stopping here first, sir. Apologies, I can't help you more with the French, but there's a few stores I could name that might deal in something like that ring. Not in the state it's in, of course, a blind beggar wouldn't want it now. But it looked like it was a decent piece when it started out. No cast marks I could see, although they may have just been worn down with the rest of it. Shame whoever owns it hasn't taken more care of it."

"Any names you could give us would be appreciated," Alfie said. He ignored the sound of the front door slamming shut behind Dominick. "As well as any establishments in town that might employ French servants."

The jeweller beamed. "I'll give you a list."

❈ ❈ ❈

"A ring for a bird? We've plenty a'those. It's mostly the womenfolk who wear rings anyways."

"No, a ring *with* a bird. With."

The pawnbroker shrugged. "If she brings it 'ere, I'd be happy to give 'er a fair price."

Alfie was going to beat the man to death with his cane.

"No." Dominick stepped forward, saving Alfie from the noose. "A ring with a bird design on it like this one. Have you seen it before?"

"Not sure I'm seeing it now," said the pawnbroker laconically. "But if you says it's a bird, I won't be one to argue. Can't give you much for it though. Now, if it's that cravat pin you're looking to sell, that's a different matter..."

❈ ❈ ❈

"Excuse me, madam. My friend and I are looking for a French woman. Do you know where we could find one? Someone older, preferably."

Alfie grasped his stinging cheek as the waitress loudly informed him that this was a respectable establishment before stomping away.

"Yes, yes. I see where I went wrong. She still didn't have to slap me. You can stop laughing anytime you like, Nick."

* * *

"You suggest I'd allow a frog in here? I assure you, sir, this hotel only employs good English men and women to serve our good English clientele. That said, my lord, I'm afraid we will be unable to accommodate you at this time. Have you tried The Primrose Inn?"

* * *

A week later and each day exactly the same as the one before it. In the morning, they set out, determined that this would be the day they learned something, *anything*, about Dominick's family. And in the evening, they returned to their room in defeat. Each new day had brought more of the same, each name on the jeweller's list bringing a moment's hope before being dashed. They then struck the name off and headed towards the next, only to have the same thing happen again. And again. And again.

Today, they'd crossed out the very last name on the list about the same time Alfie's knee buckled under him. He'd been saved from ignominy by his cane, but when Dominick hailed a coach to take them back to The Primrose Inn, he hadn't protested. Much.

As they entered their room, Alfie was surprised to see a number of letters strewn across the floor. There had been a handful over the past few days, but nothing like this.

"Would it have been that hard to hold these for us at the desk?" He sighed. "Surely slipping them under the door would've actually been more work."

He was stopped from picking them up by a tap on his shoulder. He gave Dominick a thankful smile and hobbled over to one of the beds, dropping onto it while Dominick collected the correspondence from the floor. It was just as well. If Alfie had actually bent all the way down to pick up those letters, he wasn't entirely sure he could've gotten himself upright again. He hadn't wanted to admit how much his leg had been bothering him by the end, but he'd done a poor job of hiding it.

Besides, the bed was heavenly under his aching limbs. If he had to collapse somewhere, this was an infinitely preferable spot to do so than out in the street on some fruitless pursuit. He was almost ashamed of his earlier complaints about the hotel. Clearly, he hadn't been appreciative of The Primrose Inn's charms. Either that or pain had a way of lowering his standards. Its thin walls were still a problem, however. Nothing took his mind off his sore leg more than Dominick making him sore in other places, but as long as they were staying here, they couldn't risk any of that. This inn truly was a wretched place.

"It looks like your arrival in Bath has finally been noted by the local society," Dominick said, squinting at the papers in his hand.

Alfie groaned. "I don't suppose any of them are from a Lord Bird Ring and his wife, Lady France, by any chance?"

"You tell me. I can't make heads nor tails of some of these." Dominick handed over the letters and sat down in the reading chair while Alfie sorted through them. It'd be nice if they had a fireplace to warm their sore feet, but hadn't he just decided to stop complaining? The windows all had glass in them and he didn't have to swat away rats in his sleep. The room was a palace compared to some of the places they'd lived.

Alfie huffed out a laugh as he skimmed the letters. "At least three of these are for music recitals to show off the skills of talented young women."

"That doesn't sound so bad. Might not help our search, but a bit of music's always nice."

"Nick, no. You don't understand. In this context 'talented' doesn't mean 'talented', it means 'eligible'. You have to remember that the season isn't just for throwing parties, it's for marrying off."

"Ah, so it's not that there's an earl in town they want to invite, it's that he's an unmarried one."

"Yes, and as I have all my teeth and most of my wits, I'm sure I'm considered quite a catch."

Dominick looked him over as if he wasn't sure whether to make a joke about that or agree wholeheartedly. By society's standards, Alfie certainly was a catch, but fortunately for Dominick and unfortunately for the ladies, he was already securely caught.

"I could tell them you snore in your sleep," Dominick offered, voice low so no one in the neighbouring rooms could hear.

"Oh yes, I'm sure that would help our situation immensely," Alfie said as he opened another letter and read through the contents. "And it's a lie anyway. I don't snore. *You* snore."

Dominick might have made a rude response to that, but Alfie was too busy with one of the letters towards the bottom of the pile. He read it through several times before Dominick's voice filtered back into his awareness.

"Anything interesting?"

"I'm not sure. What do you make of this?" Alfie held the letter out, but Dominick only sneered at it.

"Why don't you just tell me what it says and save me the headache."

That was only fair. Dominick could read well for someone with only a workhouse education, but Alfie had years of practice and still the elaborate scripts used for formal invitations tested his reading abilities. This one was a prime example of the lot. While he was relatively certain he knew what it said, it wouldn't be hard to convince him it was actually a map of some strange city that built its streets in spirals.

Alfie looked over the letter again. "It's an invitation to a soiree tomorrow night at the Pump Room."

"Sounds dirty."

"None of those words mean what you think they do," laughed Alfie. "A soiree is a small party, generally with music by 'talented ladies', unfortunately. And the Pump Room is one of the jewels in Bath's crown. It's where you can drink the healing waters pumped up from the ancient Roman baths from which the city takes its name. Hence, the 'Pump Room'. English creativity at its finest."

Dominick looked like he wasn't sure if Alfie was making things up or not. "It still sounds dirty. I'm not drinking anyone's bath water."

Alfie shook his head. "No, it's... It'll be easier to show you when we get there. But you *will* be drinking it. I should be drinking a glass a day while I'm here to help my leg, but from what I've heard about the taste, I am *not* going to suffer alone. But that's beside the point. The reason this caught my attention was the name of the man throwing the soiree."

Alfie cleared his throat and read off the page. "'Your presence is humbly requested by Jean-Antoine Augustin Lamourette, Marquis de Courtanvaux'. I'd say that's a French name if I ever heard one."

"And then some," Dominick agreed. "It's a start, I suppose, and unless we want to track down that Italian cook, we don't have anything else to go on."

"We could start combing through old church records," Alfie offered. "Great dusty stacks of them, all moth-eaten and covered in cobwebs. Just pages upon pages of..."

"Fine, we'll go to this fancy party," said Dominick quickly. Then he grinned. "You know I'll follow you anywhere if I'm promised some pumping."

Dominick thrust his hips up several times to illustrate the sort of pumping he meant. Impressive from a seated position, but Alfie still let out a pained sigh. It was just his luck to have had the misfortune to fall for someone who believed there were few joys greater than teasing the man he loved. "You're incorrigible."

"If that means 'incredibly witty', you're absolutely

right." Dominick was losing the battle against a delighted grin. "This pumping sooree's not until tomorrow, you said?"

"Soiree. And yes, why?"

"Then we have plenty of time to do your stretches before going down to supper tonight."

This time when Alfie sighed, Dominick didn't bother fighting back his grin.

"They can't be worse than drinking some French lord's dirty bathwater. Come along, we'll get you healthy and whole again, whether you like it or not!"

CHAPTER 4

"I think the wording on the invitation was a touch misleading," Alfie said as they handed over their hats and overcoats to a pair of liveried footmen. "A soiree implies a small affair. This…"

He trailed off as they stepped into the Pump Room. Whatever was going on, Dominick didn't think anything about it was small. Even empty, the room would've been imposing. It was vast, large enough to hold the entirety of Jimmy's pub three times over—six times if he could stack them. Fluted columns along the walls swept up to a ceiling so high, even the massive chandelier hanging from the centre couldn't banish the shadows from its furthest corners.

Just looking at the chandelier made Dominick want to turn right back around and go back to the modest comforts of the hotel. Hung so high above the floor, it was hard to get an accurate idea of its size, but it was easily taller than he was, blazing with dozens of candles, their light sparkling off not only the gold of the chandelier itself, but the thousands of crystals that hung from it like a sun surrounded by captured stars.

It wasn't the sort of thing a former prostitute from Spitalfields should even be looking at. Every time Dominick thought he'd finally grown into his place at

Alfie's side, something like this came along and made him remember where he really belonged—and it wasn't a place with gold chandeliers.

He shook the thought out of his head. Self-pity never got him anywhere. If Alfie wanted Dominick next to him, then that's where he'd be, and damn anyone, including himself, who thought otherwise.

He squared his shoulders and continued to take in the room, although he had to remind himself more than once to keep his mouth shut to keep from gawking.

The walls glowed in the chandelier's light, making their bare paint somehow more lavish than if they'd been hung with the finest tapestries and most expensive paintings. He thought he'd grown used to the extravagance Alfie's life afforded them, first at Alfie's townhouse in London, then the imposing Balcarres, but as lavish as they were, at least those places had rooms of a mostly normal size and were lit no more than they needed to be.

Two walls of the Pump Room were lined with enormous windows that let in the last rays of the fading sunset. At the far end of the room, Dominick could see a balcony with a handful of musicians all in the midst of playing. Just what they were playing, he had no idea, because between the musicians and where he stood were over a hundred people, all swirling about in a roiling mass of silk and lace. He didn't know much about fashion, but he could tell everyone was in the latest finery, their outfits walking the bleeding edge between sumptuous and ridiculous.

A gaggle of women near him burst into laughter, the feathered plumes in their hair making them resemble a flock of birds taking flight, their fans flapping like wings as they tried to fight the stifling air.

The heat of too many bodies in one place had Dominick feeling a bit light-headed already, and they'd only just arrived.

"This isn't what soirees are usually like then?" he asked.

"Not in my experience," said Alfie, accepting a glass for each of them from a passing waiter. "Although I should warn you, this is my first time in Bath. I've heard that compared to stuffy old London, this is where one comes to really enjoy himself, but if this is the Bath interpretation of a soiree, I have to wonder about some of those other invitations I received."

"Well, I'm certainly enjoying myself," Dominick muttered. He tossed back his drink, a fine champagne that deserved far better than being guzzled by him. "Come along, let's see if we can't find the French bloke from the invitation quickly. Hopefully, he'll be the spit of me, just with a great gut and grey hair."

Alfie's reply was lost when their ears were assaulted by a nasal cry.

"Freddie! I say, Freddie, that is you, isn't it?"

The look on Alfie's face immediately turned to a grimace. Two men and a woman peeled themselves from the crowd and made their way over.

The men seemed vaguely familiar, their appearances reminding Dominick of the old rhyme about Jack Sprat and his wife. One of the men was short, his stocky physique held in check by the most garish waistcoat Dominick had ever seen. The creator of the garment clearly had trouble deciding between stripes or checks and had included both, all dyed in either a mustard yellow or an orange that could be used to signal passing ships.

The man beside him was tall and skinny to the point of gauntness. That, combined with the paleness of his skin —shockingly white, even to someone who was used to English winters—gave Dominick the impression it was a skeleton waving its handkerchief in their direction.

Although the skeleton might have had better luck waving if he could raise his hand above his shoulders. His coat was so fashionably tight it could be used to restrain an inmate in an asylum. It tapered to a waist so small that even with the man's thin figure, a corset had to be involved. Dominick had no idea how he was able to breathe; if the coat wasn't enough to suffocate him, the collar he wore all the way to his chin certainly would. Acres of white linen puffed out from around the collar, his cravat tied in a knot so ornate that the fastest way out was probably to cut the damn thing off. It dimpled in the middle, creating an unflattering pucker that reminded Dominick of things best not mentioned in public, but whatever cravat pin was creating the unfortunate effect was lost in the mountains of fabric.

Thankfully, the woman beside him was dressed normally. At least, compared to the two men. Her low-bodiced dress was a white so pure it was almost blue, and it moved about her with such a lightness that it must have been sewn from the very clouds themselves. Her hair was twisted into an ornate sculpture and fixed in place with a comb in the shape of a flower—if flowers were the size of Dominick's hand and dripping with pearls.

She appeared to be in her mid-thirties and carried

herself with the grace of her years rather than trying to cling to her youth. It was altogether a very pleasing look. Then she began to climb the steps and Dominick realised with horror that her dress was so light that he could see the candlelight shining through it. Shockingly, he could even make out the silhouette of her bare legs through the fabric.

He looked away, unwilling to see what else the candlelight revealed, but a glance around the room showed she wasn't the only woman dressed this way. Christ, some of the whores he knew back in Spitalfields could learn a thing or two from these fashionable ladies about how to display their wares.

"I say, Freddie, it's been far too long! Far too long indeed." The skeleton had ceased waving his handkerchief, but appeared to be having some trouble returning it to his over-embroidered pocket. The other man stumbled up the stairs behind him, nearly knocking the half-dressed woman over. From his mumbled apology, Dominick doubted he was on his first drink of the evening. Or even his fifth.

Alfie had a fixed look on his face that a blind man might call a smile. From how white his knuckles were, Dominick worried he was about to snap his champagne glass.

"Lord Boyle, Mr. Stockton," Alfie said through gritted teeth, "what an unexpected meeting. And Stockton, this must be your lovely wife?"

"Oh yes, have you really never met? I suppose not," said the skeleton, apparently Mr. Stockton. "Freddie, this is my wife, Cordelia. Dellie, my dear, Freddie here is Lord Crawford, but of course, you must call him Freddie. He prefers it."

Dominick knew that Alfie very much did *not* prefer it. Even the mention of the dreaded nickname had Alfie looking like he'd prefer something incredibly unpleasant happen to Mr. Stockton, but he said nothing. Then Dominick noticed he was thumbing the catch on his sword cane, so before Alfie could make something incredibly unpleasant happen on his own, Dominick stepped forward.

"It's a pleasure to meet you, ma'am. I'm Dominick Trent, Lord Crawford's cousin."

"Cousin?" Mrs. Stockton turned to her husband in confusion. "I thought you said his cousin died last year?"

Alfie spoke before Mr. Stockton could answer. "I believe you're referring to Mr. St. John, who was a friend of both your husband and Lord Boyle. He was a cousin on my father's side and yes, tragically passed away last year. Mr. Trent is a distant relation on the other side of the family."

Considering their bedroom habits, Dominick didn't love the lie about them being related, however distantly, but it gave him a reason to be around Alfie that these rich toffs wouldn't question. He also didn't think the murder of Alfie's blackmailing bully of a cousin was at all tragic, but knew when to keep his gob shut.

"A good man, St. John. G-good man," Lord Boyle said, his glass already raised. His words were slurred; this wasn't his first toast of the evening either.

After everyone but Dominick had taken a drink in St. John's memory, Lord Boyle smacked his lips unpleasantly before taking the handkerchief that was hanging from Stockton's pocket and dabbing at them, all while continuing to speak. "Now what's all this Lord Boyle this,

Mr. Stockton that?"

"Forgive me," Alfie said, his smile tighter than ever. "Batty and Stokes. How could I forget?"

"Indeed!" harrumphed Lord Boyle—Batty.

The ridiculous nicknames triggered a memory in Dominick's mind. "We've met before, haven't we?"

"I say! You're right. At the club, sometime last year, wasn't it?"

Now that he thought about it, Dominick had no idea how he'd forgotten such... *distinctive* characters. But they had met shortly after he and Alfie had been reunited. Alfie had gotten him all tarted up in his first suit of fine clothes and taken him to dine at his club. In fairness, Dominick had been far too busy trying not to embarrass himself in public or ravage Alfie over the table to pay much attention to their fellow diners. The fact that someone had been trying to kill Alfie at the time had also made it hard to focus.

Now that he remembered however, it was hard to forget how much he'd disliked both men. Their boorish behaviours, bullying of Alfie disguised as comradery, and oh so casual mentions of their fancy schooling. At the time, they'd lived up to every expectation he'd had of how dreadful people in high society could be. A year later, he now knew better. Most of them were even worse.

Still, he'd try not to let that knowledge cloud his judgement of Mrs. Stockton. Either she saw something in her husband that Dominick couldn't or she'd married him for his money. Whichever it was, it was none of his business.

"How are you enjoying the soiree, Mrs. Stockton?"

Dominick asked, pleased he pronounced the word correctly.

"Oh, it's absolutely lovely. I do enjoy gatherings in these smaller venues, don't you? They're so much more personal this way."

Alfie coughed into his champagne.

Dominick agreed. "Smaller venues?"

"Oh, you don't imagine *this* is all Bath has to offer, do you?" Batty drawled, waving an arm that nearly took down a waiter. "My God, it's positively ru-rush-rustic. Freddie, what godforsaken rock has Mr. Trent been living under this whole time?"

"Cornwall," lied Alfie and Dominick in unison.

Batty swayed on his feet, clearly taken aback, but neither the shock nor the drink was enough to stop him. "Well, now that he's here amongst the cillil-civilised, you must show him all the sights. This little gathering is hardly worth our time."

Stokes was nodding along. "We rarely attend anything that isn't held in the Assembly Rooms, but the Lamourettes are dear friends."

"I haven't had a chance to meet our hosts yet," Dominick said, seizing the opportunity to change the subject to the reason for their visit. If he thought too hard about any parties larger and grander than this one, he might actually go crawl under a rock.

"Oh, but you must, you must!" Mrs. Stockton exclaimed. "They really are the kindest people and always delighted to meet someone new."

To Dominick's surprise, she then threaded her arm through his and gave him a warm smile.

"Come along, I'll introduce you and perhaps take a detour to the refreshment table along the way. There's never enough to eat at these things and I'm positively famished. Lord Crawford, will you be joining us?"

Alfie didn't get a chance to say anything before —unsurprisingly—Batty was talking again. "There'll be plenty of time for that later! P-plenty, plenty. I'm sure Freddie would much rather catch up with us first."

"Yes, my dear," said Stokes. "Why don't you and Mr. Trent run along and we'll rejoin you later."

Dominick raised an eyebrow at this. He didn't know all the rules of high society just yet, but rich or poor, he was pretty sure it was a bad idea to dismiss your wife so she could go off with a strange man. Especially if the wife in question was a pretty woman wearing little more than a nightdress. It was lucky for Stokes that Dominick was madly in love with Alfie or he might be tempted to get up to some mischief—assuming Mrs. Stockton was interested, of course.

Mrs. Stockton gave his arm a slight tug and Dominick couldn't help but glance over at Alfie. Alfie was glaring at him, the message, *Don't you dare abandon me to these louts*, clear in his eyes.

Dominick shrugged back. He'd walk through fire for Alfie—he already had, in fact. But when it came to dealing with unpleasant rich toffs, it was every man for himself. Hopefully, Alfie's wrath wouldn't be too unbearable. After all, they already couldn't fuck, how much worse could things get?

As he let Mrs. Stockton pull him away, he heard Batty drone above the noise. "R-really Freddie, do you remember that time we dragged you off to—oh, what was the name of that dreadful place again…"

As they pressed deeper into the crowd, Dominick realised that he quite literally didn't fit in to high society. In Spitalfields, his height and bulk had been a boon. When there was work to be had, he was the first picked, and most cutpurses and filchers thought twice about trying anything on a man his size, as did any clients he had who had a change of heart after getting their end away. His size had kept him safe.

In the realm of the wealthy though, all it got him was a sore head from bouncing off the roofs of carriages, unhappy sighs from tailors as they measured his shoulders, and right now, a face full of ostrich feathers from ladies' hats alongside dirty looks as he forced his way through the crush.

His guide had none of those problems. Mrs. Stockton swam through the crowd like a fish through water, laughing with acquaintances and easily dancing out of the way of those with whom she did not wish to speak. She pulled Dominick along behind her like a ruddy great anchor, all the while gaily pointing out this person or that who he absolutely had to meet later.

The one advantage of his height was that Dominick could easily track their progress towards the refreshment table and let out a sigh of relief once they finally reached it.

Mrs. Stockton laughed. "I know, I know. Now that we've made it to the promised land, there's no time to waste. Be a dear and make me up a plate of the best delicacies. I don't care what you choose as long as you take a great many of them. You'll want a glass of punch I presume? I warn you, it's quite strong. There's also lemonade if you'd prefer."

"Punch will be just fine, thank you."

Mrs. Stockton beamed. "Wonderful. I'll fetch us each a glass, then we can fortify ourselves before returning to the fray."

Dominick's shoulders loosened. Perhaps this toff nonsense wasn't so bad after all. At least, their food was usually good and their alcohol didn't burn the way gin did, which was really all he cared about. And Mrs. Stockton was pleasant company as long as he didn't look lower than her shoulders. He might actually have an enjoyable evening even if this didn't turn out to be the Frenchman he was looking for.

He contented himself with filling two small plates with morsels. By the time he'd prepared those, Mrs. Stockton had weaved her way back to him, a glass of punch in either hand, her fan dangling from a strap on her wrist. As expertly as she'd done before, she guided him over to a quieter corner of the room where they wouldn't be jostled and risk spilling something on their clothes.

Dominick frowned as he traded her the less-heavily stacked plate for a glass. "I don't mean to offend you, ma'am. But is it ah, respectable for you to be seen speaking with an unmarried man without your husband present?"

Mrs. Stockton laughed. "Oh dear, it really is your first time in Bath. You'll find that things are less restrictive here. That's part of the appeal. It's a bit of an escape from the frowning dullards and tutting grandmamas. Not that you won't still find both here. Especially if they have any eligible children to marry off, then they're like hounds after a fox. Just a warning, in case you intend on leaving

Bath a bachelor. However, if you are on the hunt yourself, I'd be happy to point out several ladies who might suit."

The face Dominick made at this was enough to make her laugh again.

"Pity," she said. "There'll be more than one broken heart tonight, I'm sure."

"Not yours though?" asked Dominick with an exaggerated waggle of his eyebrows.

She turned her laugh into an overly-affronted gasp. "Mr. Trent! I'll have you know I'm quite devoted to my Charles. And he to me. But please, if you're not in the marriage mart, do be careful once I spot our hosts. Poor Miss Lamourette has had several unsuccessful seasons and I'm certain she'll find you most interesting."

"I appreciate the warning," Dominick said, raising his glass to her in a toast. "Here's to being as uninteresting as possible."

Mrs. Stockton grinned and touched her glass to his. They spent several minutes enjoying the delicacies Dominick had collected before Mrs. Stockton caught sight of someone over Dominick's shoulder and waved.

"That's the Lamourettes now. I'll make introductions."

Dominick took a last sip of punch to fortify him before setting down his empty glass and plate. Within moments they'd been whisked away by a waiter. Very neat. He then focused his attention on the group of people Mrs. Stockton was heading towards. Once he finished yelling at Dominick for abandoning him, Alfie would want a full report on this new lead, so he'd best remember every detail.

The group they approached was once again made up of two men and a woman, but even from a glance Dominick could tell he would like these men far more than he did Batty and Stokes. For one, neither of them was wearing anything bright enough to burn his eyes. Upon reaching them, Mrs. Stockton leaned in and kissed the other woman on either cheek, then to Dominick's surprise, did the same to the men as well.

"Ah, Madame Stockton, it is so wonderful to see you! It has been far too long." The older of the two men exclaimed. He had a French accent so thick it was almost farcical, every "s" becoming a "z". *It iz zo wonderful to zee you!*

Mrs. Stockton laughed. "It's been two hours, if that, you silly old man. Or was our company really so forgettable?"

The man put a leg forward and sketched a deep bow. "*Pardon moi*, it was not my intention to speak so poorly after such wonderful dinner conversation. Allow me to invite you and your charming husband to dine with us again in repayment for my thoughtless words."

Her eyes twinkled. "Same day as always?"

The old man bowed again. "*Exactement*. But speaking of rudeness, you have not introduced us to your guest!"

"My sincere apologies! Monsieur Courtanvaux, this is Mr. Dominick Trent, cousin to a dear friend of my husband, the Earl of Crawford. Mr. Trent, this is Jean-Antoine Augustin Lamourette, Marquis de Courtanvaux."

Then Mrs. Stockton indicated the two younger people. "And these are the marquis' children, Henri Maximilian and Adelaide Marie."

Dominick gave an awkward half bow. Alfie had taught him all the silly ways English aristos preferred to be greeted, but he wasn't sure about this French nonsense.

"Pleased to meet you all."

Would he ever feel truly comfortable in this sort of company? Sometimes even Alfie didn't, and he had years more practice than Dominick. Perhaps when they were both old men and were allowed to sit at the edges of the room, gossiping to each other and ignored by all the younger, more fashionable society. The thought made him smile. The thought of still being with Alfie when they were old and grey sounded like a lifetime well spent. Although if the damned little fool kept getting them involved in murders, Dominick was going to go grey a long time before he got old.

He wondered if the man in front of him, the marquis, was grey yet. He certainly seemed old enough, but it was impossible to tell under the powdered wig he wore. His full face of ghostly white makeup also made it hard to judge his age. He had more yards of lace at his throat, wrists, and even on his shoes than Dominick had ever seen on a woman—certainly more than any of the half-dressed women tonight. The cut of his clothes was very fine, but his overall appearance made Dominick think of paintings of people fifty years ago. Had the marquis really been wearing the same clothes for that long, or had he instructed some poor tailor to recreate the style? Or perhaps the revolution and subsequent years of turmoil had set French fashions back several decades.

One look at the marquis' children put that last thought to rest. His daughter was in a dress very similar to Mrs. Stockton's, although possibly even more sheer and more low cut. He refused to judge exactly how much lower cut it might be, despite the efforts of a jewelled flower to catch his eye. The broach winked at him from between a pair of admittedly lovely breasts that were almost entirely on show.

In comparison, the son was dressed in a manner that wasn't likely to cause a riot. Smartly tailored, he wore only black and white with no oversized collars or fussy trim to get in the way. His cravat was even tied with a simple mail coach knot, the only knot Dominick could consistently reproduce himself.

"I hope I'm not disrupting your party, sir." Dominick addressed the marquis. He didn't know if you called a marquis "sir," but he was damned if he knew what else to call him. "Alfie—that is, my cousin, the Earl of Crawford—was invited and I followed along."

"Nonsense, nonsense," the marquis replied. "The more the merrier? That is what you say, is it not?"

"Exactly, uh, sir. How long have you been in England? Your English is quite good."

The marquis' daughter laughed. "Oh, I'd say so! You've been here, what? Some thirty years, papa?"

She turned to Dominick. "My brother and I were both born here, before you ask. So, while my brother is terribly tedious and insists on being 'Monsieur Henri', I prefer the English '*Miss* Lamourette'."

She winked at him. "Or perhaps 'Miss Adelaide' once we're better acquainted."

"Adelaide!" hissed her brother before Dominick could respond. Whatever else he said to her was in French, but Dominick didn't have to speak the language to know when someone was being called a shameless hussy. From the way she rolled her eyes and sighed dramatically, Miss Lamourette was hardly taking the name-calling to heart.

"Stop being such a bore, Henri," she replied in English, likely for the benefit of her audience. "I don't know why we even bother with these parties if you're going to act like that."

"I wonder myself," replied her brother, throwing their father a look Dominick couldn't read.

The moment stretched into awkward silence that even the surge of noise from the other partygoers couldn't fill.

"Tell me, Monsieur Trent," said Monsieur Henri, "are you a republican or a monarchist?"

Dominick noticed the man's accent was far thicker than his sister's although not nearly as impenetrable as his father's. Christ though, what a loaded question that was, especially from a Frenchman. The two women seemed to realise the same, sharing a look as Miss Lamourette slapped her brother's arm. But that didn't stop them all from awaiting his answer.

Dominick struggled to find that answer, looking for something to say that didn't give even odds to him being thrown out on his arse. He shouldn't have left Alfie with Stokes and Batty; he could see that now. This was his punishment.

The group was still staring at him, waiting, so he opened his mouth, not entirely sure what was going to come out of it.

Fortunately, that was when the screaming began.

CHAPTER 5

"So, Freddie," Stokes drawled, his nasal voice scraping up Alfie's spine. "You must tell us absolutely everything that's happened since we last saw you."

Alfie set his empty champagne glass down, pleased when a full one was whisked into his hand almost immediately. His thanks to the waiter was heartfelt.

"Not much to say, I'm afraid," said Alfie. *Except for all the murder, blackmail, attempts on my life, gunshot wounds, and falling in love with the most wonderful man in the world.* "Spent some time visiting the family seat in Scotland, then was back in London for a bit earlier this year, and now I'm here."

"And you couldn't have picked a better time to arrive!" Stokes exclaimed. "Fortifying yourself for the marriage mart, eh?"

Alfie concealed his grimace behind his glass. "I'm not sure about that."

Stokes laughed. "Happens to us all in the end, no use fighting it. Who knows, you might just get lucky. I wasn't certain about Cordelia at the start, you know, and I'm sure she felt the same about me! But we decided to give it a try. And wouldn't you know? I positively couldn't be happier. She really is the most marvellous woman, and grows more beautiful with every year. I say, for all I love a night gadding about, really the best part of it is seeing her when I get home."

Alfie knew exactly what he meant, sometimes he looked at Dominick and couldn't believe how lucky he was to have him. He recanted some of his meaner thoughts about Stokes. The man might be an arrogant, irritating fop, but at least he was a sincere one.

"It's not like you to admit something so unfashionable as being in love with your wife," teased Alfie.

Batty let out a snort at that. "It's enough to turn your stomach. Worse, he keeps trying to force the rest of us into matrimonial bliss as well. Bastard has just about worn me down too."

"You'll be thanking me once you're married and less of a miserable old sot." Stokes said, clearly unperturbed by his friend's rudeness. "What say we take a turn about the room, see if there aren't any beauties who might convince our Freddie he's sure enough?"

"Or desperate enough," mumbled Batty. But a fresh drink convinced him to follow Stokes down into the melee, even if his steps were unsteady.

Nearly an hour later, Alfie was cursing Dominick's name under his breath. Stokes and Batty seemed intent on acquainting him with absolutely everyone, not just the beauties, but seemingly the entire city of Bath. There were too many names and faces for him to remember a single one. His face hurt from forcing a smile as they made introduction after introduction and his leg had begun to ache, seemingly in sympathy. It wasn't anywhere near the level of burning agony he'd felt after a night working at The Rose, but it was enough to make everything that much more unpleasant. Worse of all, the currents of people moving about the room kept him separate from Dominick, so Alfie couldn't even lean on him, or even better, find a way to make him suffer just as much.

Finally, he decided that admitting weakness might just be worth it for the chance to sit down. Although even in this, he was thwarted.

"Rest, you say?" Stokes cried in a pitch that made several people nearby flinch. "My word, Freddie, it's like you don't even know where you are! Come, come, we'll get you something far better than rest. And you must tell us how you injured yourself, I'm sure it's just the most fascinating story!"

Fortunately, Stokes was more enamoured of hearing himself speak than actually waiting for Alfie's reply and Batty more interested in the contents of his glass. Since they'd run into each other, he'd had four glasses to Alfie's two. Batty had earned himself more than one nasty look colliding with other attendees as he lurched after Stokes, his meandering path clearing more than enough space for Alfie and his cane to follow.

After what seemed like another full circuit around the room, they ended up in an alcove about halfway along the wall of windows. The protruding windows of the alcove no doubt provided a wonderful view during the day, but now only a few torches illuminated the scene below.

Alfie squinted down at the shimmering surface. "Is that water?"

"My good man!" Stokes clapped him on the shoulder. "Not just any water, those are the baths of Bath! You simply must take a plunge if you haven't already. They say if the process doesn't kill you, you'll live to be a hundred."

"It can't be that bad," Alfie protested.

"They do say it cured the Regent'sss gout." Batty slurred.

Stoke shrugged. "Only his gout? Well, it's still worth trying. Freddie, do let me know what day you plan on going. I will ensure not to schedule anything I particularly want you to attend that evening. Last time I went, I nearly boiled in the pot and didn't stop boiling until the next day!"

Alfie stared down at the dark water. It might be worth boiling if it meant an end to the constant ache in his leg. Some days were better than others, but the pain was always there.

It would definitely be worth boiling to get Dominick to stop nagging him about his exercises. Yes, he always felt better after doing them, but if he was going to be spending his time getting sweaty and sore with Dominick, there were more fun ways to go about it.

He turned away from the window to make some reply, but as he did, a knot of people beside them cleared and he saw what made the Pump Room so famous.

In the centre of the alcove stood a large fountain, its pale marble glittering in the candlelight. From a waist-high basin rose four metal fish sculpted mid-leap, their wide mouths open to catch streams of water which poured from beneath the lid of a large urn decorated with carved garlands and sea shells. The fountain might have been taken from any nobleman's garden, save for the white crust that had built up over the scales of the fish. Stepping closer, Alfie could see that it wasn't the marble itself that glittered, but a coating of white crystals blooming in patches over the stone.

"If you wanted proof of the healing minerals in the water, you needn't look any closer," said Stokes. "Some tedious bookish sort explained to me once how it worked, but all I know is that despite how foul the water tastes, anything that leaves behind such purified remains must also have a purifying effect on the body.

"Are you sure it's safe?" Alfie couldn't help asking. "There are plenty of pure white things which shouldn't be ingested. Arsenic powder, for one."

Both Stokes and Batty laughed, but Alfie still wasn't sure.

Over the course of his life, he'd eaten plenty of things he probably shouldn't have, from workhouse gruel to homebrewed Spitalfields gin, but he'd never seen anything like this before. He scratched at one of the fish and some of the crust flaked off into his palm, looking as plain as table salt.

"Quite safe," said Stokes, collecting two glasses from a table beside the fountain and filling them nearly to the brim. He handed one each to Alfie and Batty before filling another glass for himself. "A full glass of this a day and you'll be flinging that cane into the river as you dance back to Scotland."

Batty had not yet finished the contents of his current drink and he tossed that back before wiping his mouth with Stokes' handkerchief.

Wiping away the taste of the debilitating alcohol before drinking the invigorating waters? Alfie wondered idly, most of his attention on his glass. Removed from the fountain, the water was hardly more appealing, white clouds swirling through it like thinned milk.

Stokes and Batty raised their glasses in a toast and Alfie felt he had no choice but to do the same.

"Here's to what ails you," said Stokes.

The clink of their three glasses was lost in the din of the room. Alfie swallowed his down as quickly as possible. He caught a whiff of rotten eggs. The warm water was salty and faintly bitter, but far less terrible than the horror stories he'd heard. Perhaps being subjected to Janie's cooking on a regular basis had built up his tolerance for unappetising refreshments.

"Well," said Stokes, "not so bad, eh?"

"I suppose not," Alfie admitted. "Still, I'm not sure I'm entirely convinced—"

"I can't feel m'legs," muttered Batty. Then he collapsed facedown into the fountain.

The screaming began almost immediately.

Alfie was still frozen in shock when the first lady to witness Batty's collapse began to shriek, but the smash of her glass as it hit the floor, spraying healing water everywhere, was enough to startle him into movement. He dropped his cane without a thought, moving in unison with Stokes to grab Batty's shoulders and pull him out of the fountain. Batty slithered to the ground, his legs folding under him. Stokes was barely fast enough to catch his friend's head to keep it from cracking against the marble floor. Alfie looked on, unsure of what to do as a weak groan escaped Batty. His lips formed words, but no coherent noises emerged.

The previously cheerful din of the room was now threaded with curious whispers and panicked cries, so

Alfie had to shout to be heard at all. "Doctor! Is there a doctor?"

"He's just in his cups. No need for a doctor," said Stokes, but Alfie could hear the worry in his voice.

Batty wasn't moving at all except for the frantic rolling of his eyes and the shallow rise and fall of his chest as he panted rapidly. Then Batty's eyes caught Alfie's and stayed there, unmoving and unblinking, but the fixed terror behind them was unmistakable.

"Hold on, old man," Alfie murmured. "We'll get you help right away."

As if summoned by his words, a ripple worked its way through the attendees before splitting the crowd apart to reveal Dominick forcing his way through, a small man in neat clothing following behind him.

A sigh of relief escaped Alfie's lips as he watched Dominick none too gently shove a gawking onlooker out of his way. Whatever was happening, if Dominick was here, then they'd find some way through it.

"Are you all right?" asked Dominick immediately.

"I'm fine," Alfie replied. "It's Batty. He collapsed into the fountain and now he's barely breathing."

Dominick looked down at the fallen man as if he hadn't noticed him before. "I heard your shout. This man is a doctor, but couldn't get through the crowd. I helped."

"Doctor Mullins, thank God," breathed Stokes as the man who'd followed Dominick knelt over Batty, turning his head to the side to hover his ear just above Batty's lips.

Doctor Mullins was young for his profession, perhaps only in his early thirties, and had a face so spectacularly freckled it looked as if he'd been splattered with ink. Alfie didn't have the time to take in more of his appearance before the doctor was addressing them.

"I can't tell what's wrong with him here. I need to move him somewhere quiet. And I need my bag; it should be with my overcoat."

"I'll get him," said Dominick. He bent down, getting one arm under Batty's knees and tossing a limp arm over his shoulders. Then before anyone could offer to help, he stood with a groan, lifting Batty—if not easily, then at least more easily than many men had carried their brides on their wedding night.

Despite having repeatedly witnessed Dominick's impressive strength, Alfie couldn't help but marvel. Judging by the whispers of some of the now quieted ladies, he wasn't the only one.

One of the waiters made his way to the front of the commotion. "There's a private study just this way, sir. If you'll follow me?"

Dominick grunted and followed the waiter, the crowd parting for them. Stokes, still clearly shocked, trailed behind.

Alfie offered a hand to the crouching doctor, helping him to his feet. "Go be with your patient. I'll make sure your bag is delivered at once."

With a grateful smile, Doctor Mullins hurried off and Alfie went to track down the bag.

✳ ✳ ✳

By the time he'd found someone to retrieve the bag and lead him to the study, it had been far longer than "at once."

The barrage of concerned partygoers asking him what was happening hadn't sped things along either.

When he finally reached the study, the mood inside was sombre. Batty was reclined on a sofa, one wrist gently held in the doctor's hand as he timed Batty's pulse against his watch. Alfie set the bag on the floor beside him. Doctor Mullins nodded in thanks without breaking his count. Stokes hovered by Batty's head, wringing his hands nervously.

Sensing a warm presence at his back, Alfie whispered, "How is he?"

"I don't know," murmured Dominick. His fingers pressed lightly against the small of Alfie's back. A fleeting gesture of comfort, all that they could get away with here.

As they watched in silence, Doctor Mullins rummaged through his bag and a few moments later the smell of ammonia filled the room.

As far from the sofa as they were, Alfie still wrinkled his nose when the doctor waved the smelling salts under his patient's nose, but Batty didn't so much as flinch. This course of action was quickly abandoned and the doctor continued his examination, pouring the contents of one glass bottle after another into Batty's slack mouth, but the contents just dribbled down onto his already soaked shirt.

Doctor Mullins took Batty's wrist again. After an interminable silence, he sighed.

"I'm sorry."

Stokes let out a choked sob. He stumbled to a chair and sat there with his head in his hands, his shoulders heaving.

Alfie caught a hovering waiter by the elbow. "Go find Mrs. Stockton. And be *discreet*."

The wide-eyed man nodded and took off. Alfie felt the press of Dominick's fingers at his back once more. He gave him a soft smile and moved towards the doctor, only realising as he took his first halting steps that in all the excitement, he hadn't noticed he'd been without his cane.

"I'll have someone find it," said Dominick softly as he took Alfie's elbow and guided him to a chair of his own. Then more loudly he said, "Can you tell us what happened, Doctor?"

"It was a heart attack, wasn't it, Mullins?" sniffed Stokes. "D-damn the man. How many times did I tell him not to overindulge? And now..." He was interrupted by another volley of tears.

Doctor Mullins hesitated, wiping his spectacles carefully before answering. "That's... a possibility."

"But there are others."

The doctor looked up in surprise when Dominick spoke, his tone making it clear it wasn't a question.

"There are others," Doctor Mullins admitted slowly. "This wouldn't be the first time I've seen him drink to the point of danger. Or there's the possibility of a sudden aneurysm or apoplexy. I would need to perform some tests on the bo—on Lord Boyle to be certain. The symptoms however, this strange sudden paralysis of the limbs... They don't match those diagnoses."

A creeping tension began to rise through Alfie. "What do they match?"

"Well..." the doctor prevaricated. "I would hate to say, knowing my suspicions were only that, suspicions. And voicing them aloud might cause undue panic if I'm wrong. Of course, on the other hand, if I'm right and say nothing before it's too late…"

Dominick's voice was like a clap of thunder. "What do they match!"

Doctor Mullins took a deep breath. "If I was forced to say, and this is without any proof, mind, just a theory. I'd say he's been poisoned."

Stokes let out a gasp. Alfie's heartbeat thudded in his ears. *Poisoned? How?* He'd been with Batty and Stokes for the last hour at least, surely he would've noticed someone slipping him something. Unless it had been done right under his nose. A poisoned champagne flute? Had Batty been intentionally singled out or was he just an unlucky innocent, receiving the poisoned dose by chance?

Or was he merely the first to fall?

"Alfie!"

Dominick's face was pale and twisted with fear. He was staring with horror at Alfie's lap.

Alfie looked down and his blood went cold. Throughout everything—Batty collapsing, the following chaos, losing his cane, the rush to retrieve the doctor's bag—somehow he'd still held onto one thing.

Gripped tightly in his hand, the drinking glass gleamed innocently, a few drops of cloudy liquid still clinging to the sides.

CHAPTER 6

Dominick could only watch as the glass dropped from Alfie's fingers.

Across the room came a shrill gasp. "I drank it too!" cried Stokes. "My God, the fountain! I drank it too! Mullins, am I going to-to… God, Batty!"

In a moment, Doctor Mullins was at Stokes' side, having obviously decided it was more important to deal with his panicking patient than his calm one. Or his dead one.

Dominick didn't give the rest of them another thought, immediately crouching in front of Alfie, looking him over frantically.

"How do you feel?" he snapped, barely biting back the panic in his own voice. He put his hands on Alfie's face and looked into his eyes. He wasn't sure what he was looking for, but the doctor had done it.

"I feel fine. I think," Alfie said haltingly. "I don't know. Let me concentrate."

He batted Dominick away from his face and closed his eyes.

Dominick didn't go far, staying crouched at his feet and gripping Alfie's knees tightly. He couldn't let him go.

If Alfie was poisoned… No, he wouldn't even let himself think it. They hadn't made it through the workhouse, through Spitalfields, through burning buildings and underground prisons just for Alfie to die at some fancy party. He'd be fine. He had to be.

He squeezed Alfie's knees tighter.

"My leg hurts," Alfie said. "Which, no, you're fine, you're not making it worse. It's just the usual hurt. I don't know where my cane is. Aside from that, I feel a bit warm and my throat's rather sore."

Dominick put the back of his hand to Alfie's forehead. He was flushed, but no more than might be expected from running about in such a crowded room. Dominick could feel the sweat running along his own spine. And the sore throat could be from yelling to be heard over the onslaught of voices. If that was it, Alfie was fine.

Or was he just telling himself that? Any moment now, Alfie could slump over in a poisoned stupor.

"He's warm and has a sore throat," he called over his shoulder to Doctor Mullins.

"I'll check him in just a minute," the doctor replied distractedly.

"You'll check him now!"

Alfie laid a hand over Dominick's at his outburst. "I'm really quite sure I'm fine. You don't need to worry. Whatever happened to Batty—"

"Will not happen to you." Dominick dropped his voice so he wouldn't be overheard. "I swear to Christ, Alfie. This is not the time for pride or embarrassment or any of your damned pigheadedness. You will let the doctor examine you and when *he* says you're not poisoned, then I'll believe it. Just… if you won't do it for yourself, do it for me."

Alfie smiled slightly. "All right. For you. You always could talk me into anything."

Dominick relaxed his grip on Alfie's knees just enough to rub his thumb over Alfie's own.

"What is going on in here!" cried a voice from the doorway.

It took every ounce of Dominick's control not to flinch back guiltily.

"Dellie, you shouldn't be in here," said Stokes. "You shouldn't see this. Batty... Batty's dead."

Dominick was on his feet without thinking as Mrs. Stockton swooned. However, she regained herself at the last moment, pressing a hand against her trembling lips.

"I beg your pardon, Mrs. Stockton," said the doctor, leaving Stokes alone in his chair. "But there's been an incident. I have everything as under control as possible, but I'm afraid I must ask you to leave while we determine what has occurred here."

Mrs. Stockton was having none of it. "But my husband!"

"Now, Dellie," Stokes tried to intervene.

"I'm staying with him." Mrs. Stockton's words were final.

Dominick understood completely. He wasn't leaving Alfie either, and he'd like to see this runt of a doctor try to force him.

"Very well. I suppose I've known you too long to expect otherwise," Doctor Mullins said with the weary professionalism of a man used to wealthy clients not listening to him. "Would you at least inform someone the water to the fountain needs to be shut off, and have them *calmly* explain to the attendees that anyone who partook of the water and is feeling unwell needs to alert us immediately? And if a magistrate could be discreetly summoned, that would be for the best."

With a last look at her husband, Mrs. Stockton nodded. Rather than leave, however, she merely flagged down someone outside the door and relayed the message to them to carry out. Amidst the terror, Dominick admired her even more.

"If I may, sir," Doctor Mullins said, nudging Dominick aside. "I'll examine the other patient now."

Even though moments ago that had been exactly what he wanted, Dominick found it hard to move away from Alfie now. It was vanishingly unlikely that they would encounter *two* murderous doctors over the course of their lives, but was it really worth the risk? On the other hand, if something happened to Alfie because Dominick stood in the way of him getting care, he'd never forgive himself.

Reluctantly, he stepped back to allow Doctor Mullins to work. He remained close though, looming over the doctor in case he got it into his mind to try anything.

After what seemed like far too short a time, Doctor Mullins pronounced that whatever had happened to Lord Boyle, Stokes and Alfie were likely unharmed.

"Still," he continued, rubbing his glasses again, "I'd prefer to continue monitoring both of you. A round of purgatives and some bloodletting would be the soundest course of treatment. Best thing for removing poisons from the body and won't do them any harm if in fact they are well."

"Blood?" said Stokes.

Doctor Mullins replied, "Yes, but not too much. I can take care of that now and give you some purgatives to take when you're home, where you'll have more comfort and ah, privacy."

He then pulled from his bag a kidney-shaped dish and a small knife.

The moment Stokes saw the knife, his eyes rolled back in his head and he fainted dead away. Both Mrs. Stockton and the doctor rushed to his side, Mrs. Stockton crying and the doctor assuring her it was just a faint, nothing to be alarmed about, Stokes' pulse was steady and strong.

"Nick," Alfie hissed, pulling Dominick in. "Now's our only chance. They're distracted. Go take a look at the body before the magistrate gets here."

Dominick stared at him in disbelief. "You can't be serious."

"Of course I am. If Batty was poisoned, we've as good a chance as anyone of finding out who did it. And if I'm poisoned too, you'll—you'll want to know."

He didn't need to say any more. With one last look at Doctor Mullins as he attempted to deal with both Stocktons, Dominick made his way over to Lord Boyle's body.

It seemed disrespectful somehow to refer to the man before him as "Batty", even if it was the name he preferred in life. In death, he deserved a greater dignity.

Lord Boyle lay on the sofa as if sleeping, arms folded peacefully on his stomach. Not much of a believer, Dominick still muttered a quick prayer of forgiveness before rifling through the man's pockets.

There wasn't much to find. A small silver snuff box, which Dominick pocketed. It might contain more than just snuff but he didn't have time to examine it now. A pocketbook, which was surprisingly light. Old habits were hard to break, but Dominick returned the pocketbook and the few notes inside in case they were missed. A pocket watch with no interesting inscriptions on the case or any distinctive charms hanging from the fob also went back where it belonged. The final pocket revealed a sodden handkerchief. With a grimace, he remembered seeing Boyle wipe his mouth with it, but hopefully a dunking in the fountain would have washed the drunkard's spittle away.

Of course, the fountain water was the whole problem. If there was poison in the water, he'd have to hope it wasn't potent enough to poison him through touch alone. He'd already gotten enough of it on himself carrying Boyle out of the main hall. After a brief examination, he gingerly pushed the handkerchief back into Boyle's pocket with two fingers.

He was just in time too. Behind him, he could hear the sounds of Stokes regaining consciousness. Dominick returned to Alfie's side. Fortunately, his lover's condition seemed unchanged. He tried to assure himself that that was a good thing. If Alfie was still well after this amount of time, it meant he was strong enough to fight off whatever poison was in the water. Still, there had barely been minutes between when he'd heard the screams as Boyle collapsed and when Dominick had watched the man take his last breath. The idea that he might only have minutes left with Alfie struck him in a rush. He tightened his fingers on Alfie's shoulder.

"Alfie—"

"I know, Nick." Alfie said softly, careful of their surroundings as always. "I know. And me too. Always know that."

I love you. I love you. I love you. You aren't allowed to die. I love you.

Dominick squeezed his shoulder again.

There was a knock at the door, but before they could answer, Monsieur Courtanvaux let himself in.

"Mon Dieu!" the marquis exclaimed, and Dominick didn't have to know French to agree with him. What a sight they made. Dominick towering white-knuckled over Alfie, Mr. and Mrs. Stockton competing for who could be more vexed while poor Doctor Mullins attempted to draw blood from the correct one of them, and of course, the body of Lord Boyle on the sofa.

"Monsieur Courtanvaux," Dominick said, when it seemed like no one else was willing or able to explain. "I suppose you heard about the magistrate. And no more fountain water."

"Indeed, indeed," replied the marquis. "But I had no idea!"

"I'm afraid your soiree will have to be cancelled," added Alfie.

"The soiree can go to the devil! Ah, Monsieur Batty! Oh, the poor man! Is there nothing to be done?"

The doctor left the agitated Stocktons and joined the conversation. "I'm afraid not, my lord. Not for him at least. I need to remove Lord Crawford and Mr. Stockton to continue treatment as soon as possible, then would be happy to answer any questions the magistrate may have."

"I will have carriages sent for at once. Leave it to me." With that, the marquis was gone. Despite his panic, Dominick couldn't help but admire the man. For all his clown-like appearance, he'd been practical, to the point, and neither went into fits nor demanded details when there were more important matters at hand.

"We're staying at The Primrose Inn," Dominick told Doctor Mullins. "Will that make it harder to treat Alfie—Lord Crawford?" The thin hotel walls weren't going to offer Alfie much privacy once the purgatives took effect, but there was nothing to be done about that.

"Absolutely not!" cried Stokes, looking even paler than before, although that hardly seemed possible. "You're staying with us and that's final! If I'd known that's where you were staying, I'd have offered on sight. And I'm not dealing with this alone. Be easier on Doctor Mullins too, not riding back and forth across town. My God, what if something were to happen to me while he was busy with you! No, I won't hear of it."

Dominick didn't care how much of Stokes' generosity was for his own benefit as long as it meant Alfie would be comfortable and taken care of.

Doctor Mullins was nodding. "I'd immensely prefer to have both patients under one roof. Now, if we can, I'd like to get the two of you out of here with the minimum of movement. You've been excited enough already and I'm afraid much more might make any poison present reach the heart before it can be treated. Allow me a moment to find some men to help carry you both to the carriages.

"Just get help for Stokes, Doctor. I've got this one."

"Nick, what are you—" Alfie's words cut off abruptly as Dominick hefted him into his arms. "Oh my God, put me down at once!"

"Not a chance," Dominick said, adjusting his grip.

Despite his protestations, he could already feel Alfie relaxing against him.

"I'm only allowing this because of the doctor's orders. You will never repeat this in public again. Promise me."

"I promise," said Dominick as he made his way towards the door. "Not in public."

Then he carried Alfie to the waiting carriage, praying the entire way that this wasn't going to be the last time he held his love in his arms.

CHAPTER 7

Alfie set the basin down with shaking hands and tried not to gag again at the smell of his own sick rising from it. It wasn't the worst night of his life, but only because he'd had so many other awful ones. At least someone might not be trying to kill him specifically, for once. That had to count for something.

He didn't fight the damp cloth that was being dabbed against his mouth, nor the steady hand that held it.

"Feeling any better?" Dominick asked, wiping the cloth over Alfie's lips again.

"I feel more like I've been poisoned now than I did before. Are you sure we should trust this doctor? We haven't had much luck with them before."

Dominick stopped his ministrations. "That isn't funny."

Alfie wanted to whine. Anything to get that cool cloth against his face again. Dominick caring for him was the only thing that made this awful experience bearable. "I was only jesting. Considering the circumstances, surely you can forgive me?"

Dominick hummed. Alfie'd had a lifetime to learn how to interpret all his little sounds. This one clearly meant, "I'm very cross with you for almost dying, but also very worried, so I'll let you have your way, just this once."

He'd heard that noise a lot.

Dominick took the basin from his lap and disappeared with it, likely to exchange it for one of the clean ones the maids had left stacked outside his door. All in all, if Alfie had to recover from being possibly poisoned, then bled, then fed medicine that made everything he'd ever eaten come out one end or the other, the Stockton home was quite a nice place to do so.

He'd seen little of the exterior as they'd pulled in, just one of a long row of terraced houses. Every house on the street was identical, right down to the blazing sconces lighting their owners' return from their own nightly escapades. The interior reminded him of his old house on Bedford Square, although the decorations and furniture were much more in line with current tastes. Striped wallpaper in blues and pinks flipped past as Dominick carried him up to his room. He'd had to close his eyes to keep from being sick, which he regretted now. Perhaps Doctor Mullins wouldn't have been quite so insistent he take a purgative if Alfie had already done half the job for him.

He groaned as he reclined back against the many pillows he'd been propped up with like a doll. If only he'd found a way to keep the doctor from bleeding him as well. He knew it was for his own good. Either the bleeding or the purging should expel the poisons, but he hated how it made him feel. He was weak as a kitten and someone had swapped his brains for wadded cloth while he wasn't looking. At least there weren't any mirrors within view of his bed. Especially if he looked a tenth as bad as Dominick did.

His lover came back with another basin, his mouth pressed into a bloodless line. Dominick had no excuse to be as pale as he appeared. After all, it wasn't his blood the doctor had syphoned out. His eyes were hollow and if he didn't stop frowning, his face would stick that way. And still, he was the most beautiful man Alfie had ever seen.

"Do you need another chamber pot or just the basin?"

Alfie cringed. And what a romantic too. "Just the basin for now. I'm hoping the ah, other end of excitement is concluded for the evening."

Dominick chuckled and set the basin beside Alfie on the bed before settling into a chair he'd pulled alongside. He took Alfie's hand and with a quick glance at the closed door, pressed a kiss to the back of it.

Alfie sighed. "I suppose that's all the kisses I can hope for while we're under the Stocktons' roof."

"At least until you get a chance to borrow some tooth powder, that's for certain."

Alfie sighed again. "I feel rotten, Nick. No, no, no," he added as Dominick jerked upright, "not poisoned like Batty. I can still feel all my limbs, which is rather the problem."

"You hate feeling weak."

"Yes. Weak and foolish."

Dominick frowned. "You couldn't have known the water was poisoned."

A bubble of laughter escaped Alfie. "Couldn't I? With our luck I might as well have known. If it wasn't poison, it would have been one of the waiters running me through, or a lady shooting at you on sight."

"With dresses like those, I don't want to imagine where

a lady could store a pistol." Dominick shuddered. Then his expression softened. "It does seem awfully cruel for this to happen to you after everything else. Sorry for the mother henning. I know you can't stand it."

"It actually makes me feel better right now. But just for right now. Don't think I'm giving you free reign to keep it up after tonight."

Dominick hummed again and Alfie didn't like that noise at all.

"I mean it, Nick."

"I know," Dominick said.

The blasted man let go of Alfie's hand, curse him, but only to rinse the cloth he'd been wiping Alfie's face with earlier. Then he returned to gently stroking it over his brow. Alfie was so distracted by the soothing sensation, he almost missed what Dominick said next. "But if you keep nearly dying, I make no promises."

"If I'd actually drunk poison, we'd know by now."

"I agree, but I didn't know that at first. And we're still not completely certain. Christ, Alfie. I'm not sure how much more of this I can take. It's like you're a bloody magnet for trouble. We should sell you to the army. Then there'd be no question of where the enemy would attack. It'd always be exactly where you were!"

"I would look good in uniform," Alfie admitted. Then his stomach let out an ominous rumble. He snatched up the basin in time, but only just.

When that unpleasantness was dealt with, Dominick wiped his face and fetched yet another clean basin.

"I hate this. Distract me," Alfie commanded. From the pitying look on Dominick's face, it was perhaps just as well he wasn't in the army.

"You're hardly in a state for my usual distractions. I could see if there's something to read if you want."

The idea of trying to make out tiny printing almost had Alfie reaching for the new basin.

"No. Tell me about your night, before all the awfulness. Did you make any progress on finding the French connection to your ring?"

Dominick stared at him. "You can't honestly believe I give a damn about any of that when you might have been poisoned!"

"But I probably wasn't! You didn't see how quickly Batty dropped, Nick. One minute he was his usual loutish self and then the next he was down."

"Is that meant to make me feel better?"

Alfie huffed. "It's meant to make *me* feel better. It's meant to make me feel like the poison either wasn't in my glass, or I didn't drink enough of it, or there was an angel watching out for me, or any other explanation that would make this whole damned thing make sense! Batty seemed fine until he wasn't and if I think about how that might happen to me at any moment, I'll go mad. So, tell me about your evening or literally any other fucking thing."

The short tirade was enough to leave him out of breath. He hit a pillow in frustration. Dominick was right; Alfie hated feeling weak. That, and the lingering fear that despite all evidence to the contrary, there might still be poison floating through his body waiting to kill him and there was nothing he could do about it.

He shuddered.

"All right, love. I'm sorry," Dominick said, returning the

cool cloth to Alfie's face once more. "Where should I start?"

"Last I saw you, Mrs. Stockton was dragging you off to have her merry way with you."

"Oh, she did," Dominick said, brushing the hair back from Alfie's face. "A few times in fact. You know, they look so delicate, but these society women are really very demanding once they get you behind a potted fern."

Alfie slapped him as hard as he could, which was embarrassingly pathetic. "A married woman? You rascal. I'm sure once Stokes finishes retching up whatever innards his corset hasn't crushed, he shall be challenging you to a duel for her honour."

Dominick grinned. "I'll be in real trouble then. I'm pretty hard to miss, but him? The best marksman in the world couldn't hit a target that narrow. All he'd have to do is turn sideways and he'd disappear completely."

If Alfie was stronger, the image would make him laugh.

"In truth," Dominick continued. "I actually like Mrs. Stockton. She reminds me of some of the bawdy girls I knew in Spitalfields."

"High praise," Alfie said sincerely.

Dominick nodded. He then went on to regale Alfie with the actual events of his evening. He'd just finished describing their French hosts when there was a gentle knock at the door followed by the appearance of Doctor Mullins.

"Lord Crawford, apologies for leaving you for so long. I'm afraid Mr. Stockton required more attention than I'd anticipated."

Alfie's heart began to race. "Is it the poison?"

"Oh no, he's quite fine, quite fine. Nothing to worry

about. I just have qualms about bleeding patients when they're unconscious, and he has a rather adverse reaction to the sight of his own blood. And of course, getting him to take his medicine in such a state is also rather tricky. If only all my patients were as well-behaved as you!"

Alfie had some strong thoughts about that, but kept them to himself as he let the doctor poke and prod him until he was satisfied Alfie wasn't going to expire immediately.

He took the opportunity to examine the doctor right back. The man's freckles were the first thing he'd noticed. It was hard not to. With his fair colouring, Alfie had several of the little spots himself, but nothing like the doctor. His face was like the night sky in reverse, black constellations over pale skin. He had a pair of silver spectacles that hung slightly crooked on his nose and dark hair cut in a way that could best be described as "tidy" but with no actual discernible style. Still, the man was focused and professional as he worked, only asking Alfie questions that related directly to his health and not nattering on about himself as many of the more fashionable physicians did.

"Well," Doctor Mullins said finally, "I won't say we're out of the line of fire just yet, but your only symptoms seem to be related to the treatment itself. I don't see any of the numbness or shallow breathing poor Lord Boyle exhibited. I'd like to check on you a few times during the night, but if there's no change by breakfast, I believe we can safely say all is well. You're a very lucky man, my lord."

Alfie would be feeling luckier if he still had all his blood and stomach contents where they'd been before, but was relieved at the doctor's words. Just by looking at Dominick he could tell he was too. His shoulders weren't hunched up around his ears any more, and the tightness of his jaw had relaxed the barest fraction.

"Thank you, doctor," Alfie said. "I appreciate you going to all this trouble."

"No trouble at all," the doctor assured him. "Although I'd wish we'd met under happier circumstances. I'm well acquainted with the Stocktons and I know what a blow Lord Boyle's death will be to them. Poor man. It's hard to believe that a few hours ago we were all laughing over whether there was time for one last cigar before the soiree and now... I wish we'd had those cigars."

There wasn't really anything Alfie could say to that. He watched while Doctor Mullins packed up his bag.

"I suppose I'll see you in another few hours, Doctor. Is it all right for me to sleep until then?"

"If you feel able," the doctor said. "Oh, and Mr. Trent? Forgive me, I believe that's what Mrs. Stockton said your name was. I know we weren't exactly properly introduced. Regardless, Mrs. Stockton said the room two doors down should be prepared for you by now."

"No," Dominick said. "I'll stay here, keep an eye on him."

"I don't believe that's necessary, but as you like. I'll never chide anyone who wishes to help care for the ill or injured. Good night to you both. Until later, of course."

The doctor let himself out.

"Don't look at me that way," Dominick grumbled. "You didn't actually think I was going to abandon you tonight, did you?"

Alfie didn't bother keeping the fondness from his tone. "Not for a moment. But I know you'll take any excuse to share a bedchamber."

He expected Dominick to laugh, but instead he just looked at Alfie with eyes so serious it made his throat go tight.

"Love, there's nothing more I want to do than hold you all night, just so I know you're here. And safe."

And there was nothing that Alfie wanted more than to be held. He swallowed around the knot in his throat. "The doctor will be back. We can't risk it."

"I know," Dominick said gruffly. "I suppose a night propped up in a chair passing you basins and chamber pots will be almost as good."

He took Alfie's hand again and as he drifted into uneasy sleep, Alfie's last thought was that he was right. It almost was.

CHAPTER 8

Dominick awoke with the sun in his eyes and a crick in his neck.

Alfie was still asleep, thank God, curled up in bed with the blankets pulled up around his ears. When Dominick leaned in, the faint snores brought a smile to his face. He'd been reasonably sure some time in the night that Alfie wasn't about to die, that he'd either been lucky enough to avoid the poison or it had been violently expelled from him by Doctor Mullins. Still, proof that Alfie was safe—and that *he* was the one who snored, not Dominick—was a good way to start the day.

He shifted in his chair, hearing several joints pop as he did so. He hadn't slept much at all between his worry and the doctor's hourly visits. Doctor Mullins must be even more exhausted than Dominick himself, having two patients to worry over. The doctor had reported that Stokes was also doing well, which was a relief. Dominick didn't much care for the man, but he hardly wished him dead.

Still, he might have been able to get at least some sleep if he'd been in an actual chair and not this hellish creation. The fucking thing was too damned good at waiting until he was almost comfortable before jabbing a decorative knob into something sensitive. He didn't know much about fashion, but from the whiff of fresh varnish that still rose from it, the chair was as modern and painfully stylish as the Stocktons themselves.

The whole room was, now that he looked at it. Wallpaper so bright it hurt his eyes, furniture that would snap if he breathed on it too strongly, and everywhere small trinkets that were as expensive as they were ugly.

He took a moment to dream longingly of his soft, homely bed at Balcarres and let out a sigh. He couldn't wait until they were home and he could drag Alfie down onto it, with its thick pillows and solid wooden frame that wouldn't buckle under the activities of twenty men, never mind just two. The bed Alfie was in now had creaked ominously during a particularly violent round of vomiting. They might be out of the inn with its paper-thin walls, but anything more than a bit of passionate hand holding was still out of the question.

Ah well, if he couldn't satisfy one hunger, he'd satisfy another. With a last look at Alfie, he rose and tiptoed across the room, his mind focused on the smell of breakfast drifting up through the house.

"Going somewhere?"

Dominick paused with his hand on the doorknob. Of course it wasn't going to be that easy.

"How are you feeling?" he asked the mound of bed linens.

"Better," the linens responded. "Although I feel like I've been scrubbed through from both ends."

Dominick tried not to make a face at that unpleasant image. And people thought *he* was the uncouth one!

The mound shifted a little. "I could use some breakfast."

"I was just going to get my own," Dominick said. "I'll bring you up something. Any preferences?"

A tangle of auburn hair, still too short to curl but trying valiantly, emerged from the wriggling sheets. "Oh no, that's fine. Give me just a moment and I'll join you."

Dominick rubbed a hand over his face. "Alfie."

"I may need some help locating my breeches. I'm afraid I only have evening wear, but I assume proper dress isn't required, considering the circumstances."

"Alfie."

"Although we are going to need to stop by the hotel before we head out. I was thinking, perhaps it's time to shift our search away from the ring and focus more on looking for French servants. I'm sure word of what happened last night will have spread to all the grand houses by now. We'll be ushered in with open arms if they believe we have gossip to share."

"Alfie, what did the doctor say?"

Alfie's upper half had emerged full from the blankets, naked save for the bandage on his wrist where the doctor had bled him. He was looking around the room in a manner so exaggerated that Dominick was tempted to shout, "He's behind you!" like the pantomime it was.

It didn't take long to spot that Alfie was looking at everything except him. If all his tells were that obvious, Dominick would have to keep him away from the card tables.

"The doctor?" Alfie asked airily. Too airily. "I'm sure he said a lot of things. I was too preoccupied to listen to everything. I'm fine now though, so it doesn't matter. Say, did you have my things put away? I don't see them."

"Alfie."

Alfie let out an exasperated harrumph. "He said I needed to stay in bed for at least another day, possibly two, to get my strength back up. But honestly Nick—"

"Alfie."

"Nick." Alfie crossed his arms and scowled. It was all Dominick could do to keep his expression under control. Doubtless Alfie thought he looked like a powerful earl expressing his righteous displeasure. But Dominick had seen that same look from under that same auburn tangle pouting at him from a workhouse dormitory bed when a much younger Alfie didn't get his way.

"Alfie, you were poisoned. You're not going anywhere. I'm going to get us some food, and then I'm going to come back here and not go anywhere either until you're fully healed."

Alfie rolled his eyes. "I wasn't poisoned."

Dominick had no idea how to respond to the absolute stupidity of that statement. Did the little fool think he'd somehow forgotten the events of the last day?

"I wasn't poisoned," Alfie said again. "I'm sure my leg will be an absolute treat to walk on now, but I'm only weak because of those damned treatments. God, I hate being bled. I doubt I'd be able to fend off an overly determined kitten in this state. But Doctor Mullins just got over-excited in the chaos along with the rest of us. If we'd all been thinking rationally, I wouldn't be stuck in this damned bed feeling like the hog that's been run through a sausage-maker.

"Don't look at me like that, Nick. If the fountain was poisoned, I'd have dropped right there beside Batty. And half of the people in that room would've dropped before us. So, unless I somehow ignored a large pile of bodies in my desire to have a drink, it wasn't the water itself that was poisoned. Although that did taste foul. If that's healing water then poison might have actually improved it."

Dominick had to admit his reasoning made a certain amount of sense. "If it wasn't the water that was poisoned, then what?"

Alfie smoothed down his blankets. "I'm not sure. Perhaps it was in one of the canapes, or placed directly into his glass. Stokes handed the glasses to us. I didn't see him slip anything into Batty's, but I can't swear he didn't either."

Now Dominick was beginning to feel sick. He'd had several of the small bites offered at the soiree. Had it only been chance that he hadn't picked the poisoned treat himself? Although even more worrying was the idea they were staying in the poisoner's house right now, and with Alfie all but helpless.

"You really believe Stokes did it?" he asked. "From what the doctor said, Stokes will be fine, but he's in worse shape than you. Would he really put himself through all this?"

Alfie seemed to consider that. "He might have had no choice, if he wanted to avoid suspicion. Although I don't know if he's that good of an actor. Either way, if he's worse off than me, I doubt he'll be up to poisoning anyone else any time soon."

Alfie's face lit up in a way that meant trouble. "Which means this is the perfect opportunity to look for clues! He's stuck in his sickbed and I'm sure the rest of the household is at sixes and sevens. You start in his study. I'll take the library. If neither of us finds anything useful we can move on to—"

Dominick couldn't believe what he was hearing. Well, it was Alfie, so he bloody well could, which was worse.

"Absolutely not. You'll stay here and rest until Doctor Mullins says you can do otherwise."

Unsurprisingly, Alfie looked ready to protest. Dominick rubbed his eyes. "Love, I spent most of last night afraid you were going to die. If you won't stay in bed for Doctor Mullins' sake, will you do it for mine?"

Alfie visibly sagged. Hardly a kitten, Alfie was more like an alley cat putting its fur down when it realised there wasn't going to be a fight after all.

"Very well," he said. "But only for now. If I find my energy returned after breakfast, I make no promises."

Dominick came over and rewarded him with a kiss before pulling the displaced bed covers back up around him. "Thank you. As long as I know you won't be haring off the moment my back is turned. I swear Alfie, if I come back here with a breakfast tray to discover a rope of knotted sheets going out the window, I'm dragging you back to this bed and tying you to it."

Alfie grinned wickedly. "Promise?"

Dominick groaned. As much as he'd like to fulfil that promise, Alfie had to have the worst timing of any man alive. There were a thousand reasons that wouldn't be happening now, even if he thought either Alfie or the bed could take it without collapsing.

"How about this, then? If you're well enough to get out of bed, you're well enough to do your leg exercises."

Alfie flopped back against the pillows. "Now that you

mention it, I am rather tired."

Dominick snorted. "That's what I thought. Now, rest up. I'll bring you breakfast and see if I can't find you some books to keep you entertained. If you stay in bed all morning without complaining *and* Doctor Mullins allows it, then maybe you can get out of bed this afternoon."

Alfie looked pleased. Perhaps too pleased. Dominick began to wonder if he hadn't just been played for a fool.

"You're a menace," he muttered.

"I'm your menace," Alfie said softly, forcing Dominick to kiss him again.

Finally, he pulled away. "Sooner I'm gone, sooner I'm back with food."

"Don't rush yourself," Alfie said, curling into his blankets once more. The little liar wasn't nearly as recovered as he pretended to be. "I'm not actually all that hungry. Perhaps I will sleep a bit longer. Build my strength up for later, you know. If you want to go investigating on your own, however, you should start by..."

His last words trailed off into a snore. Dominick waited a few minutes to make sure Alfie was all right, then gently closed the door to the bedroom behind him and made his way down to breakfast.

It wasn't that hard to find. The house was laid out in much the same way Alfie's home on Bedford Square had been, and Dominick easily found his way to the breakfast room. He chuckled. A year ago, a house like this would've been overwhelming, but now he was just glad it wasn't as sprawling as Balcarres Manor.

Finding no one else in the breakfast room, he wolfed down a quick breakfast and several cups of coffee before filling a plate with pastries and a few other foods that were just as good cold as hot and made his way back up to Alfie's room.

He was still asleep when Dominick arrived, so he set the plate on the table next to the bed. After reassuring himself that all was well, he looked around for something to do. He'd never been one for inaction, especially not when there were things he was trying to avoid thinking about.

Like Alfie nearly dying.

No. Something to keep busy. He'd folded and refolded Alfie's clothes the night before trying not to think about just that. They'd still been wet and were now likely wrinkled beyond the skills of all but the best valet. If Alfie strong-armed his way down to supper, he'd just have to suffer the indignity of appearing in public in a creased shirt as the price for being a stubborn git.

Well, that was something Dominick could do at least, see if the Stocktons could send someone to their hotel for a change of clothes for Alfie. He sniffed his shirt. For them both. He should probably check on Stokes as well, if he was awake, and thank Mrs. Stockton for letting Alfie recover in her home. It was a kindness Dominick wouldn't soon forget. Perhaps he could ask her for some reading suggestions as well. Knowing Alfie, he'd be too busy complaining about his confinement to actually read a word, but Dominick would welcome any distraction. If she had any obscene works hidden away, that might keep Alfie quiet for at least five minutes.

Grinning at the thought, Dominick emerged from the room just in time to catch a passing maid.

"Mr. Stockton is still asleep, sir, and Doctor Mullins says

he's not to be disturbed," said the maid with a perfectly executed curtsey. "Mrs. Stockton is likely in the garden this time of day, if you'd like."

Dominick thanked her and made his way downstairs. The door to the garden that separated the main house from the mews behind it was exactly where it had been in the Bedford Square house. Exiting into the morning sunlight, he couldn't help but marvel.

Just beyond the door lay a terrace complete with chairs and a small table. It must be a lovely spot to dine on fine days like today, but what really made him catch his breath was the garden it overlooked.

A few steps lower than the terrace, the garden was only as wide as the townhouse itself, with high stone walls on either side for privacy from the neighbour's gardens. It stretched back further than Dominick would have expected for a home in the city. A meandering gravel path led to the back wall of a stable so criss-crossed with trellises of climbing vines that it looked like there was no building there at all, that instead the garden had decided to take an abrupt turn skyward.

While the garden couldn't compare in size to the rampant thickets and overgrown paths of Balcarres, it made up for it in the perfectly regimented order of blooms. If there was a flower out of place or a single weed in the entire garden, he'd be surprised. He didn't know much about flowers other than that they looked nice in flower sellers' baskets, but he was certain that many of those surrounding him had never once been seen in a London market. The hum of bees could be heard over the rumble of noise from the street and he watched one of the bumbling creatures loll about, covering itself in pollen before lazily flying to the next flower. They made him think of fat men in striped waistcoats, drunkenly weaving from one pub to another.

His shoes crunched along the gravel path and he drew in a deep breath through his nose, the perfumed air filling his lungs with a dozen different scents, each more lovely than the last.

"Beautiful, isn't it?"

Mrs. Stockton was sitting on a bench beside a small fountain. She was watching him with a pleased smile that did little to hide the dark circles under her eyes. Dominick wasn't the only one who'd been sitting by the bedside of a loved one all night.

"It's amazing," he admitted. "I'm not sure I've seen anything quite like it."

She smiled. "You're too kind."

She was wearing a morning dress and coat both in the same shade of fresh butter. No wonder he hadn't spotted her immediately; the colour blended in with the garden walls that were made of the same yellow-y stone as the rest of the city.

Her hair was pulled up in a neat but simple bun. It was the sort of style she could have accomplished without the help of a maid, who were likely all busy with the extra chores two unexpected sickbeds required. The bench she sat on was bordered on one side by a bed of tall purple flowers with shorter, wide-petaled pink flowers growing at their bases. On her other side, the fountain tucked against the garden wall, its bubbling waters splashing out to dampen an assortment of blooms in all shapes, from tiny blue cups that wouldn't reach the top of his shoe to waist-high stalks from which clusters of white flowers burst like stars.

Despite the beauty surrounding it, just looking at the fountain made Dominick remember the fountain at the Pump Room and its possibly poisoned waters.

"I was told you might be out here, ma'am," he said, putting on all his best manners like an ill-fitting suit. "I wanted to ask-*inquire* about your husband's health and thank you again for taking us in for the night."

She patted the bench beside her in invitation. "It was the least we could do. And Charles is as well as can be expected. Doctor Mullins said whatever poison there may have been is gone, but my husband is still quite weak from the treatments and may be abed for several days."

Dominick wasn't surprised. Stokes was so pale and thin, there couldn't have been much blood in him to begin with. He'd be surprised if the doctor had been able to bleed him of more than a few drops.

"And, of course," Mrs. Stockton continued, her face falling. "He has lost Batty. Lord Boyle was a friend of his since childhood. He will be greatly missed. By all of us."

To Dominick's horror, she began to cry. He sat beside her and offered her his handkerchief. It was a paltry comfort, but it was the best he could come up with. She took it, and after a few minutes the tears slowed.

"I'm sorry," she said. "This sounds awful, but with everything else, I haven't had a chance to think about Batty. The poor, poor man. I can hardly believe it."

Dominick waved away the soaked handkerchief when she tried to return it. "That doesn't sound awful at all. A bit hard to worry about the dead when you're busy worrying about the living."

She sniffed and wiped her eyes again. "It still feels awful."

"Tell me about the garden," Dominick said, hearing the tremble in her voice. "We could both use something to talk about that isn't awful. And it's about the farthest thing from awful I've ever seen."

She gave him a weak smile. "You're too kind. The garden. Very well. You're here at the perfect time; while the roses won't be at their peak for another month or so, everything else is at the height of its season. They're all native plants and this is the best time for them. Isn't it astounding that a foggy little island like ours is graced with so much natural beauty? I wanted a proper English country garden, scaled down for city life. None of those Italian or Mediterranean gardens with plants you have to buy again every year because they can't handle an English winter, you know?"

Dominick did not know at all, but it seemed like the sort of thing a gentleman would be supposed to know, so he nodded sagely. "I'm sure that makes things simpler for your gardener."

This startled a watery laugh out of her. "If I tell you something dreadfully shocking, will you keep it a secret?"

Dominick *did* know that gentlemen shouldn't be hearing shocking things from married women, and after her dress the night before, he wasn't sure she had many secrets left.

"I don't have a gardener," she mock-whispered. "This is all my work. I know, I know. You're scandalised. It gets worse, there's even a vegetable patch behind that shrubbery. But you mustn't say anything. No one would come visiting ever again if they knew I engaged in anything as uncouth as tending my own garden."

From the sparkle in her eye, Dominick was pretty sure it was just a jest, but he was never sure with these fancy sorts. "Your secret is safe with me."

"Oh good," Mrs. Stockton said. "It seems so silly that I should be expected to know how to arrange, paint, and embroider flowers, but to be involved at all in their growing is frowned upon. But it is something of a mania of mine. Charles is very sweet about it. He says that as long as my sunhat is fashionable, he doesn't care what I get up to under it! That man! He's so kind, and yet so silly sometimes."

Her words slowed, but if the reminder that her husband was unlikely to be in a silly mood anytime soon bothered her, she seemed determined not to show it.

"I grew up as the daughter of a farmer, you see. Well-off as far as that life is concerned, but nothing like what we have here in Bath. Now, that isn't scandalous, at least not anymore. Of course, when I married Charles, everyone whispered it was for his money, but I'm afraid I've been far too boring to bother gossiping about since."

"If only they knew you gardened," Dominick said. "That would set tongues wagging."

She laughed. "Oh, Mr. Trent. I knew I shouldn't have trusted you! You're going to extort bouquet upon bouquet from me now to keep your silence! Honestly, I'm surprised the staff told you to look for me out here and risk revealing my secret. I'm quite protective of my work, you know. I won't even let Cook pick her own radishes. She tells me what vegetables she needs for supper and I bring them. Why, if I discover you've removed so much as a single bloom without my permission, I'll be quite cross with you."

Her cheer, even if it was a bit forced, was enough to coax Dominick into smiling back. "I gave you my word. Your secret—and flowers—are safe with me. Although this one here…"

His hand hovered over a plant with saw-toothed leaves and several oddly shaped purple blooms. He wasn't actually intending on plucking it, even if Alfie deserved a bouquet for not climbing out a window to escape yet.

"I'd warn against that one in particular," Mrs. Stockton said. "It's a stinging nettle. It's quite pretty though, isn't it? There's a sermon in there somewhere about hidden dangers."

Dominick pulled his hand back. Before he could say anything more, there came the sound of the back door banging open and two familiar voices crying out at once.

"Madam Stockton! Monsieur Trent!"

"Oh, it's awful, just awful! Oh!"

"Speaking of nettles," Mrs. Stockton said under her breath as the two Lamourette siblings rushed across the garden, their elderly father either still at home or simply unable to keep up with them. Once again, Dominick wasn't sure if she was joking or not, but he wasn't given much time to dwell on it before they were set upon.

"Oh, forgive us for not waiting to be announced, but we absolutely had to see you!" Miss Lamourette exclaimed. "We heard what occurred! Papa is beside himself. Oh, for such a terrible thing to happen! And at one of his parties too! Poor Batty. But what of Stokes? Is he well?"

Dominick rose and let Miss Lamourette take his seat on the bench. If Mrs. Stockton was annoyed at having her sanctuary invaded twice in one morning, she was kind enough not to show it, taking Miss Lamourette's hand in hers and gently explaining everything they knew.

"And your cousin, Monsieur, is he well?"

Dominick turned to Monsieur Henri. "Tired, but otherwise quite well. Thank you."

Monsieur Henri nodded, then gestured with a quick jerk of his head to the side for them to step away. Dominick followed him, leaving the two women to their conversation. They didn't go far, just far enough that they couldn't be easily overheard, especially over Miss Lamourette's frequent and loud exclamations of "Oh!"

Monsieur Henri spoke softly. "My father blames himself for what happened. *Dieu merci*, as far as we know, no one else was harmed. But Lord Boyle was a friend of the family."

"Tell your father it wasn't his fault."

Monsieur Henri shrugged. "Does that ever help? He would be here now to apologise himself, but he has taken over contacting Lord Boyle's brother and making arrangements. Guilt again, but if it makes him feel better..."

Dominick knew that feeling himself. Sometimes it was easier to bury yourself in something else than to face the guilt, deserved or not. Selfishly, he wondered if that meant it would be a good time to ask the marquis for help finding his family. It would certainly keep the old man busy. And it might make him feel better about Lord Boyle's end if he could help Dominick discover his beginning.

But it felt too much like taking advantage of a terrible situation for his own benefit. He'd waited this long to find his family. He could wait a few days more. There were more pressing matters at hand. Like the fact Miss Lamourette was waving and calling his name as if she'd done so several times already.

"—Trent! Oh, Mr. Trent! Is your cousin well?"

"No need to shout," Monsieur Henri shouted back at his sister. "I have already asked. He is fine."

"Oh, wonderful!" said Miss Lamourette, hurrying over to join them, leaving Mrs. Stockton and several feet of hat ribbon trailing in her wake. "I am so looking forward to meeting him. Is he well enough for visitors? I heard you had to carry him from the room! You must be quite strong! Mrs. Stockton says dear Stokes isn't well enough yet, but I would so love to meet Lord Crawford if he's well enough. Do you know if he is? Papa would want us to be sure."

She put her hands on Dominick's arm and looked up at him imploringly. "Please?"

She went so far as to bat her eyelashes and Dominick had to fight back a laugh. He'd never been so blatant even back in his days as a whore. She did need to work on her approach though. Speaking as a professional, it wasn't a good idea to hang off one man while enquiring about another. As she gazed up at him, he completely believed that she wanted to meet the young, handsome, *unmarried* earl who needed nursing back to health, but not because her father was concerned. At least, not entirely because of her father. She might be a bit mercenary, but Dominick could respect that. It didn't make her heartless.

But Dominick had been gone some time and forgotten to get any of Alfie's promised books, so the young, handsome, unmarried earl was probably pacing the floor of his sickroom by now. Or trying to, at least. Alfie always worked himself into a horrible mood when he was laid up. As much as tying him to the bed really might be the best solution, Dominick could at least see if Alfie wanted a little company before resorting to it.

"I'll see if he's up for having visitors." Dominick said.

"Oh, Mr. Trent, you are *too* kind!"

Dominick pried himself from Miss Lamourette's clutches and headed back into the house. As he climbed the stairs, he wondered if he shouldn't warn Alfie. Healthy or not, he wasn't sure any man was well enough to bear Miss Lamourette's attentions for too long.

CHAPTER 9

"I don't care if she's downstairs in a wedding dress with banns already posted. Anything's better than sitting in here staring at the walls."

There was a lot more Alfie could say on the subject of if he was well enough to receive visitors, but he decided his energy was better spent trying to get himself upright and staying that way. Doctor Mullins had been by while Dominick was gone and cautioned against both those things, but Dominick didn't need to know that.

"It's not like you've been chained up in Newgate for years," Dominick said with a loud sigh, as if Alfie wasn't going mad trapped in this room by himself. "And remember our agreement? It's still morning."

To prove him wrong, a clock on the mantel chose that moment to strike twelve. Alfie pointed to it in vindication.

"And now it's afternoon. Nick, I've spent most of the last year recovering from one thing or another. I said you could mother hen me all you wanted last night, but I feel much better after my nap this morning. The sun is up and so too shall I be. Now, where did you hide my clothes?"

Usually, he'd be delighted at the idea of Dominick hiding his clothes to keep him in bed. But that was under rather different circumstances.

"No," said Dominick. "You're not leaving that bed. We'll

make you decent, but I don't want you fainting halfway down the stairs and cracking your fool skull open."

From the tone of his voice Alfie knew he'd already won the battle. Now he just had to convince Dominick to admit defeat. He pulled himself to his feet to look for the damned clothes himself and the room began to roll like a ship at sea. He reached out and grabbed Dominick's arm that was already reaching towards him.

When the room returned to its rightful stationary position, he grinned. "Don't be ridiculous. See? You'll obviously catch me before I fall and crack my skull. Besides, are you saying it's a better idea to let the husband-hunting daughter of a marquis into the bedchambers of an unmarried earl? If she went after you just for being the cousin of nobility, imagine what she'll do to me. I should probably just offer her my hand in marriage and get it over with now."

He could see the moment Dominick realised he was right—about the keeping her out of the bedchamber, certainly not the marriage. Naturally, Dominick would never admit it, but his grumblings about "...should have left you in the mud where I found you." were fond as he went to the dresser to fetch Alfie's things.

He helped Alfie dress in his wrinkled evening clothes from the night before with only a few more lingering touches than were strictly necessary. It shouldn't take quite so long to properly tuck a shirt into breeches, but after the night they'd had, Alfie didn't want him to let go either, even if it did mean a delay in leaving the room.

"You know," Dominick said, taking extra care to fasten each waistcoat button perfectly as Alfie held onto his shoulders for balance. "Last night, the brother, Monsieur Henri, asked me if I was a republican. They might not be after your hand at all, but your head."

Alfie considered this. "You'd think they'd go after their own father first, if they're such blood-thirsty revolutionaries. But I'll be on my guard for either eventuality. Assuming they're still there by the time we leave this room. If you're finished?"

"Not quite." Dominick clearly chose to ignore Alfie's tone, far too focused on forming some sort of respectable knot out of his wilted cravat.

Alfie waited as patiently as he was able, but another thought occurred to him. "Are you going to ask them about your ring?"

Dominick fumbled the knot completely and the cravat slithered out of his hands. "I don't think now's the right time."

"Unfortunately, I agree," Alfie slid his hands from Dominick's shoulders and cupped his face, gently pushing upwards until Dominick had no choice but to look at him. As always, his gorgeous blue eyes took Alfie's breath away, even reddened by worry and lack of sleep as they were now. "I'm still here, Nick. I'm all right."

He didn't miss how Dominick had to swallow several times before answering.

"Curse you," Dominick sniffed. "Don't you dare make me cry right before we face the lot of them."

Alfie kissed him softly, feeling Dominick relax at that simple touch of lips.

"We are going to have to talk about it at some point," Alfie whispered. His words were as much for himself as they were for Dominick. "If Doctor Mullins is right and someone slipped poison into Batty's glass, we need to find out who did it. I don't want to think about the fact it could've been my glass any more than you do, but not only is it the right thing to do, we owe it to him.

"You know, if it wasn't for Batty and Stokes carousing with my damned cousin, we might never have met again? If my cousin had tried to drag me to that boxing match by himself, I would've said 'no', but with the three of them goading me on, I couldn't refuse."

"I'm glad you didn't," said Dominick. He gave Alfie a kiss that expressed more than words ever could. Then he picked up the cravat to try again. "Enough of that. One thing at a time: cravat, coat, warding off the advances of French ladies, and only after all that can we deal with murder and *then* my past."

Alfie lifted his chin for Dominick's inexpert knot tying. This attempt wasn't much more successful than the last, but he was willing to take some of the blame as he still had his hands on Dominick's face and was rubbing lines over his cheekbones. It took less than that to distract his lover.

"We certainly live exciting lives," Alfie said with a positivity he didn't feel. "Most men would happily stop at French ladies, but we just can't leave out the murder and mysterious past, can we?"

Dominick hummed in what Alfie would pretend was agreement.

"In all seriousness though, Nick, I'm not sure I'm up for dealing with the murder part of the list right now. But if you have a chance to get any information out of them about your ring, you should. They might not know anything, but they might have French servants who do. We were sent here by a French maid who knew *something* about you, after all. We shouldn't squander the chance to see if there's another one here who knows more."

"We'll see." Dominick sighed. "And that's about as good as that knot's going to get. No, don't look in the mirror, it'll just make you swoon all over again. Now come along, get your coat on and I'll let you hold my arm all the way down the stairs. For the support you claim you don't need."

Alfie laughed, relieved that Dominick wasn't going to make him brave the stairs alone. Even if he was sure he could handle them by himself. Mostly. Probably.

"Such a gentleman."

✳ ✳ ✳

The stairs successfully descended, a footman directed them to the back terrace where the rest of the party was assembled. Dominick appeared to know the way, so Alfie followed his lead, enjoying the chance to hold onto Dominick in public without raising suspicions.

He wasn't sure what he expected from the Lamourette siblings from the little Dominick had time to tell him, but after the introductions were made and the polite sympathies for his current condition expressed, they actually seemed quite enjoyable company.

Part of it may have just been the surroundings. The terrace overlooked a lovely garden and the return of summer promised in the warmth of the sun was cooled just enough by a light breeze that Alfie couldn't help but feel giddy. That may also have been the blood loss, but he preferred to blame the weather and the pleasant company.

They were all sitting at a small table on the terrace and Alfie had to fight back a grin when he noticed the only free seats were the ones next to Miss Lamourette. Dominick helped him into his chair, then pointedly took the one between him and the French woman.

It didn't take long for Alfie to see why. While she was hardly the ravening she-wolf he'd expected from Dominick's description, she was certainly flirtatious. But he liked her despite that. She quickly proved herself lively and cheerful, and it wasn't her fault that neither of them was as available as their bachelor status would imply. There was no way to tell her she was wasting her time, but hopefully she'd take the hint and move on to greener pastures soon enough. Still, until they left Bath, he'd take extra care not to find himself alone with her behind a locked door. Just in case.

Her brother was her exact opposite. He was polite and kept up his end of the conversation well, but there was a seriousness to him that was not just the result of his solemn dress. Interestingly, he seemed to either not notice or not care about his sister's flirting, even when she put her hand on Dominick's arm and laughed at something he said that wasn't nearly that funny. Perhaps he was simply too tired of her actions to care.

He certainly wasn't the only one who was tired. As the afternoon wore on and a light luncheon was served, Alfie found himself adding more and more sugar to his tea just to stay awake. Mrs. Stockton didn't seem to be in a much better state. She'd gotten up several times to go check on her husband, turning down Miss Lamourette's offer to accompany her each time. Every time she returned, she assured them that while he was well, Stokes was still quite weak and Doctor Mullins was staying with him for the time being to be safe. Each time she sat back down, she looked a little more worn and it took her longer to rejoin the conversation.

"Such a terrible, terrible thing," Miss Lamourette said for at least the dozenth time. "And how terrible it is when there is nothing one can do but sit and think. That might be the worst of it for me. The doctor has poor Stokes to care for, Papa is handling the arrangements for poor Batty, but what are we to do? Sit and grieve? No, I can't stand it. Besides, that's not at all what Batty would have wanted."

"What do you propose instead?" asked her brother.

"Well, of course, we'll have to throw another party to make up for Papa's ruined soiree. Oh, don't look at me like that Henri! I don't mean that Batty meant to ruin the evening, it's just that you know how Papa is. We already had to hide the paper from him this morning so he wouldn't see what the society page had to say, and I imagine we'll have to do the same with his evening paper."

Monsieur Henri grimaced. "Likely for several weeks. But still, it hardly seems appropriate to plan a party now."

Miss Lamourette clapped her hands. "What about a dinner party then? This afternoon has been so wonderful, just talking with you all has been so soothing to my poor nerves. Please, say you'll all come over tonight for dinner? That won't be too scandalous will it, Henri? Just us and Papa? It would do him so much good, I know it would."

"I'm afraid it'll have to be another time," Mrs. Stockton said graciously. "Charles won't be up for dining anytime soon and I couldn't leave him all alone. I'm sure I'd be the worst guest anyway, just sitting there and fretting the whole time. When Charles is recovered though, we'd be delighted."

"I'm afraid I'm out as well," Alfie added. "It has been wonderful meeting you, even under such circumstances, but we're lucky Doctor Mullins hasn't found out I've left my bed yet. I'm certain he wouldn't approve if I left the house entirely."

In reality, Alfie would probably fall asleep facedown in the soup. They'd only been on the terrace an hour or two, but he was exhausted. Hard to believe he'd been so desperate to leave his bed a few hours before, when all he wanted to do was crawl into it now. If only Dominick could join him in bed too. Not that Alfie could stay awake long enough to take advantage of it, but he never slept better than he did by Dominick's side.

A thought occurred to him. "You know, Mr. Trent has never been to Bath before, he might enjoy seeing the city on the carriage ride over to your home."

Dominick's look of betrayal at being left to the mercies of the Lamourettes, especially Miss Lamourette, was obvious, but it was no more than he deserved for abandoning Alfie with Stokes and Batty the night before. Still, it wasn't as if revenge was his only motive.

He gave Dominick a raised eyebrow that he hoped communicated, *I'm doing this so you'll stop playing nursemaid and see if there's anyone in their household who knows about your ring, you ninny.*

From Dominick's confused squint, it seemed like the message hadn't come across.

"We can do much better than just the journey to the house," offered Henri. "Bath is truly a lovely city with a long history. Not so long as Paris or even your London, but still. Do you ride, Mr. Trent? There are still hours of daylight left. I could show you some of the sights and then you could join our father for supper. A small affair; just the four of us."

He gave his sister a look as if she would plan a royal banquet before supper time if left unattended. From the glint in her eye, Alfie was worried she might.

Dominick hesitated before responding, clearly torn. He wouldn't want to leave Alfie alone, the old fusspot. But he also hadn't had a chance to go for a real ride since they'd left Balcarres. After some initial worries, he'd taken to horseback riding as if he'd been doing it all his life. It must have truly hurt him to not to ride these last few months.

"I'm afraid I don't have the right clothes," Dominick said finally. Alfie couldn't tell if his regret was sincere or if he was just making excuses.

Mrs. Stockton chimed in before he could find out. "Why don't you go by your hotel on the way? You'll have to stay with us while Lord Crawford recovers, and we can hardly expect you both to live out of the same evening suits the entire time. I would've sent someone to get your things already, but it completely slipped my mind."

"That's understandable," Dominick said, shooting Alfie a look that *he* failed to interpret this time. "We don't want to put you out."

"Nonsense. Once he's recovered, I'm sure Charles would love the chance to catch up with you, Lord Crawford. And Mr. Trent, I wouldn't dream of sending you back to some hotel on your own when we have plenty of room here."

Mrs. Stockton sounded more animated than she had all afternoon. Alfie supposed some people enjoyed hosting. At the very least, having two guests to worry over would be some distraction from worrying about her poor husband. Or his dead friend.

"We'd be honoured, thank you," said Alfie. He turned to Dominick and tried to gently reassure him. "Go on. No reason for you to spend all day with us invalids. Get what we need from the inn and enjoy the rest of your day. Doctor Mullins is here and he'll send word if anything changes."

"You're sure?" Dominick asked, clearly not convinced.

"Absolutely."

"All right then, thank you," Dominick said to Mrs. Stockton. Then he gave Alfie a conspiratorial look. "Although I'm afraid I might forget something. Could Lord Crawford and I use your husband's study a moment to make a list?"

Clever, clever man. What an excellent excuse for him to speak with Alfie in private before they separated, and if they were quick, a way to search Stokes' study without getting caught. What they needed to discuss Alfie wasn't sure, but doubtless Dominick was worried about leaving Alfie alone while he investigated his past. As if that wasn't the entire reason they were in Bath.

"I don't know that Charles would want people in his study," Mrs. Stockton said stiffly.

"It would only take a moment," Dominick replied.

"I'm still afraid the answer is 'no'. I can have a servant fetch you a pen and paper if you'd like. Or if you do forget any of your luggage, I'm sure the hotel can have it sent over."

Odd that she wouldn't let them in Stokes' study. What might he be hiding in there? He thought back to Stokes handing Batty and him each a glass of the fountain water. Had he slipped something into one of the glasses after all? And if so, was there something in his study to prove it?

Dominick's smile didn't quite reach his eyes. "That's fine, thank you."

"Then it's settled." Monsieur Henri pushed his chair back with finality. "We will take Adelaide home to make arrangements for dinner, visiting your hotel along the way, then we will still have time for an excellent ride to work up an appetite before dinner. We have several fine horses for you to choose from."

"Oh, you can leave me out of it," Miss Lamourette said. "I'll stay here with the—What was the delightful term you used, Lord Crawford?—with the invalids. You can tell the staff to prepare an additional place at the table as easily as I can, Henri."

Alfie's heart sank. If he didn't get a nap soon, he might cry, but he was hardly going to let his guard down with Miss Lamourette still in the house. From the look on his face, Dominick was thinking the same thing, but if he thought he was hiding his excitement at getting a chance to ride, he was mistaken. Alfie wasn't going to take that away from him. He'd dealt with murders, blackmailers, and Mrs. Hirkins. He could handle one young woman by himself.

Go on. I'll be fine.

Fortunately, this time the silent communication worked. Dominick gave him the slightest nod then made his farewells to the two ladies. Within moments, he and Monsieur Henri were gone. It was only then that Alfie realised he had no idea how he was going to make his way back upstairs without Dominick's help.

"I should check on my husband. Lord Crawford, would you care to escort me?" Mrs. Stockton offered him her arm. Bless her. His exhaustion must have been more transparent than he'd thought.

He tucked his arm through hers, and between pulling down on it and pushing up on the table, was just able to leverage himself to his feet. She took a moment to adjust her sleeve, giving the Earth time to stop moving under his feet before she guided him back towards the house.

After a moment, she turned back to Miss Lamourette.

"Aren't you joining us inside?"

Miss Lamourette leaned back in her chair in a way that highlighted her long neck and more than a hint of bosom. "Oh, it's such a lovely day. I think I'll enjoy the gardens a little longer. They're so beautiful, and beauty is fleeting, you know, just like youth. I will be sure to say hello to dear Charles when I come in."

She gave them a coy smile. Mrs. Stockton's hand, which had been resting on his elbow, tightened briefly. She was easily Miss Lamourette's elder by a decade or more. Had the French woman's words about youth been a flirtation aimed at him or a slight aimed at her? Alfie was suddenly uneasy.

Miss Lamourette smiled. "I'll see you soon."

Again, Alfie wasn't sure which of them she was addressing. What he was sure of though, was that he'd made a grave mistake sending Dominick away.

CHAPTER 10

Dominick hadn't realised how much he missed riding until he was back in the saddle.

After a brief stop to acquire horses at the Lamourettes' home—yet another of the endless townhouses built of honey-coloured stone—they rode slowly through the city. Along the way, Monsieur Henri pointed out this and that particular place of interest, including a street of townhouses that formed a perfect circle. The Frenchman claimed they were owned by the *almost* wealthiest residents of Bath, then led him to a broad park crested by an even larger semicircle of the houses that belonged to the absolute wealthiest.

So much space in the middle of a city was dizzying. Dominick had become used to the broad isolation of Balcarres and knew that parts of London held open parkland. But he was more used to the parts of town where a woman in one building could pass her hat to her friend in the building across the way. Where narrow lanes were as likely to pinch shut as they were to open to another street.

Perhaps there were parts of Bath like that as well. There had to be—not everyone could live in such scenic grandeur. But those parts didn't criss-cross through Bath the way they did in London, where darkness found a way into every crease of the city. Instead, Bath was something entirely different, not quite city and not quite country. It left him wrongfooted, even as he was charmed by it.

Then Monsieur Henri's horse was charging across the open park and all thoughts fled as Dominick gave chase. Too soon, they slowed so Monsieur Henri could lead them through the city once more, but the sprint seemed to have lit something in Dominick's guide, his solemn shell cracked open just enough to let out a few flicks of flame from the fire within.

"Those are the assembly rooms," Monsieur Henri said, indicating a building only made different from those around it by the row of sham columns that ran along its front. "The most glamorous and overstuffed building in the city, where all the great and non-so-good come to see and be seen. Doubtless your cousin will want to make an appearance there once he's better."

"For a political assembly?" Dominick asked in confusion.

Monsieur Henri barked out a laugh. "Hardly that. It is where all the largest society parties are held, nearly one every night. Why would Englishmen want to engage in politics when there are parties to attend?"

This was not the first time that Monsieur Henri had made a point of not considering himself at all English, and yet his sister, who looked only a few years younger, very much did.

Of course, their father, the marquis, was French. Very French in fact. Dominick didn't have much experience with foreigners aside from a few who worked the docks, but he'd never seen a man as French as the marquis outside of satirical prints. Perhaps Monsieur Henri felt tied more to his father's past than the soil beneath his feet.

Dominick wouldn't know anything about that. If they found his family and his father turned out to be a bricklayer, would he feel like a bricklayer? Or would he still just feel like Dominick? Although, he supposed he could understand a little of being tied to the past. After all, here he was in fine clothes conversing with the son of a marquis atop horseback and yet he was still gawking at the sights like the poor boy from the workhouse he was.

He realised that while he'd been contemplating, he'd missed Monsieur Henri telling him more about the assembly rooms.

"…and then several smaller ballrooms and a card room. You see why so few people were in attendance at my father's little gathering last night, when they could be attending much more modish affairs here nearly every night."

Dominick reined in his horse in shock. Christ, if that had been a *little* gathering, he was going to do everything in his power to keep Alfie from accepting any invitations that took place at the damned assembly rooms.

"Would it be possible to go by the Pump Room?" Dominick asked. "Lord Crawford dropped his cane during the… events last night. I'd like to see if it's been found."

"We can see," said Monsieur Henri. "Would you be interested in taking in the waters as well? Perhaps not drinking them, I myself will not be doing that for some time, but who ever heard of being poisoned by taking a bath!"

❊ ❊ ❊

Looking out the windows of the Pump Room down onto the bathers below, Dominick decided that poisoned or not, there was no way he'd ever let himself be dragged into those waters.

Either word of the poisoning hadn't spread, or it wasn't enough to stop those who believed in the water's healing powers, because the large pool he looked down on was full of bathers, steam curling around them as they swam slowly or sat along the edges.

Shockingly, both men and women were bathing together. The men wore shirts and trousers made of some hideous brown fabric and women had dresses made of the same. Most bizarre of all, they all still wore their hats and bonnets. Dominick watched as one man tipped his hat to a woman as he floated by, the proud ostrich feather on her bonnet wilting in the heat. It was almost impossible to tell who was rich and who was poor just by their hats, but it seemed all ages and walks of life were welcomed. It was beyond understanding.

Christ, he'd always known aristos were mad, but that didn't explain the rest of them.

"Are any of these the one you lost, sir?"

A bewildered Dominick turned from the window to see one of the Pump Room waiters carrying an entire bushel of canes, walking sticks, and assorted staffs in his arms. A bemused Monsieur Henri stood beside him.

"Christ, are those all just from last night?"

"Yes, sir. There's quite a few things left over at the end of every evening, sir. Not all come back for them so quickly though. It is much appreciated; we're running out of room to store everything." The waiter bowed, causing more than one of the collection to clatter to the floor.

Dominick sighed. "Give me just a minute."

It took him less than that to find Alfie's cane, although he did toy with the idea of replacing it with a particularly fine ivory and gold stick that had also been left behind. The thing must have cost more than he'd made in all his years of work, but it had been so easily forgotten. He almost took it for that reason alone, but with as much trouble as Alfie kept getting them into, Dominick would prefer he carried his own cane with its sword within rather than some frippery with—Christ, were those rubies in the handle?

Alfie's cane reluctantly acquired, it was only a short ride from there to the hotel where Monsieur Henri arranged the transfer of their things to the Stocktons' house while Dominick changed into a set of clothes actually suitable for riding. He'd grown used to how uncomfortable those fancy togs were after being in them so long, but it was nice to feel like he could breathe again.

After taking a few minutes to shave and to make sure any incriminating bottles of oil were buried deeply in their luggage away from prying eyes, he found himself feeling more like things were back to the way they should be. He should probably set aside another set of formal clothes to take to the Lamourettes' home for dinner, but after being stuck in the damn things overnight, he couldn't bear the thought of being trapped in them again. Besides, perhaps the smell of horse would keep Miss Lamourette at bay.

"Ah, Mr. Trent," said Monsieur Henri as Dominick swung into the saddle, "Now I can show you the real sights of Bath!"

They rode a few more blocks through town before

crossing a bridge over the river. Immediately, the land around them opened into rolling parkland framed by hills thick with trees that rose sharply around the city, as if cradling Bath in massive hands of leaf and stone. It was all Dominick could do to keep from digging his heels in and seeing how fast his horse could fly across the ground. He felt a moment of guilt for enjoying himself on such a beautiful day while Alfie was still unwell, but hopefully his lover would be sleeping now. Dominick told him he should, so of course, that likely meant Alfie was doing the exact opposite. At least there was only so far he could go to find trouble without his cane.

As the parkland settled into a gently rising slope, Dominick waited for Monsieur Henri to lead him off in a gallop, but to his annoyance, the man settled into a pace that was hardly more than a light trot.

"It's good land for riding," Dominick said, hoping he'd take the hint.

"Very much so," Monsieur Henri replied. "And yet so few come this way. I suppose the adventurous climb Beechen Cliff to the south of town and the rest stay at home. I prefer these open areas, they're so much better for knowing your conversations won't be overheard."

A trickle of unease creeped up Dominick's spine.

Monsieur Henri continued on. "Which reminds me, we never had a chance for you to answer my question from last night."

"What question was that?" asked Dominick warily.

"Are you a republican or a monarchist?"

The words were lightly said, but Monsieur Henri had his reins gripped tightly in his hands and behind his cool demeanour, Dominick could see the fire in his eyes. He suddenly realised they'd ridden behind one of the hills, out of sight of the city, and there was still a murderer on the loose.

He cursed himself for being such an idiot. At least he'd only left Alfie with the Lamourette sister. Her flirtations couldn't be nearly as dangerous as whatever Monsieur Henri was up to. He was still waiting for Dominick's answer. Clearly there was a correct response he was supposed to give, but what was it?

As an Englishman, Dominick was obviously supposed to believe in the king over all, even if said king was a madman and the son who ran the country in his name was a lecherous sot who'd trade all their lives for another glass of port. But Henri was the son of a French noble. Did that make him more likely to agree with a monarchy? Or had he been taken in by the ideals of the now tarnished revolution? And France had a king again now, didn't it? Dominick thought they did, but he wasn't certain enough to stake his life on it.

There was always a chance that Monsieur Henri was one of those awaiting another return by Napoleon, but if he was truly that mad, then there was no sane answer Dominick could give.

He was suddenly glad he'd kept Alfie's cane with him. He twisted it as subtly as he could without dropping the reins and was relieved to feel the catch that released the blade.

"Well," he answered slowly, not willing to start a political discussion with a sword fight, even if he was willing to end it that way if necessary. "Do you mean in

France or in England?"

"Anywhere! Should a man be governed differently due to lines on a map?"

"I suppose not," Dominick said, trying to spur his horse faster without looking like he was running away. Unfortunately, Monsieur Henri kept pace. Dominick finally gave up both trying to get away from the conversation and trying to figure out what the man wanted him to say. If he hated Dominick's answer that much, Dominick could always stab him.

"I've never met a king, but most nobles I've met, aside from Lord Crawford and maybe your father, shouldn't be trusted to wipe their own arses, never mind run things. That said, I don't know they deserve to get their heads chopped off either. I was just a babe when it happened in France, but you hear stories, and I'm sure you've heard more than me. I suppose a republic's all well and good in theory, but those revolutionaries made a right mess in how they went about it. And after all that, there's a king in France again, isn't there? So, to me that says someone certainly thinks monarchy's the way to go."

Monsieur Henri levelled him with an unreadable look. "By 'someone' do you mean God?"

Dominick shrugged. "If you like."

He waited tensely, hand gripping the cane. Then to his relief, Monsieur Henri broke into a large grin.

"*Dieu et mon droit*! You English took that phrase from us for your own king's motto, because you agree. God and my right! The divine right of kings has been proven again and again, and yet there are still those who would argue! I am glad to see you are not one of them, Mr. Trent. But of course, that divine right does rely on having a rightful king on the throne. To have a son rule in England while his father still lives is an upset to the proper order of things."

"If you say so. What say we actually ride now?" Dominick said, sensing another trap about to be laid. Before Monsieur Henri could answer, Dominick kicked his horse into motion, no longer caring if it looked like he was fleeing. What was it Alfie liked to say about discretion being the better part of valour? It wasn't a motto either of them ever lived by, but he could see the appeal now.

He heard the pounding of hoofbeats behind him, but when he looked back, Monsieur Henri was grinning as he spurred his horse on. Dominick abruptly felt silly. Had he actually thought the man was going to find a way to poison him from horseback over politics?

Ridiculous. Monsieur Henri was an odd one for sure, but he'd been nothing but kind and helpful. Besides, he was French, a little oddness should be expected.

Dominick grinned back at him and let the horse have its head, trusting it to know its own speed and course.

He didn't know how long they raced, but when his horse began to slow, he eased it down to a walk, his own sides heaving with exertion as much as the animal's.

"You're quite the rider," Monsieur Henri said as his horse came to a walk beside Dominick's.

"I'm not as good as I'd like to be, but it gives me an excuse to be outdoors."

A statement like that would've been laughable to him a year ago. After the things he'd done to keep a roof over his head and a fire lit in his meagre hearth, he wouldn't have been able to imagine why anyone would want to be outdoors when they didn't have to be. Besides, all that was outside in London was the filth of other bodies also longing to be indoors, preferably with a pint in hand. That life had been his for so long, he couldn't have imagined there was any other way to live.

Then Alfie had taken him to Balcarres. He'd never seen a place so beautiful—at least when it wasn't raining, or sleeting, or both. But that was part of its charm as well. Scotland wasn't a soft beauty. It was full of thorns, rocks, and all sorts of hidden perils.

Lovely but dangerous. He had a type.

He snorted and took in the gentler beauty of the English countryside around him. There was a break in the trees ahead and he spotted something entirely unexpected.

"Is that a bloody castle?"

It certainly looked like one, the turreted tops of the walls like something out of a fairy story. As they rode closer, the front wall came into view, two round turrets on either side of a tall archway where a drawbridge should be, then two squatter, square turrets further along the walls, one in either direction, small windows clouded with grime set high into their walls. Then around the sides…

He turned to Monsieur Henri in confusion. "Where's the rest of it?"

"That's all there is," Monsieur Henri said. Then to Dominick's surprise he spat on the ground. "It is nothing but a worthless folly."

The uneasy feeling returned. Dominick had missed it, but something had happened in the last few minutes to change Monsieur Henri's mood for the worse. He was glowering up at the folly now, eyes dark with hate.

"You can see it from almost everywhere in the city. An eyesore you cannot escape."

Dominick squinted at the single wall of the castle. He couldn't see what made it so awful. Silly perhaps, but as a child he would've loved to have been able to look up at a castle on a hill, real or not.

"It doesn't seem so bad to me."

"That's because you know nothing." Monsieur Henri spat again. "It is a meeting spot, this place, where foolish girls can meet men they shouldn't be meeting. The towers on the right are solid stone, but you see these here? There are doors on the back. The round tower goes up to view the city, but the square one! A squalid room with a door that locks.

"And if the foolish girl doesn't even take the care to ensure the door is locked? Ruin. Revulsion. Her reputation becomes so bad that she is no longer who she was. After all, she says, if they are going to believe these things of me regardless, why should I not become them? Then the only one who will offer her his hand is a drunken lord who has squandered all of his money and only wants her for our father's wealth, reputation be damned."

Monsieur Henri then exploded in a barrage of angry French.

Dominick kept his mouth shut. He didn't think the man realised what he'd just said. *Our* father's wealth. The foolish girl he was talking about, was that his sister, Miss Lamourette?

It would certainly explain a few things. Dominick had known more than one woman who'd decided to live up to her bad reputation. And hadn't he done the same thing to an extent? Everyone in Spitalfields knew the trade he'd plied, but most were smart enough not to say anything due to his other occupation as a boxer.

It was harder for a woman, of course, and in some ways these wealthy women might have it the worst. No one cared if a poor girl lost her honour, especially if the choice was that or starve, but a rich one was an entirely different matter. Their money was never really theirs. Their only real coin to trade was themselves. And those that were seen as damaged goods were worse than scorned.

But if the foolish girl was Miss Lamourette, who was the drunken lord? There was only one who came immediately to mind.

"Your sister was engaged to Lord Boyle?"

Monsieur Henri stopped swearing and turned to him. A torrent of emotions washed over his face too quickly for Dominick to catch. Then his shoulders slumped.

"I should watch my words better. Gallic passion, my sister calls it. And see where that got her." Monsieur Henri sighed. "See where it got us all. Yes, they were engaged, but it had not yet been announced. We all knew it was a money match, but he was not the man she'd been caught with and was willing to marry her anyway. That was all that mattered."

Dominick couldn't hide his surprise. "She doesn't seem to be mourning him."

Monsieur Henri shook his head. "She didn't want to marry, but our father is getting older and I have my own ambitions. I cannot have my attention divided between those and worry for my sister. But now Lord Boyle is dead, the hunt begins again."

Not just dead, murdered. Dominick thought. A sister who didn't want to marry, a brother who didn't like her intended husband, and a father who might be annoyed at losing his daughter, his money, or both. Any of them might have reason to poison Batty.

What a nest of vipers.

"I'm sorry," Monsieur Henri said. "I find I am no longer in the mood to ride. Shall we head back? There will be plenty of time to refresh ourselves before dinner if we leave now."

Ah yes, Dominick had already agreed to dine with the vipers. Wonderful. But he couldn't think of a way to get out of it now.

He nodded his head and followed Monsieur Henri back to the nest.

CHAPTER 11

While Mrs. Stockton had many fine qualities, she unfortunately lacked the strength to drag a fully grown man up a flight of stairs.

However, Alfie could hardly begrudge her because at the moment, neither did he. By the fifth step, they admitted defeat and he spent several humiliating minutes sitting on the stairs waiting for a footman to be fetched.

By the time the footman arrived, Alfie was willing to consider that he'd been a bit pigheaded in insisting he was well enough to go downstairs in the first place. By the time the three of them—as Mrs. Stockton insisted on helping—got him up the stairs, he'd compiled a list of all the times he'd been too stubborn to listen to Dominick and ended up regretting it. Doubtless there were more he'd forgotten, but it was a little hard to concentrate when the stripes on the wallpaper began to spiral.

Thankfully, there was a bench right at the top of the stairs, and he spent another several minutes staring intently at his feet. He doubted there was anything left in him to cast up, but he didn't want to find out all over Mrs. Stockton's slippers. As he recovered, she kept up a soothing stream of chatter about the house and its furnishings, as if they'd stopped solely because Alfie was too enraptured by the decor to proceed further.

The kindness was welcome, as was the glass of water the footman returned with. By the time he'd finished the whole glass sip by tiny sip, he felt recovered enough to make it as far as his room without embarrassing himself.

Which was why he was as surprised as she was when he found himself asking, "Is your husband's room near? I'd like to see for myself that he's recovering well."

He hadn't missed her glances down the hall as she kept him company and the way they grew more frequent as time went on.

"Are you sure?" Mrs. Stockton asked. "It's not very far, but I'd hate for you to overburden yourself."

"The stairs were just more of a trial than I'd expected. I'm fine now." Alfie slowly rose from his chair to test the veracity of this statement. When the floor remained strictly horizontal and the wallpaper strictly vertical, he took a few tentative steps. Without his cane, his leg gave him hell, but the rest seemed to be in working order.

Without waiting to be asked, she took his arm again, pointing out interesting portraits as they made their way down the hall at a glacial pace.

"...and this is Charles' great-aunt Catherine," she finished as she reached the door to Stokes' bedroom. "We haven't got a dog, so we put her here to guard us from intruders. Although I admit she's given me a fright a time or two when I've ventured out in the middle of the night."

Alfie laughed. Mrs. Stockton really was delightful; if only he'd been fortunate enough to make her acquaintance years ago, instead of having to put up with her husband. Lord knew what she saw in him, but it took all sorts.

She rapped lightly on the door before opening it.

Apparently too lightly, because when they stepped inside it was to see Stokes in bed as promised, but with Miss Lamourette leaning over him, his hand clutched to her chest.

"Oh!" exclaimed Miss Lamourette, although notably she kept Stokes' hand where it was. "There you are! We were beginning to wonder. Doctor Mullins had to go fetch something, so I promised to keep Stokes company until he returned."

Mrs. Stockton said nothing, but under her gaze, Stokes finally freed his hand. Between his weakened state and Miss Lamourette's grip, it was quite a struggle.

"How did you get up here?" Alfie asked. It wasn't the most important question, but it was the one bothering him the most. He hadn't been so preoccupied in climbing the stairs that he would have missed Miss Lamourette charging up past them.

"Well," she said, finally having the decency to look abashed. "I saw you were having some difficulty, so I took the servants' stairs rather than bother you."

Stokes licked his lips. "Freddie, how good to see you."

"You as well," said Alfie, doing his best to ignore the tension in the room. "I'm glad to see you're recovering. I should leave you to it."

"Nonsense," said Stokes, "Stay awhile. I could use the company."

It looked like he had more company than was good for him already. Strangely though, aside from removing his hand from Miss Lamourette's hold, he wasn't at all acting like a man caught in the act. In fact, he was now smiling at his wife and offering that same hand to her. Either he was the most shameless philanderer Alfie had ever seen, or he was too dim to realise how brazenly Miss Lamourette had been flirting with him. As impossible as it seemed, knowing Stokes, it was probably the latter.

"Thank you," said Alfie. "But I'm for bed myself."

Miss Lamourette's attention immediately switched to him. "Allow me to escort you!"

"No!" Alfie shouted. "That is... No, thank you. Perhaps you could go see what's keeping Doctor Mullins? Tell him to take his time with Stokes though, I'll just be resting."

That tidily saved him from Miss Lamourette, gave her an assignment elsewhere, and gave the Stocktons privacy.

He ignored Miss Lamourette's pout as he offered a brief farewell and fled to his room as quickly as he was able. Once there, he shut the door behind him and just leaned against it for several minutes catching his breath.

Finally, the call of the bed was too irresistible to ignore. He was just pulling off his waistcoat when there was a knock on the door. He whispered a curse. It was only a matter of time before the doctor came by to check on him, but he'd hoped Stokes would have kept him busy for a few hours more so Alfie could nap.

He looked at the bed forlornly. "Come in."

"Oh, Lord Crawford, I have a treat for you!"

"Miss Lamourette!" Alfie clutched his waistcoat to his chest to protect his modesty. Despite the fact he was still wearing his shirt, it was unseemly for her to see him any less than completely dressed. And of course, there was the fact they were in his bedchamber together, alone. Lord, if Dominick got back and found out Alfie had been backed into some sort of engagement, he'd never forgive him.

"Oh, don't be that way," she said, giving him a coquettish giggle. "It's all perfectly innocent. I only came by to give you these. They're why I came upstairs in the first place, but when I realised you'd be some time, I went to check on our other patient instead."

She pulled a bouquet of flowers from behind her back. Where she'd been hiding them before, Alfie wouldn't guess.

"Every sick room should have at least a few flowers. I chose these specifically for you. Don't these blue ones match your eyes just perfectly?"

Alfie didn't know which blue ones she was referring to, nor did he care. Rather than artfully arranged, the bouquet was a collection of as many different types of flowers as could be thrown together at once. Big blue ones, small blue ones, all mixed in haphazardly with drooping reds and clusters of tiny whites. But that was irrelevant. All that mattered was that he was partially undressed in his bedroom with an unmarried woman who was giving him flowers.

"I very much appreciate the sentiment, Miss Lamourette, and the trouble you must have gone through, but I really must insist."

He gestured towards the door. In response, she thrust the flowers at him, more forcefully this time. With a sigh, he took them with the hand not holding his waistcoat and gave them a polite sniff.

"Very lovely, thank you. Now if you would please leave so I can undre—that is, I'm quite tired and would like to rest a bit before Doctor Mullins comes to see me."

"Oh, I'm sure Stokes will keep him occupied for some time yet. Mrs. Stockton is with him too, if you were worried about us being seen dishabille."

That was exactly what Alfie was worried about. He set the flowers on the table with his empty breakfast tray, and turned his back on her to pull his waistcoat and coat back on. He could solve that problem at least, then work on the solution of how to get her out of here without anyone seeing. Lord, he'd joked with Dominick earlier about her already having the banns read, now he was starting to grow concerned.

"Of course," she went on, "perhaps it is a bit improper now that I think about it. Forgive me, it's my Gallic blood you see. I hear on the continent they're much less prudish about these sorts of things. I apologise. It's only that I did so enjoy our conversation on the terrace earlier."

"I did too," said Alfie warily. "It was nice to meet both you and your brother. Perhaps once I'm better we can all meet again. All of us. Together. But unfortunately, now is not that time."

He wasn't sure he could make his message any clearer without outright saying, "Go away, you brazen trollop." From the way she beamed at him, she was either being deliberately dim or was the most obtuse woman he'd ever met. Unlike Stokes, however, this time Alfie didn't believe it was the latter for a moment.

"Yes, I would so love that!" she exclaimed. "I do wish you were better already. It's such a shame you're stuck here. You're missing out on a lovely tour. Mr. Trent is quite fortunate as Bath is such a marvellous city. Perhaps once you've recovered, I could take you around myself. And not just the city, the lands surrounding us have some of the most beautiful views. Why, there's the most charming folly that I'd absolutely love to show you."

Alfie almost laughed. She was inviting him to "view the folly" exactly as Jarrett had offered to "show Dominick the chapel" or the way Alfie himself often asked Dominick if he'd like to "visit the library". Or the gymnasium. Or Alfie's bed. Or... well, quite a few places now that he thought about it.

He tried to brush those thoughts from his mind. Getting a cockstand now was about the only thing that could make this moment more incriminating.

"Thank you for your offer, but I'm afraid that even once I'm better, I have a leg injury that precludes me from country walks." He tapped his injured leg, which was just as tired as the rest of him. If she didn't leave soon, he'd likely collapse onto the bed anyway. He dreaded to imagine what sort of invitation she might see that as.

"Oh, you poor thing!"

To Alfie's horror, Miss Lamourette reached out, her hands low with the apparent intention to get them on his leg. He skirted around her and made for the door. If she wouldn't leave the room, at least he could. But his retreat was cut off when he collided with someone in the doorway.

"Mrs. Stockton!" Miss Lamourette giggled. "I didn't see you there! I expected you to still be with your dear husband. Doctor Mullins said he was much improved, I hope? He certainly seemed so earlier."

There was a moment where Alfie wasn't sure if Mrs. Stockton was going to scream at him for having an unmarried woman in his room or at Miss Lamourette for being in the room with an unmarried man. His heart sank. This is what Miss Lamourette had wanted all along. She'd been dragging out leaving in the hopes that someone—anyone—would catch her alone with an earl. Her shameless display with Stokes earlier must have only been a distraction, or possibly, she'd planned all along to aggravate Mrs. Stockton, so that when the opportunity came to get Miss Lamourette away from her husband for good, she wouldn't turn a blind eye.

If Mrs. Stockton or Miss Lamourette's family insisted he do the right thing to protect her virtue, what would he do? Obviously, he couldn't marry her. Not for a thousand reasons, Dominick being the most obvious and best of them all. But neither could he withstand the scrutiny such a scandal might bring. His and Dominick's relationship, his earldom, by God, his entire *life* could only continue as long as no one looked too closely at it. But being caught with a marquis' daughter? How could he have been so stupid?

He looked at Mrs. Stockton in horror, ready to plead with her not to say anything. He'd offer her anything she wanted to keep quiet, to save the beautiful, wonderful, fragile life he and Dominick had built together.

But she wasn't looking at him at all. Instead, her eyes were fixed on his bedside table.

"Are those from my garden?"

"Oh, I know I should've asked." Miss Lamourette tittered. "But you were so busy helping Lord Crawford earlier, I didn't want to disturb you. I was just delivering them now when you walked in."

Mrs. Stockton looked on the brink of tears. Alfie didn't know a buttercup from a butterfly, but she clearly cared about her garden. He couldn't imagine how hurt she must be that someone had defaced it without a second thought.

Her pain was clear enough that even Miss Lamourette faltered.

"Oh dear," she said, her voice honest now in a way it hadn't been during all of her flirtations. "Oh, Cordelia, I wasn't thinking. What have I done? I'm so sorry. I don't even know how to apologise for this."

Mrs. Stockton collected herself, taking a deep breath. "Don't apologise. I suppose what's done is done. I'm just a little overwrought."

"Of course you are." Miss Lamourette rushed past Alfie without even looking at him and helped Mrs. Stockton into a chair. "Is Stokes going to be all right? What did the doctor say?"

"He'll be fine," Mrs. Stockton said, still looking at the flowers. "I was so afraid I would lose him. But it'll all be all right."

There was a knock on the open door, and Alfie looked away from the two women to see Doctor Mullins standing in the doorway.

"Not to eavesdrop," the doctor said. "But let me reassure you all that Mr. Stockton really will be just fine. All he needs is bedrest. Which I believe is what I prescribed for you as well, my lord."

Alfie tried to force a smile, still too shaken by his narrow escape moments before. He was sorry for Mrs. Stockton's pain, but thank God she cared more about her flowers than Miss Lamourette's honour. Now with both her and Doctor Mullins as chaperones, he felt a bit safer.

"Yes, I'm not very good at bedrest, I'm afraid. I was going to take another nap but..."

Fortunately, he didn't have to say any more. Doctor

Mullins gave him a commiserating look. "Well, sit down at least. We'll leave you to rest in a moment, but I thought you'd want to hear what I've found out about the poison."

Mrs. Stockton and Miss Lamourette both gasped.

"Did someone else die?" asked Miss Lamourette.

Doctor Mullins gave her a comforting smile. "Fortunately, no. I sent a note to a colleague of mine and he has been testing the water from the fountain both scientifically and by giving it to a number of stray dogs. All of whom are still barking and enjoying what was going to be my Sunday roast as a reward. If possible, he would like to take some samples of, ah—"

He caught himself and looking away from the two women, cleared his throat. "Some samples from Lord Boyle's body to be tested for poison. It is still my firm belief that he *was* poisoned, as his sudden symptoms match no natural ailment I know, but that will take some time. However, it seems we can rest assured that no one else was poisoned. And certainly not from the fountain. Lord Crawford, I do apologise for the extensive and, it now appears, unnecessary treatments."

"It's quite all right, doctor." Alfie said, not entirely sure how much he meant it. "I'm glad you took action even if none was needed. If the water had been poisoned, a little bloodletting and an unpleasant night would've been the least of my worries. Do you have any idea of where the poison came from instead? Perhaps something else he ate at the soiree? Or even earlier in the evening? Could someone have tampered with his dinner?"

At his words, the room fell into a chilly silence. Doctor Mullins was tight-lipped and the two women's expressions were stony.

"What are you implying?" Miss Lamourette asked.

"Nothing," said Alfie, confused. "I was only asking—"

"We all had dinner at the Lamourettes' home that night," Mrs. Stockton said softly. "Charles, myself, Doctor Mullins, *and* Batty."

And now Alfie had just accidentally accused one or all of them of poisoning him. Wonderful.

"I'm so sorry," he stammered. "I didn't know. I certainly don't mean to say…"

"It's because we're French, isn't it?" Miss Lamourette said. Her heated passion of a few minutes before was now icy. "Never mind that my father fled here from the revolution, or that my brother and I were born here. The foreigners must have poisoned him, is that it?"

She rose. "I have to go. I have some errands to run before heading home. And of course, I'll need to make sure the kitchen knows there'll be someone else for dinner. Unless you believe something dreadful will happen to him too?"

Dominick.

Alfie tried to swallow back his panic. He hadn't meant anything by it, but what if one of the Lamourettes *had* poisoned Batty's food? Dominick had no idea of the danger he was walking into. And Alfie had no way to warn him.

"Perhaps I could join you for dinner as well," he said quickly.

Yes, that would work. He'd intercept Dominick before the meal was served, say he felt unwell and insist Dominick take him back to the Stocktons. Perfect.

"Absolutely not!" Doctor Mullins cried. "You won't be

going anywhere but that bed! You might not have been poisoned, my lord, but you are weak."

"If you are so worried about your cousin, I'd be happy to take him a note," Miss Lamourette offered.

Alfie hesitated. On one hand, he desperately wanted to warn Dominick. On the other hand, he wasn't sure he trusted her not to throw it on the fire. Or even worse, read it herself. As tired as he was, he didn't know if he could keep his words in check and if he wrote something that seemed a bit *too* concerned with Dominick's well-being, then the best he could hope for was that she'd be offended Alfie thought she was a poisoner. At worst, he'd draw attention to them and she might start to wonder who this mysterious "cousin" of his really was.

Actually, no. At worst, she really was the poisoner and would take her ire out on Dominick if Alfie accused her.

"I'm sure it's nothing," he said, suddenly exhausted. "I'm so tired that I don't know what I'm saying."

Her mood softened in an instant. "Oh, you poor man, of course you don't. I promise I'm not offended. Gallic blood, just like I was telling you. We're a very passionate people. You rest, and don't worry about Mr. Trent. I promise I'll keep an eye on him all night."

She gave him a wink. Then with a laugh, she was saying her farewells and was out the door. The rest of them were all held in stunned silence.

"I'll let you have your privacy with the doctor," Mrs. Stockton said after a moment. She got up and picked the bouquet off the table, cradling it delicately. "And I'll find some water to put these in."

When the door closed behind her, Doctor Mullins let

out a low whistle. "Gallic blood, eh? Not to speak ill of such a highborn lady, but sometimes I'm very glad to be nothing more than a lowly doctor and beneath Miss Lamourette's notice. Just to be safe though, please don't tell her I'm unmarried."

"Would it make a difference?" Alfie asked wearily.

Doctor Mullins chuckled. "Perhaps not. But I'd rather not risk it. Now, let me take a quick look at you and then I promise I'll let you sleep. I'm aching for my own bed too."

After the brief examination, the doctor warned Alfie to be careful not to overexert himself the next few days and to send word if he began to feel unwell.

"One last thing," Doctor Mullins said as he headed out the door. "You might want to lock this behind me, in case Miss Lamourette returns!"

Alfie nodded, but did no such thing. Instead, he sat on the edge of the bed, catching himself every time he started to nod off, worrying and waiting for Dominick to walk through the door.

CHAPTER 12

For a nest of vipers, the Lamourettes' home was quite pleasant.

The furnishings lay somewhere between the worn-in comforts of Balcarres and the painfully modern Stockton home; the furniture was comfortable, and the decorations didn't hurt Dominick's eyes. There were more figurines of shepherdesses and paintings of countrysides than he'd choose for himself, but as far as the homes of aristos went, he rather liked it.

He hadn't realised until he'd left the Stockton house how pervasive the smell of the garden was there, the scent of flowers pleasant but a little overwhelming. The marquis' home smelled of tobacco and the roast duck they'd had for dinner, but nothing else.

The meal itself had been an odd affair. Miss Lamourette was in fine form, flirting with him throughout, but not nearly as aggressively as she had with Alfie. Either he was right about the smell of horse or he wasn't worth her best work as only a *cousin* to an earl.

Monsieur Henri's mood had improved since they'd returned from their ride, but there was still an air of tension about him that Dominick didn't like. Fortunately, he seemed to be using most of this restless energy to bicker with his sister, which served the double purpose of occupying him and distracting her from Dominick. This left Dominick free to converse with their father instead.

"Thank you for the lovely meal," Dominick said as a servant whisked away the last of his plates. "I'm only sorry Lord Crawford wasn't well enough to join us."

"I'm sure Mrs. Stockton is taking superb care of both him and the sickly Stokes," Monsieur Courtanvaux replied. The hiss of his accent made Dominick think once again of snakes. The Lamourettes hadn't done anything to him yet, but there was only so much he could be hissed at and not begin to worry.

A second servant came around carrying a silver box.

"Cigar, Monsieur Trent?" asked the marquis.

"Not for me, thank you. But if you're having a glass of port or some such, I'd be happy to join you."

"Ah, we have something I believe you will enjoy even more."

Monsieur Courtanvaux waved a hand and a bottle containing an amber liquid was produced. To Dominick's surprise, everyone was poured a glass, including Miss Lamourette. The only fancy parties Dominick attended had so far both ended in murders, so he wasn't entirely certain, but he thought ladies were supposed to leave the table after a dinner party so they could chat amongst themselves while the men did the same. However, since Miss Lamourette was the only lady present, he supposed it didn't make much sense to make her sit in a room by herself.

The marquis raised his glass. "*Vive le roi!*"

Dominick didn't speak French, but he saluted the toast anyway. The drink was uncommonly good, tasting of fruit and something almost like treacle, which he couldn't identify but thoroughly enjoyed. He took another sip.

"Armagnac," said Monsieur Courtanvaux with a sigh. "Only produced on a handful of vineyards in France. Do you know, the first time I had Armagnac was at the court of Versailles?"

Dominick replied the way he always did when rich people began talking about places he'd never heard of. "I'm afraid I've never been."

The Lamourettes all laughed.

"Oh, Mr. Trent, you are too much!" Miss Lamourette squealed.

"You English are all the same, you know nothing of the world outside your own little island," sneered Monsieur Henri.

Dominick wanted to ask him where he'd gone to get his worldly education, wagering good money the answer was Oxford or Cambridge, but he held his tongue.

"I mean the court of King Louis XVI at the palace of Versailles," Monsieur Courtanvaux said kindly. "A lifetime ago now, but I'll never forget that first taste. It was offered to me at a party held by Queen Marie Antoinette herself. She told me she and her *Dame du Palais* had a glass every night before bed."

"You've met a queen?" Dominick was impressed. Alfie said he'd seen the Prince Regent at a distance once, but that wasn't nearly as exciting as a real queen.

Monsieur Courtanvaux's eyes twinkled. "More than met her, for a number of years I considered her a very dear friend."

Both the younger Lamourettes groaned.

"Not this again," muttered Monsieur Henri.

"Yes, papa, I'm sure Mr. Trent would be far more interested in things going on now, not before he was even born. Did you hear, they've opened a shopping street in London with a roof over it, so you can buy all of the finest items even in the worst of weather? What a marvel! Did you visit it while you were in town, Mr. Trent?"

"I'm afraid not," Dominick said politely, leaving out the more sordid details of what he'd been up to instead. Then he turned back to Monsieur Courtanvaux. "What was she like?"

The marquis put a hand to his heart. He wasn't nearly as done up now as he'd been at the soiree. While he still wore a wig, his face was unpowdered and the expression on it was wistful. "So many unkind things I'd heard said about the queen, but the moment she spoke I knew they were all vicious lies. Monsieur Trent, if you ever meet a woman a tenth as beautiful, charming, and spirited as her, you may consider yourself lucky. To know her was to love her."

"Clearly not everyone in France agreed," muttered Monsieur Henri.

Monsieur Courtanvaux ignored his son. "Her husband, Louis XVI, I also met, but did not know nearly as well. He was a fine king, of course, but in person you almost forgot he was in the room, especially if Madame was there.

"Ah, she truly was splendid. And the palace itself, never have I seen a woman more suited to a place. Alas, for once I must agree with my son and find England lacking. For never in my many years here have I found any place that compares. I could tell you of chandeliers lit with a hundred candles each and draped in the purest crystal, ballrooms that stretched into the infinite with silver mirrors and windows wrapped in gold, gardens you could wander for days and never take the same path twice, and everywhere, art. Paintings and watercolours and sculptures, all created by the finest artists of the last several centuries, all in one gleaming palace. And even if I tell you all this, even if you picture it in your mind, it will still not be as beautiful as the real palace."

Dominick had to believe the marquis was exaggerating. It sounded like something out of a fairy tale he'd told Alfie when they were children. *Once upon a time, there was a beautiful queen who lived in a golden castle…*

"And now his brother, King Louis XVIII, leaves it to rot." Monsieur Henri threw back the last of his glass. "What the revolution could not destroy he allows to decay. I speak not only of Versailles, but all of France."

At his son's words, Monsieur Courtanvaux slammed his palm against the table. Whatever they said to each other next made Dominick glad he didn't speak French.

"You mustn't mind them." Miss Lamourette took the opportunity to slide her chair closer to Dominick's. "Really, if they thought about why they were arguing, I doubt they'd do it at all. My father misses his country as he remembers it and my brother and I grew up on his tales of court. So, now Henri has strong feelings about how the current government in France is failing, all because they cannot build a country that lives up to childhood stories."

"Couldn't you go back?" Dominick had to ask. He tried to remember what little he knew of French history. There had always been too many problems of his own for him to worry much about what was happening outside Spitalfields, never mind on some bloody continent he'd never see.

"The revolution is over," he said hesitantly, "and Napoleon is gone. If France has a king again, why don't you all just go live there? Go back to your father's... marquisdom."

She smiled. "Have you ever returned somewhere you thought you knew and found it changed? Or rather, yourself changed so much you no longer belonged?"

Her words struck closer to home than she could possibly know.

"That is what it's like for my father. He would rather live in his memories. As for Henri and I, we were born in England. Our mother, God rest her, was English. My brother may feel tied to France, but I do not. I have no interest in going there when there are already so many interesting people in England."

With this she gave Dominick a coy smile, but he was saved from replying by the marquis and his son switching back to English.

"Forgive my son, Monsieur Trent. He forgets that family discussions should be kept amongst family and not discomfort our guests."

Monsieur Henri rolled his eyes and got up to snatch the bottle of Armagnac from the sideboard where the servant had left it. He poured himself another glass, leaving the bottle on the table, almost within Dominick's reach but not quite.

They were all seated around the head of the long dining table. While it was nice to not have to shout down the length of it to carry on a conversation, between Miss Lamourette moving her chair steadily closer to his throughout the meal, and now being in the midst of the argument between father and son, the dining room was beginning to feel quite cramped. Another glass of Armagnac might have eased that, or at least made him feel better about it.

He cast about for anything to change the subject. "You have a lovely home."

"Thank you for your kind words," said the marquis. "It is nothing like the château I had in France, but it was fine enough for Louis XVIII. I did not say anything earlier, but you now sit in the same chair in which the current king of France sat when he dined with us."

Dominick's arse had been a lot of interesting places, but none of them as elevated as this. He fought back the urge to wriggle deeper into his seat. He couldn't even pretend not to be struck by the revelation. Royal buttocks had once warmed where his buttocks now warmed.

"Really?"

Monsieur Courtanvaux smiled broadly, pleased to have made such an impression on his audience. "Indeed, just a few years ago. He dined with us in 1814 on his way back home to be crowned. It was a wonderful evening, and an advantageous one for me as well. Many of his servants did not wish to make the voyage back, so now, every day I eat French meals cooked by a French chef, and when I wake up in the morning, my valet wishes me good morning in the language of my home."

Dominick froze. His ring fixed him in place like an anchor from its chain around his neck.

"You have French servants," he whispered.

Could this truly be the home the maid in London had been trying to direct him to? Did one of the servants who worked here know something about his family? A small voice inside him, long buried, spoke up. *Is my mother here?*

"They were the smart ones," Monsieur Henri muttered dismissively. "Why bother returning to a broken France and not fix it. Louis XVIII is no more than a puppet king. He lasted less than a year on the throne before fleeing Napoleon in the night, then let you English fight his battles for him. And now that he's returned? No punishments for Napoleon's followers. My father's lands still lie in the hands of the revolutionaries who took them, while Louis XVIII calls those usurpers his council, not admitting they still hold the power, not him. What point is there in restoring a king in name only?"

"You forget yourself, Henri." Monsieur Courtanvaux's tone was severe. "We were compensated for my lands. Louis XVIII made sure of that. We have a good life here, and I am far too old to deal with that nonsense."

Monsieur Henri made a rude noise. "You believe we should just accept things as they are?"

"What would you prefer? You want to execute Louis XVIII the way the revolutionaries executed his brother? His brother's wife and children?" Monsieur Courtanvaux stopped, a look of anguish on his face.

All those people he was talking about being executed, he'd known them. He'd called Marie Antoinette a dear friend just minutes ago. They'd all met their end on the guillotine. As French nobility, the marquis must have been lucky to escape with his life. How many of his friends from that golden court could say the same? Or how few?

"I know what follows the killing of a king," the marquis said tiredly. "I would not see it again. Better now to have a king, if an imperfect one, than to see France fall back into the hands of the unwashed masses."

As an unwashed mass, Dominick should probably be offended, but he was too busy trying to come up with a way to bring the conversation back around to the Lamourettes' French servants and finding some way to talk to them.

Meanwhile, a truce seemed to have been declared between father and son. Monsieur Henri passed his father the Armagnac bottle with a nod.

Miss Lamourette caught Dominick's eye. "See, they are just the same."

"Another glass, Monsieur Trent?" offered the marquis.

Dominick eagerly assented. He pushed his glass over, but when the Monsieur Courtanvaux tipped his hand to pour the bottle, something caught Dominick's eye.

On the marquis' hand were several rings, but one in particular stood out. It was a thick band of gold carved into a design with a single small emerald embedded in it. He only had a moment to look at it, but he didn't need more than that. He'd looked at the same design every day for years, run his fingers over it until it had all but worn away. Even now, that same design rested over his heart. It was a bird, its wings spread in flight. The two designs, one in cheap pewter, the other in shining gold, were exactly the same.

My ring.

From the marquis' hand, the golden version of his bird winked at him with its emerald eye.

CHAPTER 13

It was nearly midnight when Alfie awoke to the sound of the front door opening and the murmur of low voices as one of the Stocktons' servants greeted the late arrival. He unfolded himself from the library chair in which he'd spent the last several hours dozing while pretending to read, and prayed the late arrival was Dominick. He didn't let himself consider the more terrible option, that it was Doctor Mullins coming to tell them there'd been another poisoning.

To his relief, when he peered over the first-floor railing, he was met with the sight of Dominick handing his overcoat to the butler and wishing him a good night. However, rather than head immediately up the stairs, Dominick waited for the butler to depart, then let out a heavy sigh. Even from the upper floor, Alfie could see his shoulders slump the moment he thought he was alone.

"Everything all right?"

Alfie spoke softly to keep from waking up the rest of the house, but Dominick still started at the noise, glancing around wildly. Alfie raised a hand to catch his attention.

"You should be in bed." Dominick grumbled.

"Couldn't sleep," Alfie lied, deciding that was the more socially appropriate option than falling into his arms with relief. However, crying and thanking God Dominick was alive still remained a possibility. "We need to talk. Join me in the library for a nightcap?"

As Dominick climbed the stairs, Alfie could finally make out his features well enough to tell there was something deeply troubling him.

"Don't think I can sit still," Dominick said. "I don't suppose you're feeling well enough for a walk?"

"At this hour?" Whatever was troubling Dominick must be especially disquieting if he was trying to get Alfie to ignore doctor's orders.

"I found a billiard room earlier," he offered instead of a walk that would end with him tripping into the gutter. "Do you play?"

Dominick nodded. "There was a table at one of the pubs in Sp—" he cut himself off. Just because the house was quiet didn't mean there weren't listening ears.

"Let's discuss it in the billiard room," Alfie said softly. "It's this way."

The billiard room matched the rest of the house: modern, fashionable, and with vases of flowers on every flat surface except for the billiard table itself. If they were playing a proper game, he would've called for one of the servants to iron out the baize, but with the mood Dominick was in, he doubted they'd even be keeping score.

Alfie closed the door behind them and was frustrated to see it had no lock. They'd have to be careful in case some servant doing late night rounds came in, but at least they had a little privacy. He lit some extra lamps so they could actually see what they were doing.

Dominick paced around the table like a caged tiger, pulling the three ivory balls out of their pockets and rolling them around, their quiet clacks as they struck each other the only sound in the room.

"Cues or maces?" Asked Alfie, plucking one of each from the rack on the wall.

"Cues."

Unsurprising. Playing properly, maces were mostly used by women, but he had no idea what rules they played by in the hells where Dominick had learned. He returned the mace to its place and picked up another cue stick for himself.

"Shall we play to see who goes first or just—"

"Alfie, I don't give a fuck."

"We can always just sit and talk."

"I'll go first."

Alfie passed him a cue. Dominick potted the red ball in his first shot, then his own cue ball in his second, taking his time to replace each one back on the table carefully. He managed a run of four shots in all before finally missing.

"How many points do you want to play to?" Alfie doubted Dominick cared, but it was easier to ask than it was to voice the worries that had kept him up, or to tease out whatever was bothering Dominick.

Dominick shrugged. "I just need to do something while we talk. My mind was going in circles on the ride back."

"I'd offer you my usual distraction," said Alfie lowly, "but the door doesn't lock." As he went to line up his shot, he brushed closely past Dominick despite the roominess of the space.

That seemed to be enough to shake Dominick from at least some of his odd mood. He huffed out a laugh. "Another time, love. All right, I've had a... peculiar evening, but you said we needed to talk right when I walked in. You go first."

"Are you sure?" Alfie lined up a shot.

"Go ahead," Dominick replied, right as Alfie's cue made contact with the ball. Damned unsportsmanly, but Alfie was still able to pull off a losing hazard. He reset his ball and lined up his next shot. "It turns out, the Stocktons *and* Batty dined at the Lamourettes' house the night of the poisoning. I might have been a bit concerned you weren't coming back tonight."

Dominick grinned. "You were fretting."

Alfie scored a winning hazard this time, and motioned Dominick to set the red ball back where it belonged. "A bit concerned."

"You *were* fretting. Mrs. Stockton did say something to the Lamourettes at the soiree about dinner, but I didn't even think about Lord Boyle. Christ, that's why you're still up isn't it? Did you sleep at all while I was gone?"

"A bit," Alfie lied. "Doctor Mullins was there as well. Remember his talk about having one final cigar?"

"You think that's where the poisoning actually happened? Not at the soiree?"

Alfie missed his next shot. "It's possible. At least it gives us something else to look at. I doubt the magistrates are going to come up with it."

Dominick hummed and surveyed the table. Then he came around to Alfie's side and bumped him out of the way with his hip. "Any word from the magistrate or coroner while I was out?"

It took Alfie a moment to answer. Dominick must have changed into his riding clothes at the hotel. The way the tight buckskin clung to him was distracting at the best of times, but now as he leaned over the billiard table, the tails of his coat fell to either side, framing his muscular arse like the masterpiece it was.

"What? Oh, um, no. No one. I wouldn't expect them either. Most likely they'll spend time they should be investigating smoothing feathers instead, reassuring all of Bath's great and good that there's nothing to fear, while not actually doing anything to make that so."

"In fairness, we still only have Doctor Mullin's word that he was poisoned," Dominick pointed out.

Alfie was surprised. "You think he's wrong?"

Dominick shrugged. "For all we know, Doctor Mullins might be well-connected but incompetent. After all, no one else died, and it's not surprising a man of Batty's size and drinking habits might suddenly pass away. I'm sure the magistrate is thinking the same thing."

"That's true," Alfie said slowly. "But as loath as I am to listen to a doctor, until we know otherwise, we should trust the medical man's opinion and assume he's correct."

"Which means if anyone's going to find Batty's poisoner, it'll be us. Wonderful." Dominick took his shot. "And now you suspect the Lamourettes?"

Dominick walked to the other side of the table for his next shot. Alfie followed as if he was on a lead. When Dominick bent over again, he craned his neck for a better view.

Good Lord. His fingers twitched against the cue.

"I didn't say it was them. I said Batty had dinner at their house and then died of poisoning a few hours later. It might mean nothing, but you must admit it's suspicious.

Speaking of which, did you notice how agitated Mrs. Stockton got when we asked to use Stokes' study earlier? Highly suspicious to me."

"Or perhaps she just didn't trust us not to steal her husband's pocketbook while we were in there. She certainly spotted you as the shifty character you are."

Dominick missed his next shot, and Alfie moved past him, allowing his fingers to trail over those tempting buttocks for just the briefest moment. Dominick gave him an odd look, as if he was unsure if he'd felt anything or just imagined it.

"Perhaps," Alfie admitted. "But I, for one, find it shiftier that a man's closest friend dies and while he's still abed, his wife stops anyone from going to the one place where he might keep incriminating documents. Almost as if she's covering for him."

He lined up his first shot.

"I still say it's because you're shifty," Dominick said, again, just as Alfie took the shot. That time it was clearly a deliberate distraction. Very well, if he wanted a war, a war he would have.

Alfie moved around to Dominick's side for his next shot, making sure to lean over the table more than was strictly necessary. He even threw in a small wriggle as he settled into position and was rewarded by Dominick's sharp intake of breath.

"What about you?" Alfie asked. If he hit his ball at just the right angle, he might be able to sink all three. "You came in here like a cat that's been chased by a pack of hounds. Did you learn anything at the Lamourettes' house?"

"I think Monsieur Courtanvaux is my father."

Alfie's cue ball leapt off the table with the force of his hit and rolled under a sideboard.

"What? And you let me natter on instead of saying anything? What makes you so certain?"

Dominick shrugged and went to retrieve the ball. "That was a forfeit by the way. It's my turn. And I'm not certain, but he had a ring that was the spitting image of mine, except made of gold."

Alfie listened in stunned silence as Dominick recounted his day with the Lamourettes, skimming through his ride with Monsieur Henri but relaying every moment of the small dinner party. He was too shocked to even manage to grope Dominick the few times he passed by between shots.

"That's all of it I can remember," Dominick said finally. "I might have gotten a bit confused with some of the French business, there were a lot of Louises involved. But the gist is, a French servant saw my ring and told us to go to Bath, and now we're in Bath, and there's a French marquis and he's got my ring, only fancy. Your turn, by the way."

Alfie shook his head. If he was honest, he'd never expected Dominick to actually find his family. Too much time had passed and surely if they were still alive, they'd have taken Dominick back as soon as they could. The idea of abandoning him by choice was unbelievable. When he and Dominick had been torn apart as children, Alfie had cried for weeks. Now that he had Dominick back, he would never let such a thing happen again.

And if the marquis *was* Dominick's father and had been living in luxury the whole time Dominick had been suffering in the workhouse and then on his own in Spitalfields? If that turned out to be the case, Alfie wasn't sure they'd be leaving Bath without another murder.

"I said, 'It's your turn.' Alfie? Are you all right?" Dominick walked over with a worried look. Alfie immediately dropped his cue on the table and wrapped him in a hug.

Dominick stiffened momentarily, then wrapped his arms around Alfie too. Gently at first, then almost too tight. He buried his face in Alfie's neck and dug his fingers in his coat—a drowning man clinging desperately to something that might save him.

After several minutes, Dominick stepped back.

"What the servants would have thought of that," he said ruefully.

"They can go to the devil," Alfie replied. He reached up and brushed a strand of hair back from Dominick's face, not willing to abandon their closeness just yet. "What are you going to do next?"

Dominick shrugged. "Confront him, I suppose? Or at least find out if it's true. It could be a coincidence. I was invited to come calling again tomorrow, I guess I'll find out then."

"I was going to suggest we go to the abbey tomorrow and start going through church records since we weren't having much luck elsewhere, but I suppose there's no point in wasting our time now. A French man of the right age to be your father with the same sort of ring? They don't make coincidences that large."

Alfie frowned. "Wait. Nick, how old are you again?"

Dominick hummed. "If the workhouse guessed I was

born late 1789 or early 1790 then... Give me a moment... Christ, I'm nearly thirty."

Alfie tried to remember what little he knew of French history. "And you said the marquis came here fleeing the revolution? I think that was about the same time. He might have fathered you right after he arrived, or brought you over with him."

"Then why didn't he keep me?"

Alfie had never heard Dominick sound so small. His heart ached. With a glance over at the door, he pulled Dominick into another hug, and even risked pressing a kiss against his cheek. "I don't know, but we'll be damned sure to ask tomorrow. I have several other questions to put to that man as well."

"You'll come with?"

If Alfie's heart hurt before from the pain in Dominick's voice, it was in absolute agony now.

"Of course, I will. What kind of cad would I be to make you go through this alone? I look out for you. You look out for me. Same as it's always been, right?"

"Right. I love you, Alfie."

"I love you too, Nick." Alfie kissed him again. "Now come along, before I do something that will really shock the servants."

Dominick stepped back again, but at least he was able to manage a small laugh.

A companionable silence fell over them for a few minutes while Alfie took his turn. He was getting into the rhythm of the game, sinking pot after pot, but not so absorbed he didn't miss the opportunity to touch Dominick or pose proactively when the shot allowed it.

He heard Dominick make a contemplative noise and lifted his cue so the cheating bugger couldn't make him scratch again. "Yes?"

"It occurs to me, there's an upside to me being the marquis' son."

"Unconscionable wealth and a title of your own when he dies?"

"Better than that. Miss Lamourette will focus her attentions elsewhere when she finds out I'm her brother. At least, hopefully."

Alfie choked. "Nick!"

Dominick grinned. "That still leaves you in the cannon fire, though. I can even give her brotherly advice on the best ways to woo you."

"You're disgusting and a disgrace. I don't know why I associate with you."

"Must be my substantial charms. Speaking of, you can cannon my ball off the red one into the same pocket if you hit it right."

Alfie frowned down at the table. "No, I can't."

"It's tricky, but possible. Here, I'll show you. Line up to hit the red one into the far corner."

Alfie did as he was told, then a moment later a warm heavy weight was draped across his back.

"Nick," he hissed.

"Nothing for the servants to notice here, just one man helping another man with his... billiards." Dominick whispered in his ear, his voice sending shivers down Alfie's spine. His long arms wrapped around Alfie, warm hands settling over his so they were both gripping the cue. Then Dominick twisted their hands on the stick in a way that was both familiar and deeply obscene.

"Nick," he warned again, even though his heart wasn't really in it. Indeed, his heart seemed to be having trouble beating regularly, likely caused by all his blood heading rapidly southward.

"Relax," said Dominick. "It's not a difficult game. First you have to make sure you have a firm grip on your stick. Then it's just a matter of lining up to the right pocket."

Dominick pressed his hips forward against Alfie's buttocks to illustrate the point, leaving no doubt as to the pocket his stick was aiming for. He also wasn't exaggerating the substantialness of his charms. Even through their layers of clothes, Alfie could tell he was hard.

Alfie's eyes fluttered shut, the feeling of Dominick's warmth surrounding him at once comforting and overwhelming. Traces of shaving soap and the smell of horse mixed with Dominick's natural scent. Alfie took a deep breath, filling his lungs. Without thinking, he shifted back to feel Dominick's cock push against his arse.

Dominick's breath tickled the shell of his ear. His voice was unfairly deep and husky. "Once you're lined up, it's simply a matter of taking the shot."

Dominick surged his hips forward, making Alfie groan. He wished desperately that they could continue this somewhere with far fewer clothes. The billiard table was optional, but he wasn't ruling it out. If they didn't find some place with solid walls and a door that locked soon, they'd both go mad.

By some miracle, his cue actually connected with the ball, but it only rolled forward a few inches, coming to a stop without even contacting the other two, never mind sinking them.

"You missed," Alfie said, feeling the lightest touch of lips to the back of his neck before Dominick pulled away.

"Ah well, I'm sure I'll get it next time." Dominick winked. "Or does that mean it's your turn to show me a thing or two?"

Just then, the heavy sound of feet ascending the stairs reached them. Alfie busied himself returning the cues to their rack, which had the benefit of facing him away from the door, so anyone who came in wouldn't be greeted first thing by his raging cockstand. Lord, it was honestly embarrassing the effect Dominick had on him.

As they listened to see if the footsteps would come any closer, the great clock in the downstairs hall began to chime the hour.

"Christ, is it that late already?" Dominick said. "You should've been asleep hours ago. Let me get your cane. I brought it back but left it by the front door. Then straight to bed. I need you healed up for tomorrow."

Dominick headed for the door but drew himself up as he said the last words.

The last thing Alfie wanted was for his love to spend all night fretting and worrying about their meeting tomorrow with the marquis. They couldn't even share a bed so Alfie could ensure he slept, but if Dominick was going to lie awake anyway, at least he could give him something else to focus on.

"Nick?"

When he had Dominick's full attention, Alfie gestured towards the table. "That was cheating. Next time we *play*, I expect you to have come up with an adequate forfeit to make it up to me."

Feeling like a shameless wanton, Alfie slid a hand down his trousers. Dominick's eyes snapped down as the fabric outlined his erection and made very clear the sort of forfeit Alfie expected.

When Dominick looked up, his eyes were dark. "I'm sure I'll think of something. 'Night, Alfie."

"Goodnight, Nick. Sweet dreams."

CHAPTER 14

Dominick woke early the next morning. He hadn't expected to sleep much at all, but apparently worry couldn't put up much of a fight against utter exhaustion. But now that he was awake, there was no chance of him going back to sleep. Today, they were going to confront Monsieur Courtanvaux, a man who might well be his father.

It had been something he'd dreamed of his entire life, but now that the day had finally arrived, he found he kept looking for reasons for it not to be true. It had to just be nerves, surely.

He pictured the marquis' face and the face of his son, looking for any similarities to his own features. He couldn't recall the colour of the marquis' eyes, and his hair was always hidden under that damned wig. Monsieur Henri had darker colouring to both his hair and eyes than Dominick did, but that didn't necessarily mean anything if they had different mothers. He and the marquis *might* have a similar nose, but it wasn't as if Dominick had spent much time studying his own nose.

That was enough to propel him out of bed in search of a mirror. Looking into the glass, he still wasn't sure. He might be seeing only what he wanted to see, or he might be ignoring what he wanted to ignore. He'd spent his entire life wondering who his family was, what they were like, if they were still alive, and why they had abandoned him.

Up until the day he'd left the workhouse, he'd hoped they would come to take him home. But that hope had died the moment the bird ring had been put into his hand. He'd been glad Alfie had been adopted the year before, because that meant he couldn't see the way Dominick cried as he walked out of the workhouse alone, the only link to his family clutched in his fist.

He turned away from the mirror. Dwelling on the dark days that followed would do him no good. Things were better now. That was what mattered.

He dressed and got himself ready for the day. As he passed Alfie's door, he didn't risk opening it and checking on him. They had hours still until it was a proper visiting time and Alfie needed all the sleep he could get. No reason for both of them to worry themselves to bits in the interim.

What would he even say to Monsieur Courtanvaux? *Pardon me, in all your fleeing your homeland and all, I don't suppose you happened to trip and drop an infant by any chance? It might have rolled under a workhouse gate when you weren't looking, like a lost penny. Or you might have set it down and forgotten where you put it?*

If the marquis was his father, what then? Dominick had a lifetime to imagine reunions with his family, a thousand different families, a thousand different ways. But now, faced with the reality of it, he had no idea what he even wanted to happen. What excuse could possibly be good enough to make up for all the years of loneliness and pain while his father sat in Bath, throwing soirees and drinking Armagnac?

At least he'd had Alfie. That was the one bright spark in the shadow of the workhouse. He'd had Alfie. If Dominick hadn't been abandoned, they'd likely never have met.

The thought left him feeling strange. He wouldn't trade all his years with Alfie—both the terrible ones when they were children and the unspeakably good ones now—for anything. He'd accepted in the last year that risking his life to solve the occasional murder was well worth the price for keeping that brave, handsome, ridiculous man in his life. But the family who'd abandoned him wouldn't have known Alfie would turn up. For all that the workhouse had brought him the person who was the greatest joy of his life, it had also brought unforgivable misery.

And if the marquis *wasn't* his father? Perhaps the ring was merely a coincidence, or it'd been a gift from Dominick's real family, or pawned, or stolen, or any number of things that meant he had no connection to the marquis at all and no idea where to look next. Was all this searching really worth it if he knew that, one way or the other, the answers would be unhappy ones?

He shook his head. He'd have those answers soon enough. There was no use worrying himself into a state about it now, especially not on an empty stomach.

He made his way down into the breakfast room, surprised to find he wasn't the only one awake.

"Mr. Trent, good morning. I hope you're well."

"I should be saying that to you, Mr. Stockton. From what Doctor Mullins said, I didn't expect to see you up today."

Dominick wasn't a doctor by any means, but even he thought Stokes should still be in bed. The man was wrapped in a blanket with at least two different banyans underneath, one layered over the other. An untouched plate of food lay before him, and he clutched a cup in both hands as if it took all his strength to lift it.

"Stokes, please." Stokes gave him a wan smile. "And I suppose I'm as well as can be expected, considering."

"I'm sorry for your loss."

Stokes dipped his head slightly in acknowledgement. "Thank you. Batty was a dear friend. I still can't believe he's gone."

There wasn't much Dominick could say to that. When Stokes managed a sip from the cup, he took that as a sign the conversation was over and went to fill himself a plate from the sideboard. As he took a seat, he happened to glance at the cup Stokes was still holding.

"That's not more of that fountain water!"

"Indeed it is." Stokes took another sip. "Doctor Mullins informs me that Batty's… death had nothing to do with the water itself and that it's perfectly safe to drink. More than that, it's the best thing for restoring a constitution to peak health."

From the way Stokes looked even before having all the blood drained out of him, Dominick doubted his constitution had been at peak health to begin with, but it wasn't his place to judge.

"You're a braver man than me," he admitted. "I didn't want any of that stuff before all this. Pretty sure I wouldn't touch it with a barge pole now."

Stokes leaned in and his nasal voice, weakened though it was, was even more grating up close. "Well, between you and me, it seems to be about all I can keep down. I've never been much for breakfast myself, but it appears Cook hasn't taken Batty's death any better than I have."

"Lord Boyle and your cook were friends?" Dominick asked. That didn't make any sense at all. Upstairs people and downstairs people lived in such separate worlds, he'd never heard of a friendship bridging that gap. Except for Mrs. Hirkins and Alfie, but she would violently deny it if asked, probably while brandishing a spoon at Dominick with one hand and offering Alfie a plate of sweet buns with the other.

However, if the Stocktons' cook was an attractive woman, her being "friends" with Lord Boyle wasn't that unexpected. Those sorts of relationships between master and servant were all too common. In that case, Dominick's question was unforgivably rude, especially if it was true.

Fortunately, Stokes just gave a laugh that sounded practised. "No, nothing like that. What I mean is, she's still cooking as if he was liable to pop over at any moment. She's made far too much; I hope both you and Freddie are men of great appetites."

They were, but not in the way Stokes meant.

Stokes went on. "For example, take a look at this plum cake. Have you tried it?"

Dominick looked where he was pointing. The slice on Stokes' plate was completely untouched, but Dominick had cut one for himself. He took a bite.

"It's very good," he said honestly.

"Plum cake," Stokes intoned. "Is positively my favourite food in the world. It is the one thing I am willing to eat in the morning. And yet, this is the first time in years I've been able to eat it without having to guard my plate.

Because it is—was Batty's favourite as well. Cook could've made him an entire cake of his own and if my back was turned, he'd still steal mine."

Stokes looked wistful but his lips were pressed tightly together. No doubt the memories were both fond and painful. Dominick had some experience with those.

"And now, you can't even eat yours."

Stokes looked down at the slice.

"No," he said hollowly. "I can't."

Dominick knew what a man on the verge of tears sounded like. While he wouldn't begrudge Stokes for crying over his loss, Dominick didn't want to embarrass him in his own home. Hopefully, a change of topic would hold the tears back long enough for Dominick to eat his meal and make a gracious escape.

"Thank you for letting us stay with you. It seems all the good hotels are full up. Your wife gave me a tour of the garden yesterday. It's quite nice."

That seemed to bring back some of Stokes' usual mood.

"Ohhhhhh," he said, stretching the word out longer than Dominick really had patience for. "It's not just nice. It's absolutely splendid. She does all the work herself, you know. It's meant to be a secret but she tells positively everyone then swears them to secrecy. Isn't that delightful? I do love a secret everyone knows—that's the best way to keep anyone from talking about it.

"Did she show you the rest of the house? We're very proud of it. Furnished by London, decorated by Paris, as they say. I'd give you the tour myself, but I've rather tested my limits on the stairs enough for one day. I suppose that means I'm down here until after supper. Isn't that a lark?

Do have her show you the rest if she hasn't already."

Even your study? Dominick wondered. Aloud he said, "I'm afraid she hasn't had the time. After the Lamourette siblings called yesterday, I ended up spending most of the day with them."

"*Really?*" said Stokes, his tone taking on a slyness Dominick didn't like. "Which sibling took up so much of your time? The sister, I'll wager?"

Dominick saw why Alfie didn't like Stokes. It wasn't so much the things he said, but the way he said them. Dominick didn't need all his fancy lessons in manners to know that you didn't say things like that about a lady. But Stokes hadn't actually said anything at all, which made it worse. You couldn't call out a man for the things he didn't say.

"Monsieur Henri took me on a tour of Bath, then I dined with the family while Lord Crawford rested."

Or should have been resting at least.

Dominick was about ready to make his excuses to go check on Alfie again, but then he realised what a good chance for gathering information this was. Stokes knew the Lamourettes, and clearly wasn't opposed to saying—or rather, saying without saying—things that were supposed to be kept secret. Perhaps he might let slip something useful about the family.

The Lamourettes? Well, the first thing the father did after arriving in England all those years ago was abandon his child. Also, Monsieur Henri is known for slipping poison into people's drinks.

That certainly would be useful, but Dominick doubted it would be so easy.

"Do you know the Lamourettes well? You don't see many French families in this part of the world."

Stokes preened at the chance to share gossip. "Why, we've known them for absolute ages. Wonderful company. The marquis, well, you've met him. Positively fascinating, makes me wish I travelled more. I'm dying to know if all Frenchmen are that way or if he's just like that. When was the last time you saw someone in a powdered wig outside a courtroom? And his clothes! It's not as if he can't afford new styles, it must cost him even more to have those antiquated things made. His poor tailor!"

Dominick may have made an error in judgement. Now that he'd gotten Stokes started, he didn't know if he was going to be able to get him to stop. He looked over at the clock, hoping Alfie was awake and might come down to save him.

"Now, the son is a different matter entirely, but such fascinating ideas he has! Can't understand half of them, but they certainly sound exciting. And then of course there is Miss Lamourette..." Stokes' tone went knowing again. "You won't believe this, but she actually used to be meeker than a church mouse."

That startled a laugh out of Dominick. If Miss Lamourette was any animal, it was a hungry wolf.

"It's true," said a thrilled Stokes. "She used to help my wife in the garden just for the excuse to not have to go out. But then there was something of a scandal..."

"Yes, her brother mentioned something when we were riding yesterday."

Stokes looked displeased at being unable to break the salacious news himself, but quickly recovered. "Went by the folly, did you? Well, at least now you know where it is if you meet any *particular* ladies while you're in town. But yes, that was during Miss Lamourette's first season. She claims nothing actually happened, of course, and well, I'm sure we all believe her. She acted so differently afterwards though. You can see why people began to wonder.

"It was such a blow to my wife. They'd spent so much time together and I dare say they're still friends, but she'd taken the girl under her wing and it reflected badly on her. If you ask me, the girl's behaviour is all an act. She's just behaving the way everyone expects her to behave. Don't misunderstand, it's all terribly shocking and not something we as gentlemen should really be discussing, but really, we all thought her engagement to Batty would sort her out. I suppose not, now."

"She and Lord Boyle were engaged?" Dominick knew that already, but didn't want to spoil Stokes' gossiping twice in a row.

"Engaged to be engaged, I suppose you'd say. It wasn't common knowledge, but her father and Batty were working something out. It would've done wonders for Batty too.

"Are you married, Mr. Trent? You simply must try it. Matrimony really is the most marvellous concept. You get to do all—well, almost all—the same things you did as a bachelor, then you return home to find everything has been taken care of for you. I really do recommend it."

At that moment, the reason Dominick wasn't married chose to finally join the rest of the waking world.

"There you are. Good morning to you as well, Stokes. I didn't expect you to be up already." Alfie took the seat next to Dominick.

Dominick poured him a cup of tea and was adding the second spoonful of sugar when he noticed something was missing from his plate. He looked over just in time to see the rest of his slice of plum cake disappear into Alfie's mouth. He could see why Stokes was willing to indulge that behaviour from Lord Boyle while still finding it deeply annoying.

He spent an idle moment indulging in the idea of licking the taste of plums off Alfie's lip. He'd be willing to never eat another sugary treat again if it meant he could kiss the sweetness from Alfie instead. If only they were back home at Balcarres without Stokes sitting across from them.

I wonder if Batty and Stokes' relationship was actually one like ours.

He tried to push the images that brought up from his mind. He doubted it was true. After all, men *were* allowed to be close friends without going to bed with each other. A pity, they didn't know what they were missing.

But Stokes seemed genuine in his praise of marriage, which was surprisingly unfashionable of him. Or perhaps the done thing now was to be discreet about your mistresses. That made more sense than a fop like Stokes bucking convention by actually loving his wife.

At the very least, he didn't seem to be interested in men. Not only was buggery terribly unmodish, but Dominick had had enough husbands as clients to tell which ones were open to a quick fumble in the dark and which weren't. Besides, Stokes was about as sturdy as a glass figurine. A big man like Lord Boyle would've snapped him in half.

He snorted a laugh that he was barely able to cover with a cough.

"Are you all right?" asked Alfie.

"Fine. Is it time for us to call on the Lamourettes yet?"

"Almost," Alfie said, his tone serious. "Let me just have something to eat and we can go."

"Off visiting, are we?" said Stokes, rising unsteadily to his feet. "Do give them all my best. If you could do me a favour on your way out and let my wife know I'll be taking a nap in the drawing room? I'd hate to make her worry if she went upstairs and couldn't find me."

With that, he shuffled out of the room. Dominick waited until he heard the click of the drawing room door closing across the hall and not the thud of a fainting body hitting the floor. Then he got up and got himself another slice of plum cake. This one he didn't let out of his sight.

CHAPTER 15

The first time Alfie's adoptive parents, the previous Lord and Lady Crawford, had taken him to call on one of their acquaintances, Alfie had spilled tea on a priceless antique rug then been caught stuffing his pockets with sandwiches during the ensuing chaos. In his defence, at the time he'd only been out of the workhouse for a few months and seeing that much unguarded food had been too much of a temptation to ignore.

This call was shaping up to be almost as disastrous. Dominick had uttered a grand total of three words so far, to the clear confusion of their hosts. This left Alfie alone to carry such fascinating discussions of yes, the weather was fair yesterday and whether or not that might mean rain tomorrow, while Dominick hopefully worked up his courage to raise the one thing they actually wanted to discuss with the Lamourettes.

The one saving grace was that Miss Lamourette had been called away on some sort of millinery-related emergency, leaving them free to continue their conversations with her father and brother, however dull, blissfully unmolested.

"Mr. Trent told me what a lovely dinner you put on for him last night. I'm sorry to have missed it," said Alfie, when he'd fully exhausted the topic of English weather. If he had to endure the tension of waiting for Dominick to ask much longer, he was going to go mad and start stealing sandwiches again. He tried a little subtle prompting. "What was it you were telling me about the dinner?"

"It was lovely."

Another three words, doubling Dominick's total, but that still got them no closer to finding out if the marquis was his father.

Alfie understood why he might be hesitant. Dominick had wondered about his family since they'd been children; to have the moment of discovery finally upon him must be intimidating. He'd faced down men with pistols, knives, and fists larger than Alfie's head without flinching, but it seemed Dominick had finally met his match in the form of an elderly Frenchman whose wig was askew.

"I'm glad you enjoyed the meal," Monsieur Courtanvaux said with a polite but perplexed smile. "Hopefully you will be able to join us next time, Lord Crawford."

"I'd like tha—"

"Where did you get your bird ring?" Dominick's words all ran together in a confused rush.

Monsieur Courtanvaux looked somewhat taken aback at the outburst. He glanced over at his son. "Pardon?"

Dominick sat up straighter. Alfie wished he could hold his hand in support, but had to settle for sliding his foot against Dominick's under the tea table where the Lamourettes couldn't see.

"I was wondering, that is, I noticed last night, that you had a gold ring with a bird on it. Also an emerald? I was wondering where you'd gotten it."

"Ah, Monsieur Trent, you have very good eyes." The marquis seemed pleased to finally have something of interest to discuss, and if he noticed Dominick's halting manner, he was kind enough to ignore it. "This is the one you mean?"

He held out his hand. Alfie leaned forward for a better look. He'd never seen Dominick's ring when it was new, and the design on it was now worn down almost to the band, but even to his eye, it was clearly the same bird.

"Yes, that one," replied Dominick. "Where did it come from?"

"I believe you will be quite pleased by the answer. It was a gift to me from Queen Marie Antoinette herself."

"What?" cried Alfie and Dominick in unison.

"Now you've got him started," said Monsieur Henri drily. "If I have to listen to more reminisces on *the good old days*, I'm going to need something stronger than tea. Can I get you gentlemen anything?"

Alfie shook his head. Dominick didn't even seem to notice the interruption.

"I assumed it was a family heirloom," said Dominick breathlessly. "You got that from a real queen?"

Alfie couldn't even begin to guess what thoughts were racing through his head.

The marquis laughed. "A very real queen, I assure you. That is why it is one of my most prized possessions. It reminds me of my days at court, walking the gardens, discussing philosophy and the arts. Feasts every night and the exquisite balls—"

"—like nothing you've ever seen before or since." Monsieur Henri finished for him.

"Indeed." Monsieur Courtanvaux took no notice of his son's rudeness, lost in his memories. "And the lovely Madame Marie Antoinette at the centre of them all. She was very fond of games, you know, and this ring was given to me by her personally for winning an exceptionally clever puzzle. I would explain it further, so you could see how truly my brilliance deserved to be rewarded, but alas, the riddle does not translate into English."

"So, it was a prize," said Dominick. "Was it the only one of its kind?"

"*Mon Dieu*, but no. She had many made and gave them as gifts to her closest friends."

The wind went out of Dominick's sails and he sagged back into the sofa. Alfie was just as disappointed. They'd been so sure that the marquis was at least linked to Dominick's family. But now, who knew how many rings they'd have to track down, and how many had been lost forever when those closest friends had faced the guillotine.

Still, the maid in London had told them to go to Bath. There had to be something here, the coincidence was too great otherwise.

Monsieur Courtanvaux continued on, unaware of their turmoil. "*Oui*, she was very fond of birds. Song birds, hunting birds, it made no difference to her. I think… I think she was not always happy, and found the thought of a little bird flying away comforting. Or perhaps I am seeing things differently now, knowing all that came to pass. It was a very long time ago."

They all lapsed into silence at that, each left in the company of his own thoughts and the ghost of a murdered queen.

"Did she have the rings made for anyone else?" Dominick asked finally. "Perhaps ones not made of gold?"

"She did," said Monsieur Courtanvaux with a tone of surprise. "It became something of her unofficial emblem, used to mark those closest to her. Gold for her friends, courtiers, and noble ladies, and silver for her handmaids and most trusted servants."

"What about pewter?"

Alfie didn't see anything shocking in Dominick's question. It was what his ring was made of, after all, and if there were tiers of who received gold and silver rings, pewter seemed the next obvious rung down. But both Lamourettes recoiled as if they'd been slapped.

"What did you say?" whispered Monsieur Henri, his father too taken aback to speak.

Dominick sounded as confused as Alfie. "I only asked if any pewter rings had been made."

"Now there is a story!" said Monsieur Henri excitedly. Before any of them could react, he ran from the room.

The marquis was looking decidedly unwell. Alfie set his teacup on the table in case the man required assistance. "Are you all right?"

The marquis shook his head. "*Non.* That is, no, I am well. It is just... that question brought back memories I have not thought about in a long time."

Before Alfie or Dominick could question him further, Monsieur Henri returned to the room with a book clutched in his hands. "Why do you ask about a pewter ring in particular? Why not iron or brass?"

Alfie looked over at Dominick. This was his story to tell.

"I..." Dominick hesitated. "I thought I'd seen a similar

ring once, only it was made out of pewter, so it had worn down over time."

Monsieur Courtanvaux exclaimed something in startled French.

His son leaned forward eagerly. "You saw it? This ring my father has, but in pewter? Where? Here in England?"

Dominick looked uneasy. "London, probably. Does it matter?"

"Does it matter? Does it *matter*? Father, you knew Marie Antoinette. Would you tell us the story of her pewter jewels?"

Monsieur Courtanvaux did not share his son's enthusiasm for the story, but it was clear his time at Versailles had been dear to his heart. "Usually, you say you are sick of them, Henri, but now you ask me to tell my old court tales? Very well, but only because Lord Crawford and Monsieur Trent are better listeners than my children.

"As I said, Madame was not always happy in her life as a queen. They said she had a lust for expensive clothes and jewels, but the opposite was true. I believe, given the choice, she would've happily given it all up for a quiet life in the country. So much so, she had a small village built on the grounds of Versailles, and sometimes she would have her maids dress her in their clothes, and they would all pretend to be shepherdesses and washerwomen in the little village. It was a rare honour to be invited to join them. I myself was asked once and believe I made a very fine butcher.

"Of course, a queen could not be seen without her jewels, but what shepherdess wears diamonds? So she had pewter copies of her favourites made."

"Including a pewter copy of the bird ring," whispered

Dominick.

"*Oui.* If a queen could not wear her jewels, then neither could her courtiers. She had a small chest containing perfect replicas in pewter to exchange for the duration of the game.

"Oh, that chest was almost as marvellous as the little village! I remember once, a *duc,* who had been granted permission to join her on a Wednesday, had only on the Tuesday received from the jeweller a new signet ring he had commissioned. Not wanting to surrender his new prize, he slipped it into his pocket when the chest was brought out. His other items he exchanged, but when he turned away, Marie Antoinette exclaimed, 'Monsieur, you have forgotten something!' and presented him with a pewter version of his signet ring that had been delivered to her on the Monday.

"All the great jewellery of France was kept in that chest —or at least their replicas, worthless pewter as they were. But although there was one of everything within, Madame insisted that there *be* only one. Including only one pewter ring like my golden bird in a size that fit a man's hand."

Monsieur Courtanvaux held up his hand and the golden bird obliged by gleaming brightly. In the light from the window, the shining wings gave the illusion of flapping ever so gently as the marquis twisted his hand back and forth.

Enraptured, Alfie asked, "Why only one?"

Monsieur Courtanvaux gave a small smile. "I think it was Madame's way of reminding the men who visited her village of their place. The village was a sanctuary for her and her ladies. For a man to be a guest there was a privilege, but he was still only a guest. He could no more complain about wearing a ring that had been on another man's hand than a guest at a hotel could complain of a mattress that had been slept on before. There were many *golden* bird rings, but there was only one Marie Antoinette."

The marquis sighed. "The greatest men in France all wore that pewter bird at one time or another. But like them, that ring is long lost. Thank you for indulging an old man's stories, but the one Monsieur Trent saw must only have been a similar design."

A cryptic smile played over Monsieur Henri's face. "I would not be so sure. And that is where the story truly becomes interesting. Do you know the tale of the 'Lost Dauphin'?"

The question surprised a laugh out of Alfie. "Has another one shown up? It's only been two months since the last one was in the papers. They're increasing."

Dominick looked at him quizzically. "The Lost Dauphin?"

The marquis spat. "Charlatans!"

"It's a rumour," Alfie explained. "Every so often someone turns up claiming to be one of the children of Louis XVI. I can't remember which one."

"Louis Charles," said Monsieur Courtanvaux softly. The marquis slouched in his seat, fingers gently brushing over the ring on his hand.

"Yes." His son nodded. "Born in 1785, Louis Charles became heir to the throne after his older brother died, and was even King Louis XVII of France for a few brief years after his father's execution, although he ruled from a windowless cell.

"You see, in 1789, the entire French royal family was imprisoned by revolutionaries. At first, their accommodations were restrictive, but in accordance with their status. As the revolution continued, this changed. Six cruel years later, Louis Charles, now a sickly child scarred by years of mistreatment, died in prison. Most agree it was from illness while others whisper of poison. But some say Louis Charles did not die at all. Instead, they believe he was spirited away by royal sympathisers and the body of another child was left in his place."

"Which is when the charlatans began," said Alfie with a sympathetic nod towards Monsieur Courtanvaux. It had to be terrible for the poor man to hear such things said about people he'd once known. But even without the personal connection, Alfie found the Lost Dauphin pretenders vile.

Alfie continued the story. "Almost immediately, people started coming forward claiming their children were actually Louis Charles, the so-called Lost Dauphin. Every single one of them has proved to be lying, although in some cases not before swindling vast amounts of money from those who want to believe. They still appear from time to time, although all adults now, claiming the title for themselves. If I recall correctly, the last one didn't even speak French."

"But what does that have to do with the ring?" Dominick asked. "I—that is, I know the man who owned the pewter ring I saw was younger than that. If you think he was the real dauphin, you're mad. And he didn't seem the type to go about pretending he was."

Alfie took a moment to do some calculations. If Louis Charles had been born in 1785, that would've made him four or five years older than Dominick. Not a lot of difference for an adult, but Dominick was brought to the workhouse as a baby. Even as negligent as they were, the nurses there would've been able to tell the difference between an infant and a five-year-old. If Monsieur Henri was implying the owner of the ring—*Dominick*—was the Lost Dauphin, then Dominick was right, he was mad.

Monsieur Henri grinned and tapped his fingers in a quick tattoo over the book he'd so hurriedly gone to fetch.

"The pewter ring has absolutely nothing to do with the Lost Dauphin. At least, nothing to do with Louis Charles. But you see, I have recently received this book. Smuggled out of France, it is purportedly by one of the doctors who served the royal family during their imprisonment. Listen."

Monsieur Henri opened the book and flicked through several pages before finding what he was looking for. "The book says Marie Antoinette was not allowed any of her jewels during her imprisonment other than 'a few worthless trinkets'. This was to keep her from bribing her guards, but what man would be bribed by a pewter ring?

"But that is not all. Here is why the book is banned in France. While she and her husband were kept separate following their imprisonment, according to this, the queen was already with child. Since she was still allowed to have her maids and other servants attend her at this time, she gave birth in secret. She then entrusted the baby to one of her maids who was able to smuggle him out. The maid was also given what few trinkets the queen still possessed in a small chest, in the hope they might pay for the escape from France.

"From here the maid disappears and the doctor doesn't know what happened to her or the babe."

Monsieur Henri slammed the book closed. "Don't you see? If a child of Louis XVI and Marie Antoinette still lives, then his uncle who currently rules should not be on the throne. That child is the rightful king of France."

Dominick had gone very still.

Alfie didn't know what to say. It had been almost beyond belief when they'd thought that Dominick's father might be a marquis, but if what Monsieur Henri was implying was true…

"That's impossible," Dominick whispered.

But in his heart, Alfie knew it wasn't. He did the calculations again. Monsieur Henri said the royal family was imprisoned sometime in 1789. If the queen was with child at the time, the baby would've been born in 1789 or 1790.

Exactly the same as Dominick.

Escaping France at the time would've been expensive, and a single woman with a child would've found it hard to find work in London. She might have had to give up the child in hopes she could retrieve it later when she could afford to care for it.

But could still just be a coincidence. Perhaps it was chance that Dominick was the same age as the royal child. And a coincidence he'd been left at a workhouse with a ring similar to the one held in that chest of worthless jewels. A ring of which there was only a single pewter copy. A ring that had been recognised by a French maid working at a hotel known to employ former royal servants. A French maid who had directed them to Bath, where they found a

French aristocrat with the same ring in gold and who knew its origins.

It could still just be a coincidence.

"Nick?"

But Dominick wasn't looking at him, he was staring wide-eyed at Monsieur Courtanvaux, who was staring right back, his face blank with shock.

"It's you," the marquis whispered.

Wordlessly, Dominick reached into his collar and pulled out his ring. He held it out for them all to see. In the sunlight streaming in through the drawing room windows, it was a sad little thing, scratched and worn, of value only to its owner. *A worthless trinket.*

The marquis extended his shaking hand so the two rings were side by side. One gleamed in the sun, its golden bird winking a jewelled eye as it took flight. The other bird was faded and dull, but there could be no question.

They were identical.

For a moment, all time stopped, the world stunned into stillness around them. Then Monsieur Henri moved, dropping into a deep bow before Dominick.

"Your Majesty."

CHAPTER 16

Dominick stared helplessly at himself in the mirror. When he was in Spitalfields, his life had been simple. Cold, miserable, and frequently painful, but simple. Coming to live with Alfie had complicated his life, mostly for the better. But now? He looked down at the long strip of fabric on the dresser before him. He was supposed to twist the linen into some sort of cravat knot, but right now it was one more complication than his mind could handle.

After Monsieur Henri had called him *that*, things had happened very quickly.

Monsieur Henri spouted a lot of political nonsense Dominick didn't understand while his father had tried to get him to stop making a fuss. Fortunately, they began to argue and slipped into French at that point, so Dominick hadn't had to listen anymore. Not that he could before that anyway. All he could hear through their argument and the ride back to the Stocktons' home with Alfie afterwards was the word *King… King… King… King… King* repeating in an endless loop until the word lost all meaning and just became another sound he couldn't understand.

He shook himself, trying to get the word out of his mind and realised there was another repetitive sound, although this one was real. After another round of knocking on his door, it creaked open and he watched in the mirror as Alfie slipped inside.

"Are you all right?"

Dominick looked back down at the cloth. "When I'm crowned, the first thing I'm going to do is outlaw cravats."

Alfie's voice was alarmed. "Nick?"

"No, I am not all right. Christ, I can't even think."

"I don't know what to say. It might still all just be a horrible misunderstanding."

A bubble of tentative hope formed in Dominick's chest. "You really think so?"

Alfie's hesitation said it all. The bubble burst.

"It might be?" Alfie said tentatively. "We still haven't been to every pawnbroker in Bath yet. One of them may know of another bird ring? Or there was that Italian cook we heard about who might turn out to be French. We could expand the search to the surrounding villages. The maid back in London might not have known Batheaston and Bath were different places. Or she was mad and this has been a wild-goose chase all along. The rings and the story of the lost heir and the dates all matching up could just be —"

"A coincidence?" Dominick finished.

He was desperately hoping Alfie would say something along the lines of, "Of course! Isn't it obvious?"

But instead, Alfie just opened and closed his mouth a few times with no sound coming out. He sat down heavily on the edge of Dominick's bed. "I don't see how it could be. If it was just one coincidence, perhaps, but all of them together? We can keep searching if you want but..."

"But it's the same ring."

It was. There was no use fighting it. Their search

for Dominick's family had come to an end in the most unexpected way.

"My God, Dominick," whispered Alfie. "You're a king."

"Worse than that, I'm French."

Alfie buried his face in his hands and let out a long groan. That didn't seem to help much, as after a moment he flopped back onto the bed and stared up at the canopy. "What are we going to do, Nick?"

"*We.*" The band of steel and dread that had been tightening around Dominick's heart loosened just a fraction. Alfie wasn't abandoning him. He wasn't going to have to face this alone. Not that he actually believed Alfie would be so fickle, but he was too terrified to be rational about things right now, so the reassurance was welcome.

"We could catch a mail coach to the coast, then book passage on the first ship we find."

Alfie propped himself up on his elbows. Dominick had meant it as a jest, but Alfie's face was completely serious. "Say the word. Say one word and we'll go."

For one brief, beautiful second, Dominick let himself be tempted. Hadn't he always wanted to go on a grand adventure? But now that he was living one, it didn't seem quite so appealing.

Then he shook his head. "There'll be time for that later. Even if... even if I am who they say I am, they can't expect a whole country to just agree to pop a crown on my head."

Alfie nodded rapidly, apparently as desperate as Dominick to find some way around this. "You're right. After all, no one accepted all those Lost Dauphin impersonators. Even if it is true and you're—I still can't believe it—and you're the rightful king of France, they're not going to overthrow their current government just on the proof of the marquis' word about the ring and a fantastic story about a secret child."

Alfie warmed to his topic, his words rushing out. "No, of course not. Instead, you'll be a *cause célèbre* for a week, then a laughingstock for another week once people come to their senses, then entirely forgotten."

It sounded too good to be true, even with the week of mockery. "Are you certain?"

Alfie stretched his arms above his head and let out a relieved sigh. When he looked back at Dominick, he was smiling. "Now that I think about it, I honestly am. I know you don't read the papers, but hardly a week goes by without some other lost prince turning up or a shipwrecked queen of Javasu or some heir to a title discovered in Australia. Every single one of them has their moment in the sun, then is soundly decried for being a charlatan and vanishes into obscurity."

"But I actually am a lost prince."

Alfie waved a hand, his lack of concern making Dominick feel better. "That hardly matters. Even if it is true, after all the others, no one is going to believe it."

The idea was comforting. Dominick might not be able to accept the fact he was a king, but at least he wasn't going to actually *be* a king.

"Now," said Alfie, rising to his feet, "I see Your Majesty has forgone the use of a valet to dress to meet his court. Might he require some assistance?"

"You're going to be an absolute pest about this aren't you?" Dominick asked, feeling a bit better despite Alfie's antics, definitely not because of them.

"I would never dare… my liege."

"Then come help me with this damned cravat. Why are we getting dressed up again? I wasn't exactly paying attention."

"No, I rather expect you had a lot on your mind." Alfie walked over to Dominick and draped the cravat around his neck. "Monsieur Henri wants us to come back for a small dinner gathering with some acquaintances. Lift your chin up. He called it the something-or-other society, but I'm sure that's just a name. I know the Stocktons are coming, but no household could be expected to throw together a supper for more than a handful of people with only a few hours' notice."

Alfie squinted at his work. This close, Dominick could smell the citrusy tang of the soap the Stocktons used rising with the warmth of Alfie's body. It combined with the smell of hair oil and that indefinable scent of Alfie's that had always meant *home*. He had to fight very hard not to kiss the little lines that appeared in Alfie's brow when he frowned.

Alfie frowned harder at the cravat. "That should be presentable enough. Although I do foresee one problem."

Dominick slumped until his head rested on Alfie's shoulder. It was far too intimate a gesture, but at the moment, that was at the very bottom of his list of worries.

"Now what?" His question was muffled by Alfie's coat.

A hand came up and carded soothingly through his hair. "Well, we're not going to be able to tell people we're cousins anymore. We're going to have to make up some story about you actually being the ward of a distant relative or something. Bad enough people believe *you're* royalty—don't drag me down with you!"

* * *

"Is it too late to catch that mail coach?"

The 'small dinner gathering' at the Lamourettes' house might be serving dinner, but it certainly wasn't small. Considering how many people had been at their "soiree", Dominick probably shouldn't be surprised, but seeing dozens of people crowded into the townhouse was more than he was prepared to face.

Unfortunately, before they could turn and run, Miss Lamourette spotted them.

"Your Majesty!" she all but shrieked, running over to them and dropping into a curtsy so deep that parts of her that should remain covered were at risk of falling out of her gown. Heads turned at her exclamation and Dominick could see a few other members of the society bowing where they stood. Apparently, word had spread. He was already tired of it and wished they would skip to the mockery stage as soon as possible. At least he knew how to handle that.

"And Lord Crawford," Miss Lamourette added as if only just noticing him. "So good of you both to join us. My brother has been telling everyone about your thrilling story. Oh, I'll never forgive myself for not being there the moment the truth was revealed! Was it terribly shocking or had you suspected all along? May I see the ring? Are you wearing it now?"

To Dominick's surprise, she then grabbed both his hands, not even bothering to mask her disappointment at finding them bare of rings. Still, she took advantage of the situation and used her grip to all but wrench him away from Alfie. Fortunately, Alfie refused to be wrenched from, following along behind them despite her best efforts.

"Oh, but there are just so many people you must meet, Your Majesty! Now over here we have—"

"No more majesty nonsense, please. Just 'Mr. Trent' is fine."

Dominick thought that would put her off a bit, but instead she let out a dreamy sigh. "So noble!"

She then proceeded to introduce him to every single person in the room. By the third set of bows Dominick stopped trying to remember names and faces. If there was someone actually important here, he was sure Alfie would give him a nudge.

Finally, his eyes landed on a familiar face.

"Doctor Mullins!" He shook the doctor's hand, feeling only a little like a man rolling towards the edge of a cliff and grasping at anything to keep from going over. "It's so good to see you! Look, Lord Crawford is here as well. He's doing much better."

Alfie took his cue to step forward, pushing Miss Lamourette gently but firmly out of the way as he did so.

The doctor smiled kindly and from the twinkle in his eye, Alfie's manoeuvre had not gone unnoticed.

"Lord Crawford, I'm glad to see you're doing well. But do be sure to take a seat if this crowd gets to be too much. The Lily Society members can be a rambunctious lot, and your—Well, I suppose he's not actually your cousin, is he? —Mr. Trent here has them all in quite a state."

"Mr. Trent is the ward of a distant relation," Alfie

said, the lie they'd practised rolling believably off his lips. "'Cousin' was just simpler to say. Although apparently not any longer."

Dominick gave a tight smile. "The Lily Society? You're all gardeners like Mrs. Stockton?"

Doctor Mullins laughed. "Let you in on her big secret, has she? No, lily as in the *fleur de lis*. You couldn't have chanced upon a more sympathetic audience. All the members gathered here support a strong monarchy in France. Stronger even than the current king's position."

Doctor Mullins tapped his lapel and Dominick noticed a small pin in the shape of a flower. Looking around, he noticed for the first time several other people wearing similar pins or brooches, one woman even sporting a large lily-shaped comb in her hair.

"I'm surprised Monsieur Henri didn't give you the full manifesto," the doctor continued.

"He said something about it," said Alfie. "But as you can imagine, there was a lot to take in."

As if summoned by his name, Dominick spotted Monsieur Henri making his way through the throng.

Dominick leaned over to Alfie, hoping the noise of the crowd would be enough to cover his words, even as he felt the weight of eyes on his back. "I can't handle any more of the Lamourettes right now. Could you?"

Alfie gave him a decidedly unhappy look. "Could I sacrifice myself to the cause? I suppose so, but you owe me *two* forfeits now."

With that Alfie straightened. "Doctor Mullins, it was a pleasure to see you in better circumstances. If you'll excuse me, I must go greet our hosts."

Doctor Mullins was giving Dominick a look that was part concerned and part knowing. "You look a bit overwhelmed, Mr. Trent. There's a terrace behind that set of curtains. I can't promise peace and quiet for long, but at least you'll get some fresh air."

As they stepped outside, Dominick drank in the cool night air as if it was water.

"Thank you, I didn't realise how much I needed that."

"Well, interpreting a patient's symptoms and effecting a cure is my profession, after all," said Doctor Mullins as he cleaned his spectacles with a bit of cloth. "And I can use a break myself. I'm as much for king and country as the next man, but to be honest, I get a bit lost in Society conversations. Mr. Stockton was very, very generous in supporting my practice when I was first starting out, and it would've been rude to turn down his offer of membership."

"He doesn't seem like the sort of man to go in for politics."

Doctor Mullins returned the spectacles to his nose and gave Dominick a meaningful look over them. "It's very fashionable at the moment to have grand ideals."

Well, that explained it. If someone told Stokes that it was fashionable to climb buildings naked, Bath Abbey would have a new gargoyle by morning.

"Besides," continued the doctor, "the Stocktons and the Lamourettes have known each other for ages. I'm sure when Monsieur Henri was getting this society together, Mr. Stockton could no more refuse than I. Lord Boyle did, although I was never sure if that was for ideological reasons, or merely because those two loved to argue."

Now, that was interesting. If the Lamourettes were so

passionate about this club and Lord Boyle refused to join, could there be a motive for murder in there somewhere? Perhaps the society wasn't as inoffensive as Doctor Mullins made it sound. If they were some sort of radicals and Lord Boyle disagreed, or even threatened to report them, then slipping something into his soup might have seemed like a necessary evil to protect the cause.

All just supposition, but it still made him wary.

"How is Mr. Stockton, by the way?" asked Doctor Mullins. "I don't mean physically. I mean as far as Lord Boyle's death? Aside from his wife, I'm not sure there was a person on Earth he cared for more."

"As well as can be expected," Dominick said, parroting Stokes' own words. "Speaking of which, is there any further progress on the poison?"

Doctor Mullins' mouth twisted in frustration. "Damnedably no. My colleague, the expert, hasn't been able to give me a definitive answer and keeps pushing me to write Lord Boyle's family and ask them if they wouldn't mind sending him some of his organs for testing. He's as sure as I am that it *is* poison though, he just doesn't know which one.

"I spoke to the coroner. Lord Boyle's heart was in good condition and there were no other obvious causes of death. He's willing to say in his report that it was just one of those times where people drop dead for no reason. He says it can't have been poison, because he had none of the tell-tale signs of arsenic ingestion, but there are so many other poisons in the world that science has not yet given us a way to test for!"

Dominick was taken aback at the ferocity of Doctor

Mullins feelings on the matter, never mind the image of organs being mailed through the post.

The doctor cleared his throat and looked abashed. "Forgive me, that was uncalled for."

Dominick shrugged. "I've heard worse."

He'd been carrying something in his pocket since the night of Lord Boyle's murder, unsure of who to trust with it. He still wasn't completely sure about the doctor, but if nothing else, he seemed sincere in his desire to identify the poison that killed Lord Boyle. There was still a chance that he'd committed the murder himself and wanted a way to prove it *had* been a murder without saying, "I know because I did it." But they were short on options.

With a quick glance back to make sure no one was peeping at them through the curtains, Dominick pulled the snuffbox from his pocket and handed it over.

"I don't know if this had anything to do with his death but I... found this by Lord Boyle when he collapsed. It must have fallen out of his pocket. I don't know if you can be poisoned by snuff, but it might be worth testing."

Doctor Mullins clutched the snuffbox to his chest, his eyes bright. "It's certainly worth trying! My friend is going to be so excited. If you'll excuse me, I must get this to him at once, he'd never forgive me for delaying scientific experimentation just for the sake of a dinner party."

Dominick barely had time to wish the doctor a good evening before he was rushing off. He did note that this mysterious tester of poisons was first "my colleague" and then "my friend". Curious, but he didn't have long to wonder about it as Doctor Mullins' departure seemed to have opened the floodgates and people began to spill out onto the terrace.

Dominick was forced into several conversations with strangers he'd apparently already met about what his economic policies would be, whatever those were, before he was able to make another escape.

"There you are!" came a nasal cry. For once, Dominick was glad to hear it.

"Mrs. Stockton, Stokes, how honestly wonderful to see you." It was true. At least he usually knew what the Stocktons were talking about, even if it came at the price of having to actually hear Stokes' voice.

Now that he was looking for them, he couldn't miss the lilies each of them wore. Mrs. Stockton had a delicate gold lily pinned just below her bust where it couldn't help but catch the eye, and her husband wore an enamelled cravat pin so large, Dominick was surprised he wasn't constantly falling forward, dragged down by its weight.

"I'm sorry we didn't ride over with you," said Mrs. Stockton. "I did so want to get here early and help get everything in order."

"Didn't Cordelia do a marvellous job?" asked Stokes. "Imagine putting together something like this for the entire society on such short notice."

"It's very impressive. I'm surprised you didn't mention the Lily Society earlier, Mrs. Stockton, given your love of flowers."

She touched her pin. "Well, they're not really the same things, are they? Although I must admit, I'm glad the society chose such a pleasing emblem. A lily makes it easy to recognise other members without looking garish. And imagine how impossible it would be to find matching jewellery if their emblem was some nasty animal like a badger or a stoat!"

"If that was the case, we wouldn't be members," said Stokes drily. Dominick wasn't sure if he was joking or not. "But it really is the most just cause. Don't you agree, Your M—never mind, you still wish to be called 'Mr. Trent', of course. Very admirable."

Just when Dominick had been hoping for a break from the political talk. He wished more every minute that he and Alfie had bolted when they had the chance. "I've only understood a little. Something about the French monarchy?"

Stokes let out an excited noise, then immediately schooled his face into droll aloofness.

"I'm sure Monsieur Henri will be displeased he didn't get to explain it all himself, but as future monarch, you'll need to understand these things as soon as possible. As you know, your father, Louis XVI reigned before the revolution."

Your father.

Until Stokes said it, it hadn't really struck Dominick that all these grand figures whose names would go down in history were actually his family. Christ, he wouldn't be written about the same way, would he? His life reduced to names and dates for bored schoolboys to memorise? He'd rather be forgotten.

Alfie'd assured him that he'd be discounted and dismissed, but the more he listened to this society talk, the more he began to worry. And if his name was recorded in the history books, would Alfie's be as well? Or would only one of them be remembered?

Oblivious to Dominick's concerns, Stokes continued on.

"That whole unpleasantness with the revolution was dreadful for all involved. My sincerest condolences on your loss. But your family weren't the only ones to suffer. Monsieur Courtanvaux was one of the lucky nobles to escape with his life, but he arrived penniless on these shores. My father gave him some money to get by, and when he received compensation for his lost lands, I dare say that generosity was repaid to us a thousandfold. But what those who call themselves republicans don't understand is that the common people suffered as well."

Stokes said "republicans" the same way Dominick might say, "Guess how I discovered the rotting mouse carcass the cat left in my boot?"

"Then came the years of Napoleon, and I don't have to tell you how that just made everything worse. And now your uncle Louis XVIII is on the throne." Stokes paused. "Although I suppose technically you would be the eighteenth. Will you take Louis as your regnal name or go with something else? A matter for another time, but something to be thinking about. Regardless, the French people go through all that upheaval just for what? To end up with a king again? Or do they?"

Dominick was feeling distinctly lost. "It sounds like it?"

"Nooooo." Stokes dragged out the word until Dominick's hackles rose at the unpleasant sound. "Because your uncle is a weak king. He decides nothing for himself and rules only as he is told to rule. It's barbaric. Now, I'm not one to say specifically what's to be done—I leave that to our friend Monsieur Henri. But mark my word, if nothing changes, there will be another revolution. What France needs is a stable monarch, strong, unimpeachable, like we have in England."

Dominick barely caught his bark of laughter in time. Good God, Stokes actually meant it. No wonder Batty argued with him. England had a madman for a king and lush for a regent. Although, if Stokes was right and this Louis XVIII was even worse than that, no wonder all these people wanted Dominick to be king.

The idea sat uneasily in his gut. Surely they weren't right? Could he really be the best of bad options?

"Mr. Trent," Mrs. Stockton cut in, "are you unwell?"

Dominick took a moment to catch his breath. "Thank you, no, I'm afraid it's just the soiree all over again. The first half I mean, with too many people."

She smiled at him kindly. "Then perhaps the solution is the same. Enough of all this talk and time for some refreshment. I'm afraid the Lamourettes don't have a table capable of seating all of us, but a buffet has been arranged. Would you care to accompany me?"

Dominick took her offered arm gratefully. He knew from experience how much a hot meal could make everything better.

She turned to her husband. "Will you be joining us, dear?"

Stokes smiled. His ghastly pallor would probably be improved by a good meal or two, but he just shook his head. "I'm fine. You two run along. But mind your manners, Dellie. You're dining with a king!"

Several people around them tittered, proving they'd been eavesdropping, but Dominick didn't get a chance to tell them what he thought about that before Miss

Lamourette came rushing up. As Alfie wasn't being towed along in her wake, Dominick assumed she'd abandoned him for larger prey. Just his luck. After all, why angle to be an earl's wife, when she could be a queen?

She pouted when she saw Mrs. Stockton's arm in his. "Oh, I was just coming to tell you Henri wanted us all to come in. I'd hoped we'd go in together but I see someone else got there first."

She went up to Stokes and grabbed his arm imploringly. "Oh, my dear Stokes, we've been cruelly abandoned! Whatever shall we do?"

Mrs. Stockton's grip on Dominick's arm tightened.

"I'm afraid there's only one thing for it, Miss Adelaide," Stokes said, raising his voice so the assembled group on the terrace could hear. This had the unfortunate effect of making his voice so grating it could chip glass. "If your brother has requested we all return inside, then we must obey. Would you do me the honour of walking in with me?"

Miss Lamourette giggled and took his arm.

Having commanded their attendance, it appeared Monsieur Henri wasn't going to let Dominick eat without hearing whatever the announcement was. The man was standing on the staircase in the main hall, a few steps up so he could look out over the crowd. When he spotted Dominick, he motioned him forward.

The last place Dominick wanted to be was in front of all the society. At least when he'd been amongst them, they could only sneak glances at him. Now, they'd have every right to stare. The only good thing about it was he saw Alfie by the stairwell as well, talking to a seated Monsieur Courtanvaux. The marquis was in his full powdered face and wig again tonight, but he looked tired, the white makeup gathering in the creases of his face and making him appear even older.

He left Mrs. Stockton with her husband and—narrowly escaping the clutching hands of Miss Lamourette—detoured over to the marquis.

"Monsieur Courtanvaux, apologies for not thanking you yet for welcoming us back into your home. I'm afraid I keep getting diverted."

"It's quite all right," the marquis said. "Lord Crawford has been keeping me company, and this whole gathering is my son's idea. I'm merely providing the home."

Alfie and Dominick had just enough time to share a commiserating look before Monsieur Henri began tapping his glass to get everyone's attention.

"Ladies and gentlemen, by now you have all heard about the historical moment that brings us here together. By chance, fate, or divine intervention, the true heir to the throne of France has been delivered to us, living for years unknowing of the royal blood in his veins. The indisputable proof is in the form of a ring he wears, a ring that only the true son of Marie Antoinette could possess, as proven both by documented sources and my own father's account. Mr. Trent, will you raise your hand and show us that ring now?"

Dominick froze as every eye in the room focused on him. "It—it doesn't fit," he stammered.

It was true. He hadn't been able to wear the ring at all since his last boxing match with Bill "The Bodysnatcher" Nunn. It'd already been tight before that, but after the fight, his knuckles had been too damaged to try. Even after they'd healed, the swelling had never completely gone away.

One fight too many, he supposed. Of course, if Alfie hadn't stopped that fight, it might have been his last in more ways than one. So really, it was better this way all around. The ring was safer on a chain around his neck than it was with him wearing it on his finger and Alfie certainly liked his big hands.

A little louder so everyone could hear, he said. "I promise, the ring is somewhere secure." He wasn't about to admit to having it under his shirt and give Miss Lamourette an excuse to tear it off.

If Monsieur Henri was disappointed by Dominick's lack of showmanship, he didn't let on, instead continuing with even more passion in his voice.

"So, now it becomes clear that the man who currently sits upon the throne of France was never meant to rule. This is why he does nothing, and why the French people suffer as this puppet is jerked about by his true masters. But I am not here to advocate the deposing of a monarch, however false."

An unhappy murmur went through the crowd.

"My God," whispered Alfie. "They really want that."

Monsieur Henri raised his hands. "I know, I know. There are those of you who believe this is the only way. But my father can attest to the suffering that is caused by the execution of a king. That is one solution, but there are others.

"In many ways, we in England suffer the same as our French brethren. Are not the unfit given power here as there? Are our sisters and mothers not left unprotected from unscrupulous men? Do we not watch our kings decline and worry what chaos will be loosed when they've gone? Here in England, the Prince Regent is king in all but name, but he has no legitimate heir. The same is true in France. In both countries, the line of succession is muddied with brothers ruling where there are no sons. Like the regent, Louis XVIII has no legitimate sons, so who shall rule when he dies? Another brother? And so, we take another step away from the true line of succession.

"Here is what I put to you. We wage a war to put Mr. Trent on the throne. Not on the battlefield, but in halls of embassies and the minds of the people. The people of France want a return to order, not more bloodshed. They want the true king of France on the throne, not as Louis XVIII's replacement, but as his successor. This way the line of succession continues unbroken, having only briefly wandered from its path before being corrected. In addition, this gives Mr. Trent time to learn the things he should have been taught since birth, such as politics and diplomacy."

"And French," Dominick muttered.

Alfie kicked him. Dominick glanced over, but was arrested by the look on Alfie's face. "What is it?"

Alfie's eyes were wide. He was flicking the catch on his cane open and closed, something Dominick had only seen him do when he was truly scared.

"Nick, what he's saying... It makes sense. A direct continuation of the royal bloodline, a peaceful transfer of power to a rightful heir, returning things back to the way they *should* be. People like those sorts of things. They like those sorts of things a lot."

Dominick looked over his shoulder. Behind him, the Lily Society was nodding along, transfixed by Monsieur Henri's words.

Alfie took a deep breath. "I thought this was going to blow over in a matter of weeks. But this plan might work. It makes sense. It would be popular with both the monarchists and the more reasonable republicans. It could take years to build up enough support for it but when Louis XVIII dies… Nick, they might actually make you king."

"They might indeed." Monsieur Henri beamed down at them from the stairs. His eyes held a fire seen only in fanatics and madmen. "In fact, they almost certainly will."

He raised the glass he held. Behind him, Dominick heard the rustle of fabric as the rest of the Lily Society did the same.

"A toast," Monsieur Henri cried. "*Vive le roi!* Long live the king!"

CHAPTER 17

The ride back to the townhouse was silent.

The Stocktons had remained at the Lamourettes' party, but after that toast, neither Alfie nor Dominick could stand another moment.

A footman let them in, bowing as he did so. Even though he'd bowed every time someone entered or exited, this time Alfie saw Dominick hesitate before continuing on into the house. Alfie followed him up the stairs and didn't even consider going to his own room.

As he shut the door to Dominick's room behind them both, he heard him let out a sigh.

"Alfie..."

"Hush," said Alfie, checking the lock on the door and putting a chair under the knob for good measure. "I don't care what it looks like to them. I'm not leaving you alone tonight."

Dominick didn't argue, which only worried Alfie more. He hadn't seen his lover like this very often, but each time it was because he was struggling under the weight of something immensely awful. The last time had been after Helen's murder. At least then, he'd been able to focus his attention on finding her killer. Now? It wasn't as if Dominick could undo who his parents were or forget learning the truth about them. Even if he could, there was a house full of people who'd just learned who he was. Short of praying for the earth to open up and swallow up all of Bath, there wasn't anything Dominick could do.

But there were a few things Alfie could.

He pulled Dominick's overcoat off his unresisting shoulders, then did the same with his coat underneath. Cravat, waistcoat, and shirt were next to follow.

His hands hesitated over the thin chain around Dominick's neck and the ring that hung from it. If he removed it, he would only draw attention to its existence, but to leave it on and remove the rest seemed unfair when it was the cause of Dominick's current misery.

In the end, he left it where it was. Dominick was so used to wearing it, its absence would be more noticeable than leaving it alone. Besides, whatever the ring itself might mean about Dominick's past and their future, it was such a part of him that he wouldn't look like Alfie's Nick without it.

He guided Dominick over to the bed and pressed his shoulder gently to get him to sit so he could get at the rest of him. Dominick followed his instructions without protest, lifting one leg and then the other when Alfie directed, but he wasn't paying any real attention, his eyes focused not on Alfie, but on some vague place Alfie couldn't see.

Shoes and stockings, breeches and drawers. He had Dominick fully stripped and was guiding him again, this time between the bedsheets. He then quickly stripped off himself and crawled in behind him, curling up against Dominick's warm back and wrapping his arms around him. He always felt safe and protected when Dominick held him this way, and willed all that love and security into his own embrace.

One part of his body took immediate notice of their positions and was quick to remind Alfie of how long it'd been since they'd been naked together in a bed, but Alfie willed himself under control. Dominick was in no fit state for such activities and despite what his rebellious body might want, Alfie wasn't in the mood. This was just about comfort, in finding peace in the one place they always had —with each other.

He held Dominick and when his shoulders started to shake with silent sobs, Alfie held him all the tighter, resting his head between Dominick's shoulder blades.

In fairy tales, when the poor orphan boy is revealed to be the long-lost prince and the people cheer, the boy is overjoyed and lives happily ever after. But real life wasn't a fairy tale. After the initial shock of learning Dominick's origins had worn off, Alfie hadn't been too concerned, but after hearing Monsieur Henri's speech, he realised everything was going to change.

Once, his adoptive father had taken him to Parliament to see how it functioned. That day he'd seen the difference between men who spoke to be heard and men who spoke to be believed. It was that second group of men whose ideas were made into laws.

Monsieur Henri spoke just like them. Alfie wasn't sure whether or not he could actually make Dominick king. But he could make people *want* Dominick to be king, to believe he *should* be king, and there was no happily ever after to that story. There was only danger and responsibility and a lifetime of looking over their shoulders.

Assuming Alfie was able to stay with Dominick at all. Kings needed heirs. And while Alfie could give Dominick his heart, soul, and life, that was the one thing he couldn't give him.

He ran his hand up and down Dominick's arm, hoping at least one of them could be soothed.

Finally, the body against his stopped shaking. Dominick sniffed, and wiped his face with the corner of the sheet. He lay there quietly, but Alfie could tell he wasn't asleep. The silence in the room was unbearable. Alfie wasn't sure what to say, but he couldn't just let them lie there, stewing in their misery.

"Once upon a time, a very long time ago…"

Dominick snorted weakly. His voice was thick. "I'm the one who tells the stories."

"Then I've more than earned my turn. Once upon a time, a very long time ago, there was a brother and sister who lived all alone in the woods with their father. Then one day—"

"And stepmother."

"What?"

"And stepmother. It's the stepmother who convinces the father to leave them in the woods."

Alfie considered that. Dominick was right, there was a stepmother. This was why Dominick had been the one to tell stories when they were children, Alfie could never remember the details. He'd only chosen this fairy tale because it was the only one he could think of that didn't have royalty popping up in it.

Perhaps it was childish, two grown men curled up in the dark telling bedtime stories, but it made him remember their time together as children, and right now, they both needed the reminder that they'd gotten through terrible things together before. They would get through this.

Somehow.

"They lived alone in the woods with their father and stepmother. Then one day, the stepmother convinced the father to leave the children in the woods. But fortunately for the children, when their father took them into the woods, they brought some breadcrumbs with them."

"Stones."

"What?"

"The first time, they bring stones and follow them home. The second time it's breadcrumbs." Dominick's voice was a little stronger now.

Alfie continued telling the story, with Dominick interjecting every time he got something wrong. With each interruption he sounded more like himself and if Alfie made some mistakes on purpose, that was his secret to keep.

By the time they got to the end, Dominick had taken over completely. "And so, with the treasure they took from the witch's house, Hansel and Gretel lived happily ever after. The end."

With the story over, the silence returned, but this time, it didn't feel quite so terrible. Dominick leaned back against him and Alfie could feel his body grow heavy as he settled into sleep.

He kissed Dominick's shoulder. "We'll figure it all out too. Sleep now."

After Dominick fell asleep, Alfie lay there for several

hours, memorising the feel of Dominick in his arms. Just in case.

*   *   *

In the morning, Alfie slipped out of bed before the servants rose and made his way back to his room. There he mussed the sheets until he deemed their appearance sufficiently slept in, then changed quickly. Within minutes, he was knocking on Dominick's door.

A confused and bleary Dominick opened the door after several more rounds of knocking, eyes squinted and his still-naked body barely wrapped in a banyan. It was just as well it was Alfie at the door and not a maid with a pitcher of hot water.

"Get dressed, we're headed out."

Dominick blinked at him as his sleep-addled mind slowly parsed the words. "Are we catching the mail coach after all?"

Alfie hesitated. That hadn't been his plan but, "Do you want to?"

Dominick seemed to actually be considering it. Alfie mentally ran through a list of the essentials they'd need to bring into exile, how much in funds he could acquire on short notice, and who he trusted enough to contact for more later.

"No," Dominick said finally. "Not before breakfast at least."

Alfie tried not to let the relief show on his face. He'd meant what he said the night before about figuring it out together, but he was glad they weren't resorting to running from their problems just yet. "Go get dressed then. We're going out for breakfast. I've barely seen any of Bath yet outside pawnbrokers and jewellery shops. I want you to give me the full tour."

Dominick grumbled something about having only seen it once himself, but went to dress. By the time they made it down to the Stocktons' stables, he was almost in a good mood. Horses tended to have that effect on him. Alfie even witnessed a small smile when one of the mares ate a handful of oats from Dominick's palm. He wasn't sure how long his leg was going to allow him to stay on top of such a beast, but he felt sufficiently recovered from his poison treatments that he wasn't going to swoon and fall off.

Breakfast earned two more smiles, one when a waiter placed a fragrant cup of chocolate in front of Dominick, and one when Alfie pointed out a truly ghastly hat on a passerby. Another smile was earned when Dominick pointed out the entrance to the famous Roman baths as they rode by and Alfie demanded they stop for a soak. But there was something about this smile he didn't fully trust.

"Are you sure you want to do that, Alfie?"

"What, why? It's supposed to be good for my leg. Just because the waters didn't agree with my insides doesn't mean they won't agree with my outsides."

Dominick's smile wavered. Damn. The whole point of this day was to distract him from the awfulness of the night before, not to remind him instead of the awfulness of Batty's poisoning.

But Dominick rallied and gave a shrug that was even more suspicious in its nonchalance. "If you want."

* * *

In his imaginings, Alfie had assumed the baths were a place of decadence, where he and Dominick could lounge like the ancient Romans, swathed only in towels while eating from bowls of figs as the steam from the pools billowed around them. Perhaps they would have their own private enclave draped in billowing white linens where no one could see what they got up to inside.

That image was promptly dashed when the bath attendant handed him a brown pile of clothing and pointed his way to the changing stalls. It was worth it though, because when he emerged with his arms held out stiffly to the sides to touch as little of the itchy shirt to his body as possible, Dominick laughed so hard he had to sit down, then kept laughing every time he got another look at Alfie.

It seemed the only way to get him to stop was to conceal the awful bathing outfit, so Alfie stepped into the steaming waters, taking in the other patrons who bobbed around him and lined the edges of the pool. Despite the clothing, it was actually quite pleasant. He'd never seen so much hot water in his life and marvelled at the novelty of being able to stretch out in it rather than being hunched over in a small bathing tub. He sunk in all the way past his shoulders and groaned. No wonder people said the waters were healing; he could actually feel the knots in his back begin to work themselves loose. He drifted over to an empty spot along the wall. By the time he reached it, his leg already felt better than it had in months.

He closed his eyes, but the sound of splashing announced Dominick's approach.

"You were right," Alfie said. "This was a terrible idea. I regret this fully."

"I don't," Dominick replied. "I'm going to cherish the sight of you in that outfit for the rest of my life."

He started laughing again. Alfie cracked open an eye to get a look at him. Even in identically hideous bathing garb, Dominick was breathtaking. His skin was flushed from the heat and beads of water clung to his skin. When he looked back at Alfie, he was radiating such pure happiness that Alfie was tempted to steal the damned bathing suit just to bring it out again on gloomy days.

He gave Dominick a small splash, just because he could. "No, I mean it's a terrible idea because I'm never going to be content with lukewarm bathwater again. Could we have one of these put in at Balcarres?"

"I'll bet if you got Mrs. Hirkins to try it once, she'd find a way to have one installed, even if she had to crack open the ground herself to make the hot spring."

Alfie closed his eye again and grinned. "I don't doubt it."

He floated contentedly for a while, letting the healing waters do their work and listening half-heartedly to the chatter around them. Then there was movement next to him, and a wave of water struck him in the face. Alfie spluttered, but when he turned to look at Dominick he was facing away, the picture of innocence. So, Alfie did the only reasonable thing. He splashed him back.

Dominick turned and gave him one more smile—no, this wasn't a smile, it was a wicked, evil *grin*—and then the battle began.

*　*　*

"I can't believe you got kicked out of the baths!" Alfie chuckled as the rented coach bounced along the road back to the Stockton home. Between the heat of the baths and the excitement of the day, he was ready for a nap.

"Me!" Dominick protested. "That's not how I remember it!"

After a thorough drenching and a very stern talking to by the manager of the baths, they'd dried off and ridden a bit more around the city, finally ending up at a perfectly cosy pub for lunch. Unfortunately, the ride had undone all the bath's good work on Alfie's leg, so they'd rented a carriage and paid to have the horses led back home. All in all, it'd been one of the best days Alfie could remember in a long time. He wasn't sure how long it'd been since he'd felt this content. Likely not since they'd left Balcarres.

He used the privacy of the carriage to give Dominick's thigh a slap and leave his hand there. "Of course it was you. They're not going to toss out an earl, especially when he's only defending himself from watery attacks. I only left when they threw you out so you wouldn't feel alone."

Dominick gave a rude gesture. "Well, aren't you kind? And that bit when you pushed me under was just defending yourself was it?"

Alfie grinned at the memory. "That never happened. You're making it up."

"Lies and slander!" Dominick knocked his shoulder against Alfie's. "That sort of talk will be considered treason when I become king."

The last word dropped through the carriage like a stone, dragging their good cheer down with it. *When Dominick became king.* The very thing they'd both been trying so hard not to think about.

"At least you'll have no shortage of hot water at your palace," Alfie said softly. "You could probably even have a bath like that built, even without Mrs. Hirkins' help."

Dominick shifted so Alfie's hand slid from his thigh. "I'll make it my first royal decree."

The butler was already opening the door to the townhouse when they arrived and they were almost bowled over by Stokes as he exited.

"Ah, Freddie! Mr. Trent!" Stokes said with a chuckle. "Well, 'Trent' for now, I suppose. We were wondering where you were. It's fine to swear off today, but do let us know in future. Lots to discuss, lots to plan. Which reminds me, I'm off to my tailor. Would you care to join me, or do you already have appropriate outfits for Thursday?"

Despite Stokes' airy demeanour, there were still dark circles under his eyes. Batty's death hadn't been forgotten, merely set aside at the prospect of purchasing new frippery.

"Thursday?" Alfie asked. The sound of Stokes' voice was enough to make the knots in his back reknit one by one.

Stokes flicked an invisible bit of lint from his sleeve. "I forgot, you left early. Yes, well, you see, last night the Lamourettes were rather hoping Mr. Trent would formally announce himself as the rightful heir to the throne of France and state his intent to take back what was rightfully his. When the current king's reign comes to a peaceful end, of course." Stokes added in a rush.

"But when that didn't happen, Cordelia said it only made sense to hold the next gathering here since you're already staying with us. Quite the feather in her cap that is! Because it's best to get things moving as quickly as possible, Thursday was agreed upon in your absence. Now the whole house is in an uproar trying to get things ready in time."

There went Alfie's nap.

Stokes continued. "I've been thrown from my own home and told not to return until I have an outfit appropriate for the occasion. Still, it will all be worth it if you have an historic announcement for us Thursday. Eh, Your Majesty?"

If the cheer of the good day had been dragged down in the carriage, now it was thoroughly drowned.

With a tip of his hat, Stokes stepped into the carriage they'd just left and gave the driver his direction. Alfie watched it trundle off, taking all their previous happiness with it.

CHAPTER 18

"Well, this feels familiar." Alfie said from his seat on Dominick's bed as he watched him struggle with his cravat again.

Dominick scowled at him in the mirror. It wasn't his fault this bloody knot required a dozen bloody folds and twists that had to be done just right. It was like one of those courtly dances going on under his chin, all twists and twirls. The problem was, he could never remember any of the steps and the whole thing just ended in a mess.

He grumbled as the knot unwound itself for the third time. "Don't these people have anything better to do than throw bloody parties?"

"They're all wealthy so, not really." Alfie shrugged. "Do you require assistance?"

"I can do it, just give me a minute."

The night of the dreaded Thursday party had finally arrived and Dominick still didn't know what he was going to say to the Lily Society. The Stocktons had a writing table and stacks of paper brought up to his room so Dominick could compose a speech befitting the historic moment, but aside from a few rude drawings he'd immediately thrown in the fire, he hadn't touched any of it.

He really only had two choices of what to say, "Fine, I'll be king," or "Bugger off". Either way, it was going to be a short speech.

The problem was, he still wasn't sure which he was going to choose. He'd spent the last several days pointedly trying not to think about it and failing miserably. He and Alfie had gone to the baths again a few times, keeping their splashing to a minimum, but mostly Dominick had just found himself wandering the streets of Bath alone, trying to make sense of it all.

He'd spent a full day trying to work out if Lord Boyle's death could somehow be related, but no one involved had even known he was in Bath at the time, never mind that he was a royal heir. It didn't get him any closer to solving the murder, but at least it reassured his conscience. But if he declared himself as king and it caused some sort of civil war, how many lives would be lost on his account then?

He jerked at the tap on his shoulder. Alfie was standing beside him, looking him over with obvious concern.

"I said your name half a dozen times but you didn't answer."

"Sorry," Dominick said. "I was elsewhere."

Alfie took the cravat from him and in a matter of moments, had magically produced the perfect knot. "You've been elsewhere a lot lately."

"Sorry," Dominick said again. "I've been neglecting you, haven't I?"

"Dreadfully," Alfie replied, tugging Dominick's waistcoat smooth. "And we're going to have another conversation at some point about you not just running off when there's something you don't want to talk about. If you remember, the last time you did that I ended up cutting off all my hair. Let's not find out how much more dramatic I can be."

He handed Dominick his coat. "Unfortunately, we have more pressing concerns at the moment, so our talk will have to wait. Are you ready?"

No.

Dominick didn't say the word aloud, but he might as well have. Alfie gave him a long, searching look, then let out a heavy sigh. "Right."

Then Alfie began walking around the room, examining various pieces of furniture and shaking his head.

"Snap like twigs," he muttered under his breath. He examined the bed carefully, looking back and forth between it and Dominick before glancing at the clock on the mantle. "Not enough time for that."

"What are you doing?" asked Dominick.

"Can you get those curtains?" Alfie replied.

Bemused, Dominick did as he was asked, pulling the heavy drapes closed and blocking out the setting sun. The room was immediately plunged into twilight, the only light coming from the low fire in the hearth and the few lamps that had already been lit. He heard a scraping noise behind him and turned in time to see Alfie sliding a chair under the door handle, the same as he'd done the night he'd stayed. He tested the door several times until he was finally content before facing Dominick with a pleased grin.

Dominick couldn't help but grin back. "Are we barricading ourselves in?"

"Only for a little while," Alfie said cryptically, but before Dominick could question him further, Alfie was striding across the room.

He pushed Dominick back against the wall and then

he was upon him. Dominick's mouth opened instinctively as Alfie's lips found his. The kiss was searing, the weeks since they'd had the privacy to do this properly providing kindling for the wildfire that rushed through him. The strokes of Alfie's tongue against his own were pure heat, the wet slide overwhelming after so long without. Dominick couldn't bear it and he couldn't stop either, sucking on Alfie's tongue until his lover keened.

Dominick gave him a quick bite to the lip in reprimand. "Shush. You want them to hear you?"

"You shush." Alfie's eyes were blown wide with lust. Pulling him in closer revealed Dominick wasn't the only one affected by the kiss. "This was a terrible idea."

"This was your idea," Dominick reminded him, taking the opportunity to lick his way up Alfie's jaw. His freshly shaved skin was smooth; Dominick preferred when he had a bit of stubble, but the way Alfie shuddered and grasped Dominick's waist tightly more than made up for it.

"I have, ah, many terrible ideas." Alfie gasped. "You should do a better job of stopping me."

"I rather enjoyed this one." Dominick chuckled, then gave Alfie's earlobe a nip for good measure. "I suppose we'd better head downstairs now."

Alfie pulled his head back. Dominick assumed he would immediately start getting them back to rights, but instead Alfie's hands slid lower, gripping Dominick's buttocks. He levelled Dominick with a flat stare.

"Nick, you think I went to all that trouble for a sodding kiss? One of us is getting fucked against that wall in the next five minutes and I don't care who."

"Christ!"

Alfie was blushing. How could he say such filthy things so confidently and still be blushing?

"Shush. You want them to hear you?" Alfie grinned, his pink cheeks setting off the red in his hair.

"My menace," Dominick said fondly.

He kissed Alfie again, this time no less passionate than the first. When they finally parted for air, he managed to gasp, "We're expected any moment. We don't have time."

"I could use my mouth," Alfie offered, as if the suggestion alone wasn't enough to make Dominick's cock twitch. It was already hard and pressing painfully against his breeches. If Alfie was going to keep saying such things, Dominick wouldn't be letting either of them go down to the party at all. From the gleam in his eye, the little pest knew it too.

"Or we could use hands." Alfie shrugged. "Whatever's amenable."

"I'll show you amenable," Dominick growled, but the effect was rather ruined by how frantically he hauled Alfie back in, kissing him and running his hands over whatever parts of him Dominick could reach. With all their damned clothes in the way, it wasn't much, and even this much movement was enough to strain the fabric of his fancy coat.

"I wish I had time to get you naked," he sighed.

Alfie's hands slid forward and rested on the fall of Dominick's breeches. "We'll have all the time in the world when we get back to Balcarres," he said as he began undoing the buttons one by one.

Dominick hissed when his cock was exposed to the cool air of the room, but almost immediately, Alfie had his hands on him, moving them with the same sure strokes he'd used to ravish Dominick's mouth. The sensation was almost too rough at first, the dry rub veering away from pleasure towards pain, but on each upstroke, Alfie collected more of the fluid leaking from the head of his cock until Dominick could almost weep with pleasure.

Then Alfie gently squeezed his bollocks, rolling them expertly in his palm. It'd been far too long, because Dominick was already on the verge of spending and he'd been too distracted by his own pleasure to even think of Alfie's.

"You don't have to," Alfie said as Dominick wormed his hands between the tight press of their bodies and clumsily started on Alfie's buttons. "This for you."

"Bugger that for a lark," Dominick swore as the confounded buttons resisted him at every turn. "I want you."

Alfie's grip tightened at his words, making Dominick go briefly cross eyed with how good it felt. His lips grazed Dominick's ear.

"Then have me."

Dominick bit back a groan, all too aware of where they were and exactly how many people were waiting for them downstairs.

Finally, he defeated the buttons of Alfie's fall. Alfie's cock sprang free, beautiful as always, curving upward and already wet at the tip. His shirt hem brushed Dominick's hand as he greedily reached for him, damp from where it'd been trapped between Alfie's cock and his breeches.

They quickly found their rhythm, matching stroke for stroke as they panted open-mouthed against each other's lips. Every now and then, Dominick added a little twist just to be rewarded with the way Alfie gasped his name as his hips jerked.

"Oh fuck," Alfie whispered, his voice rough. "Wait, wait, I have an idea."

Dominick didn't want to wait, not even for whatever terrible, brilliant, irresistible idea Alfie had this time, but Alfie was nudging him aside, taking Dominick's place on the wall between the two windows. With a wink, Alfie shouldered his way out of his coat before shimmying his breeches down his thighs and gathering his shirt up around his waist. Then he turned around, resting his elbows against the wall and jutting his hips back so his arse was deliciously bare and on display.

"Well?" Alfie asked, looking at Dominick over his shoulder.

Dominick licked his lips at the sight before him. He stroked a hand down Alfie's flank, his calloused palm catching on the soft skin.

"I thought we didn't have time for that?" Dominick asked.

"No, no, I mean," Alfie waved a hand unhelpfully. "Do it between the thighs."

This time, it was Dominick who keened. "Fuck, love."

"Spit in your hand and slick yourself up so it'll be smoother."

Dominick didn't need telling twice. This wasn't something they did very often and usually it was on their sides in a soft bed, Alfie's thighs so slippery with oil they were like silk. So to have him like this, spit slick and up against a wall, even if it was a wall in a fancy townhouse, had Dominick squeezing his cock tightly to keep things from being over before they could begin.

Alfie's thighs clenched around him as perfectly as if they'd been made for this and this alone. Dominick pressed forward slowly, enjoying the glide. Then he bent his knees, changing the angle until the head of his cock bumped against Alfie's bollocks.

Alfie swore, so Dominick did it again, pleased when Alfie dropped his head forward against his arm and reached down with his other hand to stroke himself as Dominick thrust. He smoothed his hands soothingly down Alfie's thighs, the short hairs tickling his palms. Then he felt the twisted scar beneath his fingers.

"How's your leg?"

"Sod my leg."

"Alfie."

"It's fine. Just… just hurry."

Dominick did, gripping Alfie's hips firmly and driving forward. Alfie cried out so loudly that Dominick froze, listening for the sound of footsteps that would signal he'd been heard.

"Sorry," Alfie whispered.

Still listening, Dominick waited a moment more before replying. "No harm done. Do you need me to gag you?"

He'd meant it in jest, but Alfie shivered under him.

"Oh Christ, love. I don't deserve you." Dominick fumbled off his cravat, trying to forget how long it'd taken to get it just right, and passed it forward. The sight of Alfie wadding it up and shoving it between his teeth would be seared into his memory forever.

After that, he drove forward again and again in total

abandon, Alfie's muffled cries spurring him faster. Even through the gag, recognised the noises his lover made when he was about to spend. The idea of Alfie streaking the wallpaper with his come was unspeakably sinful, but at the last moment, Alfie pulled the gag from his mouth, biting down on his own arm as he spent into the cravat.

His entire body tensed as he did, his thighs gripping Dominick's cock as sweetly as his arse. Dominick barely had time for Alfie to sigh and sag against the wall before he felt the tell-tale tingling at the base of his spine.

He gritted his teeth. "Pass it here."

Alfie fumbled the cravat into his hand just in time for Dominick to wrap the wet fabric around himself.

That's Alfie's come, he thought. Then stars burst at the edges of his vision as his climax struck him, not once or twice, but in pulse after pulse. He fell forward, burying his face in the back of Alfie's neck, breathing in the sweat-hot scent of him as his short curls tickled Dominick's nose.

Finally, Alfie's muffled voice drifted through to him. "Tell me you're burning that."

Dominick glanced down at the ruined cravat. "I don't know, I could say it was the latest French fashion. Start a trend."

Alfie's shoulders began to shake under him, and for a moment Dominick worried until Alfie let out a howl of laughter.

"Shh," Dominick said, already laughing himself. "We didn't go through all that just for you to ruin things now."

Alfie muffled himself with his arm again. Dominick closed his eyes, resting his chest against Alfie's back and basking in the feeling of the man he loved, happy and sated.

Finally, Alfie's laughter petered out. Dominick wiped the insides of his legs with the cleanest part of the cravat before going over and, as Alfie watched, tossing the damn thing on the fire. Then between the two of them they got Alfie returned to some semblance of order. His shirtsleeve was damp with spit where he'd bitten down, but fortunately that was the worst of it and would be covered by his coat.

For a man who'd just been frigged against a wall half-dressed, Alfie looked remarkably unlike a man who'd just been frigged against a wall half-dressed. He sat watching from the bed as Dominick set the room to rights and fetched a fresh cravat.

"Come here," said Alfie softly. "If they have to wait for you to tie that, they'll have found a new long-lost heir before we get down there."

Dominick settled on the bed next to him and lifted his chin while Alfie repeated his witchcraft, producing another perfectly tied knot. He helped Alfie to his feet and they looked each other over for any signs of what they'd been up to.

"What should I do?" Dominick finally asked.

"About what? You look fine, not a hair out of place."

"About them." Dominick cocked his head towards the door. From the constant rapping on the front door of the townhouse to the increasing murmur of voices drifting up the stairs, the sounds of the Lily Society arriving had been building to a dull roar. Likely, they wouldn't have heard Alfie even without the gag.

"About what they want me to say tonight. Whether I'll

be king or not."

Alfie averted his eyes and began fussing with the lines of Dominick's coat. With the dinner party being held just downstairs, they weren't going to need overcoats, but Dominick wished he had more layers to put on. A full suit of armour would be ideal.

"I think you have to make this decision on your own, Nick. I didn't have a choice in becoming an earl. They just took me from the workhouse and told me that would happen. Aside from leaving you to suffer alone, I don't regret the life their decision gave me, but it wasn't easy. It still isn't easy sometimes, and I'm only a minor noble with peaceful holdings and no real political influence. In the great scheme of things, I'm still much closer to being that muddy orphan boy than I ever will be to being a king."

If Alfie, who'd spent so many years learning all the ways of court and the rules of society still felt that way, what chance did Dominick have when he still swore he could feel Spitalfields dirt under his nails?

"But you do have a choice," Alfie said, smoothing his hands down Dominick's labels. The motion was more soothing than it had any right to be. "And you can change your mind too. At any point, whether it's now or on the ship to France, just say the word and I'll have us on the next mail coach."

Dominick smiled, even if the jest had worn itself thin. "You won't find many mail coaches aboard ships."

"I'd still do it," Alfie said firmly. Dominick believed him.

"How about this?" Alfie offered. "We go down tonight, let them fawn all over you for a bit, then tomorrow, we catch that mail coach—or preferably, arrange for a well-sprung carriage—but instead of running off to some foreign land to start new lives trading furs, or herding cattle, or whatever it is people do in the colonies, we instead go back home to Balcarres. Then we continue to live our lives there as we wish. And if at some point someone knocks on our door with an orb and sceptre, we can either see how good you look in an ermine robe or set the barn cats on the buggers to run them off. You can decide then."

Dominick sagged a little against Alfie's hands. He always had a way of making trouble seem less troublesome. Even if he was usually the cause of it.

"There now," said Alfie, looking pleased with himself. "Doesn't that sound better?"

"Much."

"Good." Alfie gave him a gentle shove. "If you hadn't kept running off on me, I could have told you all that days ago. Now, come along. One last dinner party, then we never need to see any of these people again if you don't want to. And if things get too bad, I have this."

Alfie plucked up his sword cane and gave it a jaunty twirl. With his devilish grin and perfectly cut suit, he looked every inch the dashing hero he was. Dominick could never let him know the effect that had on him.

"Save it for the music hall," Dominick said, but he gave Alfie a well-deserved kiss anyway. "And I'm holding you to that. The first sign of trouble and you're cutting us a path to freedom."

"Of course," Alfie grinned. "I'm Lord Alfie of the Mud, after all. Protector of kings, lovers, fools, and annoying men who are all of those things at once!"

CHAPTER 19

Lord Alfie of the Lies, Dominick thought. He'd been sending pleading looks towards Alfie all through dinner and the damned man still wasn't holding Miss Lamourette at sword point.

"Oh, Mr. Trent, that is most insightful!" Miss Lamourette exclaimed with a hand to her breast and much batting of the eyes.

Dominick hadn't said anything more than, "These parsnips are good," but he supposed she'd take what she could get. He was amused by how thoroughly she'd thrown over Alfie in favour of him. Clearly Alfie was right, an earl was nothing compared to a king. While she'd been seated between the two of them, she'd only thrown a few flirtatious words to Alfie the entire meal. Dominick supposed he couldn't blame her, after all, *he'd* been the one saying "insightful", "brilliant", and "most fascinating" things all night.

"Thank you, Mr. Trent. I'm glad you're enjoying them," Mrs. Stockton said from his other side. Her husband beside her at the head of the table had taken perhaps three bites of his meal. From the way he kept pressing his hand to his side, Dominick wondered if he'd over-tightened his corset to look his best for the evening.

Mrs. Stockton continued. "The parsnips are from our

very own garden. Unfortunately, it's the wrong season for many of our vegetables, but I'm sure you will be delighted to try them all once they ripen."

How wrong you are, Dominick thought, taking a sip of wine. *I'm going to be back in Balcarres choking down another one of Janie's overcooked monstrosities long before anything else in that garden ripens. And I'll be all the better for it.*

So far, the dinner hadn't been nearly as bad as he'd feared. Being introduced to members of the society he hadn't met yet, and reintroduced to those he had, had been as unpleasant as all the fussy social occasions seemed to be, but it was nice to get to see Monsieur Courtanvaux again, even if his children were driving Dominick mad.

Miss Lamourette draped herself all over him the moment he came downstairs, to the point he'd been afraid the lily necklace she was wearing was going to dip into his soup. He'd tried to foist her off on Alfie, Stokes, and any other man in shouting distance just to be able to get through a single course, but while she had charming words for them all, her focus quickly reverted back to her main target.

Her brother wasn't any refuge either. Even saying hello to Monsieur Henri was enough to get him ranting about all sorts of political things Dominick didn't have the faintest clue about. In contrast, their father was a sanctuary of reason and calm, even if he was wearing enough wig powder to make Dominick sneeze.

It seemed that everyone assumed Dominick was going to wait until after dinner to make his grand pronouncement, so at least he and Alfie would have full bellies if they had to make a quick escape from a displeased mob. Or an overly pleased one. Dominick still hadn't decided exactly what he was going to say.

He snuck a glance at Alfie around Miss Lamourette, not an easy thing to do since she seemed intent on taking up as much of Dominick's attention as possible. But seeing Alfie calmly eating his dinner while nodding at something one of the other diners said was enough to reassure Dominick. If Alfie was relaxed enough to set his knife back down after cutting his beef, rather than clutching it in case of attack, then things were likely to be fine.

With this thought in mind, he leaned back so the servants could remove his dinner plates and replace them with dessert. Since he was still watching Alfie, he got to see the moment when his face lit with delight as a crystal bowl of syllabub was placed before him. The frothy concoction of white wine and lemon was his favourite dessert in the entire world and Alfie was waiting about as patiently as a hound on a hunt for everyone else to be served their portions so he could eat.

Something tickled Dominick's hair and he batted it away absently. A moment later, something heavy settled on his head and a cheer went up around the table. Confused, he reached up to see what it was and was horrified to feel the sharp angles of a crown.

He pushed back from the table and jumped to his feet, the violence of the motion sending his chair skittering back until it tipped and crashed to the floor with a loud bang. If everyone wasn't looking at him before, they were now. Without even thinking, he knocked the crown away.

I don't want this.

The realisation was as sudden as it was inevitable. He

didn't want it. Any of it. Hell, he was barely able to tolerate pretending to be an earl's cousin, and these people wanted him to act like a king? He didn't care if he was born to rule. Let his uncle keep the damned throne and all of France too. However bad Louis XVIII was and however much worse whoever they found to succeed him was going to be, he couldn't do a worse job of it than Dominick would. And even if Dominick could learn to be a king the way he'd learned how to ride, hold a teacup, and not to tell bawdy jokes to anyone with a "Sir" in front of their name unless they told one first—even if he could learn, he didn't want to.

The crown rolled down the length of the dining room, a battered thing of tin and paste jewels like might be found in a theatre trunk. Then with a wobble it changed its course and rolled under the dinner table.

Dominick looked around wide-eyed to see everyone staring at him. Several other society members had leapt to their feet as well. So had Alfie, who held his sword cane in both hands, the blade still sheathed but the catch undone.

"Are you well, sir?" said a voice from behind him. He spun around to see the concerned face of Doctor Mullins.

It took a moment before Dominick was able to speak.

"Fine," he finally said. *Aside from the racing heart and feeling of being a cornered fox.* "I'm fine. Just... startled."

Doctor Mullins gave him a commiserating smile. "Yes, this all must be rather abrupt. My apologies, I saw them coming but didn't have time to intervene." He gave a pointed look to a number of lily pin-sporting young men who Dominick assumed had been the ones to crown him. "While I'm sure this was just a well-intentioned bit of fun, I don't believe it's the proper procedure for a royal coronation."

A few titters went up amongst the crowd before a hunt for the crown under the table began. Soon everyone turned their attention from Dominick as several society members fought playfully over it as if it were an actual crown. The table cheered for the eventual victor and conversation started up again, the moment of tension over. Dominick realised he'd been clenching his fists, thumbs on the outside the way Jimmy had taught him to fight. He shook them out.

Alfie was still standing with the cane in his hands. At Dominick's look, he raised his eyebrows and mouthed, "Mail coach?"

As tempted as he was, Dominick shook his head, and motioned for him to sit. Alfie did so slowly and Dominick noticed he kept one hand on his cane, the handle still unlatched.

"Here you go," said Doctor Mullins. He and two repentant looking men righted Dominick's chair.

He sat back down with a muttered thanks and still-frayed nerves. Almost immediately, another unwanted weight was upon him, this time in the form of Miss Lamourette as she seated herself directly in his lap.

"Miss Lamourette!" he hissed.

"Oh, it's quite all right," she giggled. "Besides, in all the excitement, I'm afraid I knocked over my dessert. Might I have some of yours?"

Without waiting for his answer, she dipped her spoon into the sweet treat, moaning indecently as she sucked it off the spoon with an audible pop. She shifted in his lap, her buttocks pressing dangerously close to a place he didn't want them to be, and went back for another spoonful. This one she licked off with delicate kitten licks, looking at Dominick coyly through her lashes as she did so.

Christ, he'd known subtler Covent Garden whores. Even Jarrett at his most obscene couldn't hold a candle to her.

"Oh, that's divine," she purred. "The aniseed is unexpected, but I find a bit of bitterness makes everything else so much sweeter, don't you agree?"

She ran her finger around the edge of the bowl, bringing up a healthy dollop of syllabub. "Care for a taste?"

Dominick declined.

Undeterred, she popped her finger into her mouth, pursing her lips around it.

I wonder if she'd be willing to teach Alfie a trick or two, Dominick thought, and had to bite his lip to keep from laughing. Then he remembered Alfie's position against the wall a few hours earlier. Clearly the man was already a master wanton and needed no further instruction in the art of seduction. Although Dominick was fully willing to help him practise his skills any time he wanted.

"She's at it again," he heard someone whisper. He looked around, but it could have come from any one of the disapproving faces looking his way. Well, looking Miss Lamourette's way, but considering she was doing her best to get Dominick to sire a royal heir with her right there at the dinner table, it was much the same thing.

❋ ❋ ❋

When the ladies withdrew after dinner, Dominick had never been more relieved. Port and cigars were passed around, but as the minutes ticked by the conversation amongst the men began to slow, stopping entirely every time Dominick opened his mouth so much as to ask for another drink. He knew what they were all expecting from him, and knew there was only so much longer he could put it off.

Finally, Monsieur Henri spoke up, "Stokes, with your permission, perhaps it is time for us to rejoin the ladies so they might also hear any announcements that are to be made?"

"A capital idea," Stokes agreed. Unable to bend over due to his tight lacing, he rocked forward several times before finally getting to his feet with the assistance of the table. The rest of the men followed suit, but when they turned into the drawing room Dominick hesitated.

Alfie touched his elbow gently. "Nick?"

"Go on ahead," Dominick said. "I'm just going to get some air first."

Alfie frowned. "Do you want me to come with you?"

"No, I'll be fine. I just need a moment."

"All right," Alfie relented at last, giving his elbow a quick squeeze before letting go. "But remember what I said about cutting off all my hair last time. Either you run off with me or not at all. Promise?" A thread of seriousness wove through his light words.

"I promise. Now go in and make up some excuses for me."

"I always do."

With one last squeeze, Alfie left and Dominick made his

way out onto the terrace.

The night air was cool, but not so cold he needed his overcoat. After the warmth of so many bodies in one room, he welcomed it, feeling the chill soothe his overheated face. He took several deep breaths, drinking it in until he almost felt normal. It was a cloudy evening, but here and there a few stars peeked through, the lights from the house behind him not enough to hide their shine.

In the dimness, the garden lost all its colour, becoming a sea of twisting shapes in shadows and greys. When the moon came out from behind a cloud, the white flowers glowed with an eerie light before fading again as the moon was covered once more. The whole thing made him think of the story Alfie had so poorly told him of the haunted forest inhabited by a witch.

"Oh, here you are, Mr. Trent."

Miss Lamourette wasn't exactly the hag from the fairy tale, but her voice still sent chills up Dominick's spine.

"I'll be just a moment, Miss Lamourette. Please go back inside."

"But it's such a lovely night. Sh-surely, it's even better enjoyed with company."

Dominick sighed. He hadn't wanted to cause a scene earlier, but even he knew that the daughter of a marquis should not be out alone at night with a man, especially if she already had a... tarnished reputation. The last thing this cesspool of a situation needed was any sort of accusations being made.

He didn't need to hear the slight slur to her words to know she'd been drinking all evening as well, which could only make the situation even worse.

"Miss Lamourette—"

"It's so cold out tonight! L-look at me, I'm trembling." With that she tucked herself against Dominick's side, nudging his arm as if she expected him to wrap it around her. If so, she was sorely disappointed.

But for all her false pretences, her shivers were real enough. Dominick could feel them even through his coat. So be it. If she wanted to be outside in a dress that was little more than a glorified nightgown, that was her choice.

It was also her choice if she wanted to throw herself at him. He was done trying to protect her virtue. He wasn't her father or brother to tell her how to behave, and if anyone did see them, she was the one who would face the bulk of the outrage, not him. It wasn't fair, but that was how the world worked.

It was a pity too. She was actually quite a charming girl when she forgot to flirt. Pretty, too. Dominick had been with both men and women in his past, not just as a prostitute, but for his own enjoyment as well. But while he was fond of both, he *loved* Alfie and it would take more than a bit o'muslin to tempt him away from that. Let some other man more receptive to her attentions enjoy them.

If she would only act like herself, he could see where they might become friends. He certainly admired her courage, turning a damaged reputation into the determination to go after what she wanted, be that an earl or a king.

A king.

He'd put this off long enough. Time to go back in and seal his fate.

He turned to face her and offered her his arm. In the

low light, her pupils were blown wide, her eyes almost completely black.

"I'm going back in. Care for an escort?"

She surged forward and kissed him.

It wasn't much of a kiss, barely more than a press of lips, their noses colliding at the abrupt angle. He stepped back immediately, wanting no part of this, but she clung to him even as he tried to shake her off.

Anger swelled in him as well as shame. How many people had treated his body like they could do whatever they wanted with him? How many years had he been forced to swallow back his feelings as he was kissed, fondled, and fucked by people he didn't want, just so he could afford a meal? Those days should be behind him, but here it was, happening again. He wasn't a king; he was still just a whore. Even though it was only a kiss, it still made him feel just as dirty as it used to.

He shook her again, more violently this time, but still her hands gripped his labels. When he grabbed them, ready to throw her off, he was shocked to find her hands were like iron. When he finally tore her away, they stayed curled in tight claws. He held her by her wrists, his fury still rising. He could feel the cruel words building on his tongue when the look on her face stopped him. She didn't look pleased or triumphant; she looked terrified.

Of course she did; he was a large, angry man. Even if she'd been the one to cause his anger, she was right to be terrified. He wouldn't harm her, but there was no way for her to know that. He'd known that same fear when he was smaller, and was rarely lucky enough to be around men who wouldn't harm him. Recognising it in her now was enough to cool his rage, but not completely extinguish it.

He loosened his grip. "Hey now, I'm not going to hurt you."

She still looked up at him, terrified and unmoving. It was more than just fear of him keeping her still. Something was wrong.

"What is it?" he asked.

She worked her mouth several times, as if she wasn't able to get it to open. Finally she stuttered out, "S-spinning."

Then she collapsed.

He barely caught her in time to keep her head from striking the flagstones. He sat heavily, rolling her over so her head was cradled in his lap.

She stared up at him, eyes blown wide and brimming with terror. The shivers he'd felt before were her only movement aside from the quick rise and fall of her chest, each breath more shallow than the last.

"I've got you. It'll be all right." Then he shouted, "Help! Help! Send the doctor! Help!"

Within moments, the doors to the terrace burst open and a flood of people spilled out into the night. At the head of the pack was Doctor Mullins, who immediately dropped to his knees beside Dominick.

"When did this start?"

"Barely a minute ago. She was shivering before that, but I just thought she was cold."

"I need light!" Doctor Mullins shouted. "And my bag!"

"What's happening?" Monsieur Henri pushed his way to the front of the crowd, behind him was his father, his white makeup glowing with a ghostly light.

"She collapsed," said Dominick. He glanced at Doctor Mullins. "Just like Lord Boyle."

It wasn't really a question, but Doctor Mullins gave him a brisk nod in answer anyway. And just like Lord Boyle, she was going to die.

Dominick swallowed, then looked down at Miss Lamourette. "You'll be fine. I've got you. Doctor Mullins is here. He'll get you sorted in no time."

Monsieur Henri stumbled forward and knelt to take her clenched hand in his. "All is well, Adelaide. All is well."

Her lily necklace rose and fell rapidly with each laboured breath. Then it stilled.

A silence fell over the stunned society. Then there was a sound, an animalistic cry. Dominick had never heard a banshee before, the ghostly wail of lament at the moment of death, but that was the sound being wrenched from Monsieur Courtanvaux now.

He howled again, the grief and pain in it bringing tears to Dominick's eyes. More than one person began to cry. Then the murmurs began.

"Just like Batty..."

"...my God, but if it was..."

"...poison..."

"You saw how she..."

"Poison."

"...but it was *his* dessert."

"...Nick? Nick, set her down, there's nothing more you can do."

Alfie lifted Dominick's arms from around Miss Lamourette, then with Doctor Mullins help, he softly laid her on the terrace.

"Alfie," Dominick whispered. "My syllabub. She said it tasted bitter."

There was a long pause before Alfie answered. "Mine didn't."

Poison. It was true. But the deadly dose hadn't been in her dessert. It'd been in Dominick's. She wasn't supposed to be lying there dead. He was.

The whispers grew louder and louder. Someone had taken the marquis inside, but his muffled wails could still be heard over the din. There was an ugly, shuddering sound. Dominick looked over at Monsieur Henri. His face was wet with tears. He gave another awful, wet sob and stood.

"Society!" Monsieur Henri called out, his voice cracking with emotion. "My sister is dead! Murdered! Poisoned!"

He stopped then and took in a rattling breath, grimacing at the pain of saying the words aloud. Then he raised his head and once more Dominick could see the zealot's fire in his eyes.

"But more than that, my sister was assassinated! For she was not the target of this crime. The vile poisoner meant to kill the king! We all saw her eat from his bowl! That was a divine twist of fate. She did not know it, but her actions saved his life, and saved the dream—*her* dream of a better France! My sister is dead so he may live, so our dream may live! She dies a true martyr to the cause. The first to fall in the name of the true king.

"Brethren, will her death be in vain? Or will you stand with me and in her name, in honour of her sacrifice, return the rightful heir to the throne of France? *Vive le roi! Vive le roi! Vive le roi!*"

The rest of the society took up the chant, their voices filling the garden and spilling over the walls.

Dominick looked down at the body of Miss Lamourette and with a shaking hand, gently closed her eyes.

CHAPTER 20

The day of Miss Lamourette's funeral was sunny and bright. Birds twittered as they swooped through the air, and the last of the spring flowers had finally come into bloom, dotting the hillsides around Bath with patches of yellow and purple.

It was cruel, Alfie thought. The weather should be as miserable as the rest of them were. At least it had the decency not to be warm. He wrapped his overcoat more closely around him as the wind huffed out its last few breaths of winter.

The days since her death had been a blur of quiet chaos. They hadn't seen the marquis and his son at all, but Mrs. Stockton acted as a go-between for the two households, helping the Lamourettes make burial arrangements while she and her husband mourned another of their circle lost.

The funeral service had taken place at Bath Abbey, with its soaring arches and countless stained-glass windows whose light dotted the black-clad mourners in patches of inappropriately bright colours. Alfie thought that Miss Lamourette would've liked that. With her reputation, he'd worried the vast nave would be mostly empty, but instead it'd seemed like all of Bath society was there. Clearly, nothing cleaned a reputation like an untimely death. Or maybe they were there to gawk at the spectacle. By sending

Batty's body to his family, Bath had been denied the chance to whisper over the funeral of a murder victim.

How excited they must be to have a second opportunity, he thought bitterly.

He and Dominick had stayed towards the back, unwilling to intrude on the family's grief. But they were not so far away that they couldn't see how stiffly Monsieur Henri held himself as he was offered condolence after condolence or the way the marquis had aged ten years in just a few days.

Afterwards, he'd followed a silent Dominick out and wasn't surprised when instead of following the crowds north towards the fashionable end of town where the many gatherings were being held ostensibly in Miss Lamourette's honour, he headed due east instead. Within a few blocks, they were crossing over the river that marked the edges of the city and were soon surrounded by lush greenery. Dominick's pace slowed once they were out of the city proper, allowing Alfie to mostly keep up as the ground steadily rose beneath them.

He was worried about Dominick. He'd been far too quiet since Miss Lamourette's death, doing little more than nodding when Doctor Mullins confirmed she'd been poisoned as well, as if that wasn't obvious to everyone. When he closed his eyes at night, Alfie could still see the look on Dominick's face when they'd found him cradling her body on the terrace. The pain there was enough to break Alfie's own heart. He couldn't imagine how Dominick felt. Couldn't imagine and hadn't been told, leaving him no choice but to wonder and worry.

"Give me a moment," Alfie said as the path hit a rocky

patch and he needed to calculate exactly where to place his cane to best support him. He'd mostly recovered from Doctor Mullins' treatments but he hadn't been prepared for a hike through the countryside.

"Sorry," Dominick said. He offered a hand which Alfie took more because he wanted to than because he needed it. Once Alfie was over the difficult section, Dominick didn't continue on, instead he just stood there looking down at their hands.

In a better world, Alfie could have kissed the misery off his face, but instead he just squeezed the hand in his. "Do you want to talk about it?"

"She shouldn't have died."

"I know," Alfie said, squeezing again. "It was awful. I'm sure the magistrate is doing everything he can to find out what happened. And if he isn't, we certainly will. For her father and brother at least, even if there's nothing we can do for her."

Dominick shook his head and began to walk again, slower than before. His hand slipped from Alfie's, but his pace was easy enough for Alfie to match, so he brushed their shoulders together as often as he could, hoping that would provide some comfort.

"What I mean," Dominick said again, when they'd walked several minutes in silence, "is she shouldn't have died. It was supposed to be me."

This time it was Alfie who couldn't move forward. He'd been telling himself for days that it wasn't true, that it had all been a mistaken assumption on their parts. But she'd said Dominick's syllabub tasted bitter.

Dominick stilled, but he didn't look at Alfie, directing

his gaze instead behind him. Alfie turned to see what he was looking at, and realised they'd climbed high enough to have the whole city of Bath laid out before them. Spiralling streets coiled beneath the grey slate roofs of the buildings that ran along them, their yellow stone gleaming like gold in the crisp light. From this height, it looked so very small, a child's model of a city, rather than one large enough to contain all the horror of the last few weeks.

"I've been thinking about it." Dominick huffed. "All I've done is think about it. The poisoning had to happen sometime during the dinner party, nothing else makes sense. But when?"

"I don't know," Alfie admitted. "This may sound awful, but I suppose I'd hoped someone handed her a glass of poison at some point and her comment about the syllabub was just a coincidence."

"A coincidence. We seem to be drowning in those lately," Dominick said darkly.

Alfie sighed. As much as he hated to admit it, it was another coincidence too unlikely to be true. "I suppose it's too much to hope that you weren't intentionally targeted?"

"What do you mean?"

"Well," Alfie said. "Batty's death was so arbitrary. Even if it wasn't in the fountain water, if he was poisoned at the soiree and not at dinner, there were scores of people there. No one could have known who would eat the poisoned sweetmeat or whatever it was. And as for Miss Lamourette, the syllabubs were all brought out on large trays, nothing to distinguish one bowl from another. It may have just been random chance they were the ones to end up dead."

Dominick nodded. "I thought the same at first. But then

I thought about it a little more. Lord Boyle might have been on the verge of bankruptcy, but he was still a lord, and then there is a second poisoning at a dinner to celebrate... someone of even higher social standing."

A king. A dinner to celebrate a king. You're a king, Nick, and you still can't believe it. I still can't believe it.

Alfie couldn't hold still a moment longer. If they were going to have this talk, they were going to have it walking so he could focus on the ache in his leg and not everything else.

"You believe they were assassinations?" he said, when he heard Dominick's footsteps catch up to him. "Someone murdering the aristocracy one at a time?"

"It makes sense. There were a lot of people with funny politics at that dinner with us. Not just wanting to overthrow a French king, that's bad enough, but doing the same here, or other strange ideas. If some of them were happy talking treason, then why not be willing to act on it? I haven't figured out yet why Lord Boyle was targeted, but we know he was against the Lily Society. He could have easily caught our murderer's eye. Perhaps they got into an argument about—what was all that nonsense? Absolute monarchies and correctional monarchies?"

"Constitutional monarchies." Alfie hated where this conversation was going. "Or perhaps the killer doesn't like the idea of a monarchy at all, so when a king falls neatly into his lap, he sets his cap at a bit of regicide. And what, pays the cook and one of the footmen to poison a bowl of syllabub in the kitchen and make sure it was delivered to you?"

Dominick shook his head. "It didn't happen in the

kitchen."

"I don't understand."

"It's like this: Assuming our killer is one of the society members, there's only one way he could have ensured my bowl contained the poison and not his own. You remember the commotion just as it was being served? Those damn fools with their tin crown?"

Alfie remembered. When he'd heard Dominick's shout, he'd been ready to take on whatever danger was at hand. But he'd had no idea the real danger was sitting in a crystal bowl. "You're saying our assassin put something in your food when we were distracted?"

"Had to have. I certainly wasn't watching my bowl and I doubt anyone else was either, especially once the damned crown rolled under the table and they all went after it. Miss Lamourette was all over me after that point, so it couldn't have happened later. I didn't get a bite of it myself. All that moaning and spoon licking." Dominick smiled fondly. "She really was a shameless hussy. God rest her."

Meanwhile, Alfie's stomach was roiling. Not just at the thought of someone trying to kill Dominick, unfortunately, he had far too much experience with that already. But to do it in such an awful way, dropping something in his food then sitting back to watch him eat it, knowing he was going to die. What had they thought when Miss Lamourette had slipped that first deadly spoonful into her mouth instead? Of course, they weren't going to yell, "Don't! It's poisoned!" and doom themselves to the gallows. But they could have caused another distraction, thrown something, feigned illness, anything. Instead, they'd said nothing and let an innocent woman die.

"Oh God, she was killed right in front of us and we didn't even know."

Dominick nodded.

They reached the crest of the hill. Up here, the wind was even colder than in the protected confines of the city. It blew more strongly too, flapping Alfie's coattails against his legs. He shuddered, but not just from the cold. "It's so horrible, Nick."

"I know."

"If she hadn't done all that. If it'd been you—"

Dominick cut him off. "I know. Her father and brother, I couldn't even bear to look at them at the funeral. They have to blame me. How could they not? I know, I know, that it wasn't my fault but… That's why I had to get out of there. If only for a bit. I should have told you before, but I wanted to think it all out first."

"I understand." Alfie truly did. He was sure there was even more to it than that, Dominick having to face coming so close to death once again, only to have someone else unknowingly take his place and die so horribly in his arms. He still wished Dominick had said something though, let Alfie share his burden. But they weren't at Balcarres where the walls were thick and the servants were few, they had to be careful.

Dominick was looking back over Bath again, his brow furrowed and gaze somewhere even further away than the city below.

Alfie stepped closer, letting the shared heat of their bodies warm a long line down their sides as he too looked out, lost in his own thoughts. Finally, his gaze began to wander from the city to the countryside around them. He jerked his head back in shock.

"Is that a castle?"

"Something like that." Dominick snorted. Then he tilted his head to the side. "Fragile thing, isn't it? Life. You never really know how close yours is to being snuffed out."

Alfie didn't know what he was meant to say to that. It was certainly true, Miss Lamourette's tragically short life was proof enough, not to mention their many close scrapes.

Fortunately, Dominick didn't seem to be waiting for his response. Instead, he just nodded to himself. "Best not to waste it. Alfie, stroll around and make sure no one's about. There's a door on the back of one of those short square towers. In five minutes if the coast is clear, knock three times then go in."

"What on Earth?"

Dominick grinned. "Five minutes, remember!"

Then he took off towards the castle without further explanation. Alfie sighed, and began a slow loop of the area as he counted off the minutes.

Roughly five minutes later, assured there was no one else about, Alfie stood under the archway of the castle. While there was only one standing wall, it was far too neat to be a ruin. It must instead be some rich man's folly, built to improve the view from his house. He looked down the hill to Bath, where he could make out any number of grand homes whose owner might have constructed it. He hoped the rest of them enjoyed the view as well.

What in God's name was Dominick up to anyway? He was nowhere to be found, the close-mouthed bastard, so Alfie supposed he had no choice but to carry out the rest of his orders. He found the door on the back of one of the short towers, ignoring the door beside it attached to one of the taller, circular ones, and knocked three times.

There was no response. Alfie rolled his eyes. Whatever scheme Dominick was running had better be worth it. He tucked his cane into the crook of his arm and pulled on the door handle. It was surprisingly heavy and caught in the tall grass that grew all around the folly, leaving enough space for Alfie to walk through, but opening no further. With a deep breath, he stepped inside.

"Nick?" The room was dim, a scarce amount of light filtering in from two dirty windows at the top of the tower, too narrow to be climbed through, and too high for even someone on horseback to look in. A little more light made it around him through the open doorway and when his eyes adjusted, he slammed the door shut behind him.

The room was warm, almost stuffy without the wind to cut through it. It was small too, likely smaller than some of the closets at Balcarres even, but more than enough room for a man to walk around in. Or lie down in, which Dominick was currently proving from where he was sprawled on a pile of blankets in the middle of the room, completely naked.

"Make sure to lock it too," Dominick said wickedly. He ran a hand slowly up his inner thigh. Alfie whipped around, focussing all his attention on bolting the door to make sure he did it right. He stuffed a handkerchief into the keyhole for good measure. When his breathing had returned to something approaching normal, he spun back around, his forgotten cane striking the wall as he did so and clattering to the stone floor.

"What in God's name are you doing, Nick?"

Dominick raised an eyebrow at that before pointedly moving his hand from his thigh to grip his cock, giving it several long, tantalisingly slow strokes. He was half-hard already, his other hand tucked behind his head like the wanton he was. Alfie's mouth watered.

Dominick's voice was a rumble that went right to Alfie's core. "I'd say that's obvious." He looked down at himself. "Very obvious."

Alfie ignored his leer. "What if I'd been someone else?"

"Then they'd be in for a right treat." He grinned up at Alfie. "I believe I owe you a forfeit after our billiards game?"

Alfie licked his lips. "Two."

Dominick hummed and ran his fingers over the head of his cock, moisture beading up under his palm. "Care to make it three?"

Alfie groaned and sank to his knees. However, rather than putting his mouth where Dominick obviously wanted it, he crawled up the length of his body until he was hovering over Dominick instead, his hands planted above Dominick's shoulders.

"Hello, you," Dominick said softly.

Alfie couldn't help it. He dipped his head down and gave Dominick a long, deep, and utterly thorough kiss. This wasn't one of the quick stolen kisses they'd been forced to survive on the last few days, or even the devouring kisses of the other night. Too much had happened since. Alfie needed to feel Dominick, to prove to himself that he was really alive. Dominick seemed happy to reassure him, opening his mouth immediately and coaxing Alfie's tongue inside with a gentle sucking that went straight to

Alfie's cock.

When he ran out of air, Alfie pulled back, only for Dominick to drag him back down, gripping Alfie's short hair fiercely, too used to being able to manoeuvre him by his curls. His tongue was a welcome invader, licking across the roof of Alfie's mouth. Something about that particular move never failed to make Alfie shudder.

Finally, exhausted from days of fear and grief, his body couldn't take any more of the pleasure. His elbows buckled, banging his nose against Dominick's cheek painfully and dropping him down onto Dominick's inviting chest.

He lay there panting, suddenly aware of how painfully tight his trousers had become.

"Christ, I've missed you."

Dominick's hand that had been tangled in his hair draped across his back, and he worked his other arm out from between them, slinging it low and possessive over Alfie's hip.

"You had me just the other day."

"Not properly."

Alfie shifted into a more comfortable spot on Dominick's chest, nuzzling into the golden hair there. He wondered if Dominick even realised he was still wearing his bird ring.

"How did you even know about this place?" Alfie asked.

"I came here with Monsieur Henri."

Alfie raised his head and fixed Dominick with a look.

"Not *here* here, you daft ninny. We rode by it that first day after you'd been not-quite-poisoned and were supposed to be resting. He mentioned it had a reputation as a *meeting place*."

Alfie jerked up. "My God, this is the folly Miss Lamourette invited me to!"

Dominick chuckled. "Did she now? I can't blame her for trying. Poor brash girl." His tone grew more wistful. "It sounded like she was caught here herself once. Forgot to lock the door."

"Where her reputation began." Alfie remembered Dominick telling him what Monsieur Henri had said. He carefully pulled himself out of Dominick's grasp and rose to double check the door. Still locked, and firmly.

He looked around the room again, doing his best to ignore Dominick this time, even as every fibre of his being screamed at him that Dominick was *right there* and *naked*.

Thick stone walls to muffle any sound, high windows with smeared glass for light but no chance at being spotted or heard if anyone came this way. It wasn't exactly one of their velvet-draped beds back home, but it would do.

He wrinkled his nose. "I don't love the thought of what might be on those blankets."

"Ah, see, I thought you might say that. That's why I laid my overcoat down on top. If it gets too ruined, I'll just say I dropped it in the mud and left it where it fell. A chilly walk back will be worth it."

Alfie laughed. "Thought of everything, have you?"

"Not quite," Dominick said. "I hadn't planned ahead, so I was worried our options might be limited. Good thing I found this."

He held up a small glass bottle. Alfie couldn't tell exactly what was inside, but it looked viscous and slick.

Dominick winked. "I guess we're not the only ones."

Alfie would have a reply to that, if his mouth

wasn't completely dry. Instead, he began tugging at his overcoat. His coat followed next—why were the damn things cut so tight—then the rest of his clothing. In other circumstances, he might have made a show of it for Dominick, but it'd been weeks since they'd been able to be together properly. If he didn't get Dominick's naked body against his own soon, he might actually die.

It didn't help that Dominick was putting on a show for him instead, touching himself on all of Alfie's favourite places as Alfie cursed his damned buttons. Dominick ran fingers down the side of his own neck, then through his chest hair to circle his nipples, then lower.

"Stop that, damn you," Alfie hissed. "Or this will be a swift and disappointing rendezvous."

He should've known better.

"Excited, are we?" Dominick purred. Then in one smooth motion, he rolled up on his knees and yanked Alfie's half-open trousers down, taking his drawers with them. That was all the warning Alfie had before Dominick's mouth was on him, surrounding his cock in gloriously wet heat.

His hips jerked of their own accord, but Dominick only groaned, pressing himself deeper until he'd taken Alfie all the way to the root, his throat fluttering around Alfie's cock. Alfie bit his wrist to stifle his cry, then remembered where they were. He could make as much noise as he wanted, or as much as Dominick could wring from him. The latter was quite a bit more.

"Oh fuck, oh fuck. Nick, please!"

Dominick pulled back with a pleased hum, the vibrations lighting sparks in front of Alfie's eyes. Then he took Alfie back in again until his nose was pressed against Alfie's pubic hair, his hot exhalations tickling across his skin. Alfie didn't think he'd ever master this trick himself, especially considering how thick Dominick's cock was, but God, he was glad Dominick had.

Dominick gripped his hips, controlling Alfie's movements backwards and forwards into his mouth. It was all Alfie could do to stay upright. He leaned forward, curling his body over Dominick's and holding onto his shoulders for dear life.

"Oh God, Nick, you're beautiful like this. Don't stop, don't stop!"

Dominick kept it up for several torturous minutes, then sat back on his heels. He looked up at Alfie, the tip of Alfie's cock resting against his lips. His mouth was swollen and his chin shining with his own spit and Alfie's pre-spend. He looked like a fallen angel. Then he stuck out his tongue and licked.

Alfie hissed. He was so sensitive, he couldn't tell if the feeling was pleasure or pain. He'd forgotten fallen angels were devils.

"Wicked." He panted. "Wicked, evil, t-terrible bastard."

Dominick licked him again. And again. Even if Alfie wanted to squirm away, he couldn't, Dominick's grip crushingly tight, his thumbs digging into Alfie's skin.

There'll be bruises tomorrow, he thought desperately. *Even if they're hidden under my clothes, I'll know they're there. He'll know they're there.*

And still Dominick toyed with him, bringing him close to the brink, then backing off. Alfie couldn't take it anymore, but neither, he suddenly realised, could his leg.

"Nick, Nick," he gasped.

Dominick pulled back. "It's all right. Come for me, love."

Alfie was so, so close, but that wasn't it. "No, my leg."

The shudders he'd first attributed to lust were growing violent now.

"Ah, I see. Easy there, I've got you."

And he did. Dominick eased Alfie down onto the pile of blankets. The fine wool of the overcoat was a welcome relief, surrounding him in Dominick's scent and drowning out whatever else the tattered blankets might have smelled of.

Dominick pressed himself against Alfie's side, and dropped a kiss on his shoulder. "I suppose the long walk uphill didn't help."

"Was it that or was it you trying to suck my soul out through my cock?"

He felt Dominick's grin rather than saw it. "Hard to tell. Want me to try again and see?"

Yes, yes, yes, yes!

"Actually," Alfie said, knowing he was blushing. After everything they'd done together, he shouldn't still have such a reaction to dirty words. "I was hoping I could fuck you. If you didn't mind. Or rather, I want you to ride on me. If you want that too."

Dominick let out a strangled noise.

"Nick?"

Dominick gulped. "Christ, the mouth on you."

"You like my mouth."

"Nothing but trouble," Dominick muttered, clearly more to himself than Alfie. "Should have left you in the gutter where I found you. All right, move, move. Where's that damned oil?"

"Oh. I thought you were ah, ready to go already."

Dominick stopped his searching to stare at him. "I only had a five-minute head start! You think I made sure this room was empty, piled the blankets, found the oil, got naked *and* stretched myself all in five minutes? I'm damned good, but I can't work miracles!"

Alfie laughed. "I suppose not. Would you like some help?"

Dominick fumbled the retrieved bottle and dropped his chin against his chest. He let out a heavy sigh, then moved to place his mouth at the base of Alfie's neck, just below what would be covered by his collar and bit him.

"Wicked. Evil. Terrible. Bastard." Dominick parroted back, punctuating each word with a bite. He slung a leg over Alfie's chest and shuffled up so his knees were tucked into Alfie's armpits and slapped the bottle into his hand. "Go ahead, you villain, do your worst."

Alfie did, slicking one finger and reaching around Dominick. He took his time pushing into him, enjoying the tight pressure of Dominick's arse. He stroked his finger over the velvety walls and reached for the spot that made Dominick writhe and curse. He couldn't quite get it from this angle, but their position afforded him other delights. As he slid a second finger in, he craned his neck forward and licked a stripe up Dominick's cock.

"Christ!" Dominick shouted. He bent over, the change in angle making them both gasp, and did something to the blankets behind Alfie's head. When he leaned his head back, Alfie realised Dominick had pulled them into a pillow of sorts. A surge of fondness momentarily overrode the want.

However, the want redoubled its strength and in no time, Dominick was shuffling back, three of Alfie's fingers slipping from his body as he poured more of the oil over Alfie's cock and positioned himself above it. His eyes twinkled in the low light.

"Ready?" He asked.

"Just a moment."

Dominick raised an eyebrow, but waited. He was glorious like this, skin flushed with want and a small smile, just for Alfie, toying around the edges of his mouth. It was more than just how he looked, however. It was the way he responded to Alfie, taking such care when his leg couldn't continue as they were, arranging this nest and sacrificing his overcoat to the cause, knowing it would make Alfie more comfortable. It was all the little things he did every day, knowing how Alfie took his tea, telling him stories, and just being there when Alfie needed him.

And all he asked in return was for Alfie to do those exact same things for him. As if there was anything else Alfie would rather devote his life to doing.

"I'm madly in love with you, you know?" Alfie whispered.

Dominick's grin widened. "You just realised now?"

"No, but it bears repeating."

Dominick leaned down and dropped a feather-light kiss against his lips. "Then it's a good thing I'm madly in love with you too."

He brushed his nose against Alfie's. "Ready now?"

The instant Alfie nodded, Dominick dropped himself down, burying Alfie almost to the hilt.

Alfie's whole body rose off the blankets, pinned to the ground only by the weight of Dominick on top of him. Dominick let out a sound that wasn't human, sitting bolt upright, his beautiful body mostly out of Alfie's reach. He clawed his hands into the coat instead as Dominick lifted up on his knees until only the last inch of Alfie's cock was inside him. Then Dominick dropped himself again and again, his bollocks slapping against Alfie's groin, the obscene sound echoing around the room with their curses and cries.

The next few minutes existed only in flashes of sensation. Dominick with his head thrown back, sweat beading on his chest and dripping down onto Alfie. The sound of flesh against flesh as Dominick rode him, the bounce of his ring against his chest setting the pace as his hips rolled in perfect synchronicity with Alfie's own, coming together each time in sharp bursts of unspeakable pleasure. Dominick's shouts as Alfie scrambled for any part of him he could reach, raking his nails up Dominick's thighs and leaving marks of his own.

Then Dominick cried out one final time and his body clamped down around him. Alfie felt a hot splash of liquid and looked down just in time to see Dominick's cock jerk in his fist as he came all over Alfie's stomach.

Then his vision whited out as his own orgasm struck him. All Alfie could do was gasp as wave after wave of pleasure crashed over him.

When he came back to himself, he had no idea how much time had passed. The air was still hot and stank of sex. Dominick was still straddling him, his breaths harsh. Alfie tried to help as Dominick leaned forward just enough for Alfie's now softened cock to slip from his body, but found he wasn't quite able to move yet. Then Dominick crashed down onto him, and he found he had just enough strength to turn his head to kiss Dominick's temple.

"Nick?" he whispered.

Dominick rumbled out a questioning noise that was almost a word.

"You still owe me another forfeit."

CHAPTER 21

Dominick would be content to stay in this squalid, cramped, stuffy folly until the end of time. Or at least until they got hungry, whichever came first. He'd choose this tiny room with Alfie in it over a fancy manor house without him any day.

With any luck, they'd sort out this damned poisoner soon enough and then he could take Alfie back to their fancy manor house, neatly solving both problems. There was also this king nonsense to deal with, but he wasn't going to think about that right now. He'd had far too few chances in the last months to just enjoy lying with Alfie, he wasn't going to ruin this one.

What little light filtered down from the high windows didn't do a sleeping Alfie justice. Dominick had never been one for art, but when the sun lit Alfie's auburn curls just right, or the warm glow of a fire made his lips look impossibly red, he wished he could capture that look and keep it forever. It probably didn't matter though. He doubted any artist could truly capture Alfie the way Dominick saw him.

"You're thinking too loud," Alfie grumbled. "What is it?"

Dominick smiled and kissed Alfie's shoulder. "Just sentimental nonsense."

"Mm. Well, keep it down. Some of us are enjoying the quiet."

Tucked up against Alfie's side as he was, Dominick couldn't resist running his fingers over Alfie's chest and stomach, coming just close enough to ticklish areas to get Alfie to wrinkle his nose adorably, but not so close he swatted Dominick's hand away. When his fingers trailed through the rapidly cooling spend he'd shot all over Alfie, a possessive pride coiled up happily in his stomach. He'd have to take care of that soon—either clean Alfie up or mark him again.

Distracted, his fingers trailed too far down Alfie's ticklish side and he earned himself a swat. Then Alfie rolled over so he was facing him, their faces only inches away, sharing the same pillow of wadded up and thoroughly destroyed overcoat.

"I can never have any peace with you, can I?" asked Alfie, but his tone was fond.

"You're one to talk. You're the one always getting us involved in murders and such. At least my distractions are enjoyable."

"You consider the overthrow of a royal line of succession enjoyable?"

Dominick didn't answer that. In the poor light, Alfie's hair was faded to the colour of an old tuppence. It was still so short too.

I wonder how long it'll take to grow back fully.

His thoughts were interrupted by Alfie's sigh. "I'm not daft, Nick. I can tell you don't want to talk about it, but we need to anyway."

Dominick gestured between their thoroughly naked

bodies. "Now?"

"While we're in a place where we can't be overheard and there's a locked door between us and any potential interruptions? We're not going to get a better time. You can put your trousers on if it'll make you feel better."

Dominick did no such thing. That would mean moving. "All right. Go ahead."

"Do you want to be the king of France?"

"Christ, why don't you just ask directly?"

Dominick tried to roll away, but Alfie pulled him back. He left his hand on Dominick's hip, the warmth of it on his bare skin reminding him he was with the one person in the world he didn't have to hide things from. The one person who loved him and promised to keep him safe, just as he'd promised to keep Alfie safe in turn.

"It's like something out of an adventure novel, isn't it?" Alfie said. "The poor orphan who finds out he's a prince? Perhaps there will be a dragon for you to slay."

"A gothic novel is more like."

"I suppose that's true. The beautiful damsel doesn't usually die in the adventure stories." Alfie's eyes widened. "I'm sorry, that was a terrible thing to say. Tell me again you know that wasn't your fault."

Miss Lamourette's death was another thing Dominick didn't want to think about while he had Alfie in his arms. "Can we stick to one awful conversation at a time?"

Alfie nodded, his nose brushing Dominick's. "That's fair. Which awful conversation would you like to have first?"

Dominick sighed. "Miss Lamourette. Yes, I know it was only the poisoner's fault, and there was no way I could have known, but it's like Helen's murder all over again. I can't help but feel that if I'd been paying more attention, I could've stopped it from happening."

"I felt the same way after we found out Baz killed my cousin," Alfie admitted. "Although at least in that case, I could console myself knowing he had partly brought it upon himself. But neither Helen nor Miss Lamourette deserved their fates. I don't know what to tell you to make it better, except to remind you again it wasn't your fault."

"I know. And the best thing I can do is to catch Miss Lamourette's killer, the same way we caught Helen's, and make him pay. It still hurts though."

Alfie gave him a soft kiss. "You wouldn't be the man I loved if it didn't."

"Now who's sentimental?" Dominick said, but he couldn't help but be touched by Alfie's words.

Alfie gave him what was clearly meant to be a stern look, but this close just made him cross eyed.

"Speaking of the man I love..." Alfie removed his hand from Dominick's hip and moved it to his neck instead. He then followed the line of the chain down until he was resting his palm over Dominick's heart and his damned ring. "Can we move on to *this* awful conversation now?"

Dominick sighed. They did need to talk it over, but that didn't mean he couldn't hate every minute of it. The moment Monsieur Henri called him a king, he'd known that the life they'd been living was over. And now Miss Lamourette's death had given her brother and his followers a cause to rally around. There would be no quiet seclusion in Balcarres to wait things out now.

Whatever he decided, he would no longer just be some

ambiguous relation of Alfie's no one really cared about, living in some out of the way earldom. Now he'd either be a king or he'd be the man who turned down a crown. There was no way to expect the Lily Society members to keep their mouths shut. Even if he'd turned down the chance to be a king, he'd still be noticed and whispered about wherever they went. If they went home, they'd probably start receiving all sorts of unwanted visitors at Balcarres, come to either change his mind or just stare at him like a circus curiosity.

There were more terrible outcomes too, ones where people started looking too hard at his and Alfie's relationship, or began digging into the past of this so-called king and discovered his life in Spitalfields. They'd both be ruined then and he didn't know how to stop it from happening.

If he did agree to try to claim the throne, even just as a successor, there would be war. He had no doubt about that. Could he live with people dying for him in the hundreds? Thousands? What would happen if he won? He knew nothing about ruling a country.

And what would happen if he lost?

"You're thinking too loudly again," Alfie said softly. "Can I guess? You're imagining all the horrible things that might happen if you don't take the crown and all the even more horrible things that might happen if you do."

"I don't want this." Dominick could barely get the words out. He'd never felt as small as he did now.

Alfie moved his hand just enough for the ring to slip free, then he was pressing his hand back against Dominick's heart, skin to skin, nothing else between them.

"I know. I wish you didn't have to deal with this at all. I wish you weren't royalty. I wish your family wasn't dead. I wish your mother had turned out to be a laundress and your father some red-faced publican so proud to share a pint with his long-lost son. But at least now we know. There's something in that. Just think, all the times you were daunted by me being an earl, I should have been ten times more awed to be in the presence of a king!"

The jest fell flat, but Dominick appreciated the attempt. He covered Alfie's hand with his own. "I love you."

Alfie leaned forward to rest their heads against each other. Dominick closed his eyes, and just let himself take the comfort he so desperately needed.

"I love you too, Nick. And there's nothing that could ever change that. Whether you're a prince or a pauper, I'll always love you. It might be harder to be together without scrutiny if you're king, but I suppose kings can do whatever they want. The regent certainly does, and he's not even properly king yet."

"You're not worried I'll go mad with power and turn into a tyrant?"

He felt Alfie's chuckle. "Nick, you'd only accept becoming king if you thought it would make things better. You'd hate every minute of it, but if you thought you could help people, you'd do it and you'd spend your entire reign doing it. And if, *if* you ever started to turn, I'd be right there beside you to tweak your nose and remind you what fine behaviour that was from someone who always made sure we both had exactly the same number of currants in our pudding each Christmas."

Dominick smiled at the memory. He liked that vision

of the future, Alfie standing just to the side of his throne, making sure Dominick always did what was best.

But it would never be. Becoming king would mean losing Alfie. For his own good. If Dominick was on the throne, Alfie would be a dirty secret impossible to keep. His presence would weaken Dominick's rule in front of enemies and allies alike. And more dangerous than the mockery and whispers about him, Alfie's life would be at stake. Dominick might not know much about ruling, but as his own mother proved, those who loved kings died violent deaths.

And for all the good Alfie might see in him, Dominick was too bloody selfish to give him up. Not for a crown. Not for a country. Not for a kingdom.

But he couldn't help but think about those who would suffer for his selfishness. If the society was right and Louis XVIII and his brother-heir were as ill-suited to rule as they said, could Dominick really condemn an entire country of people to suffer just for the sake of his own happiness?

He knew he'd have to make a decision, and soon. But he didn't want to make it now. Not when he could still pretend it was just the two of them, Lord Alfie of the Mud and his Nick, same as it'd always been.

"Dominick, I mean it. It'll all work out. We'll find a way. Whatever you decide, I'll be there."

For just a moment, Dominick let himself believe it.

He had to swallow several times before he could speak without his voice shaking. "Of course you will. Christ, if I haven't been able to shake you yet, I doubt crossing the channel would be enough to do it."

Dominick felt a sharp sting distinctly like he'd been

swatted on his flank.

"You dare assault your king? That's treason, sir!" It was easier to joke about such things than it was to think about them.

He opened his eyes to see Alfie grinning wickedly. "And pray tell, what is the punishment for such a treasonous act?"

Dominick decided it would be better to show him.

❊ ❊ ❊

"I suppose we'd better make our way back to the Stocktons soon. We'll be missed."

"Are you sure that's a good idea?" Alfie's voice was muffled from being facedown in the overcoat, loose limbs sprawled all over the place, but he had a point.

"You think someone will try to poison me again?"

Alfie tried to roll over. It took several attempts. It was possible Dominick could have helped, but he was far too sated and sticky at the moment to feel like doing anything. Besides, watching his sex-drunk lover try to regain control of his limbs was far too entertaining.

Alfie finally rolled over onto his back which had the pleasing effect of tucking him up against Dominick where he belonged.

"You know, most people can fuck without punctuating it with conversations of kings and murders." Alfie sighed.

"So, you *do* think someone is going to try to kill me again."

Alfie scrubbed a hand over his face. "I don't believe the Stocktons will. If either of them is our poisoner, they had plenty of opportunities before the dinner party to do you in. Why wait? That said, I'm not betting your life on it a moment longer than I have to. I'll make hotel enquiries just to be safe."

Dominick shook his head. "I wouldn't do that. If they do want me dead, moving out of the house will only let them know we know. And if they don't, we'd be subjecting ourselves to a subpar hotel for nothing.

Alfie snorted. "And clearly we both require only the finest comforts," he said, patting the ruined overcoat pointedly.

"I say it would be better to stay where we are." Dominick replied. "Besides, both poisonings happened when the rest of the society was about, so odds are it's one of them."

"All right," Alfie yawned and Dominick couldn't help the ripple of pride at being the one to wear him out. "But the moment I don't like the look of the soup, we're gone. Now help me find my trousers."

Later, after seeing a wobbly Alfie out the folly door, Dominick spent the minutes before it would be his turn to leave tidying up and making sure they hadn't left anything incriminating behind. He bundled up his ruined overcoat to be *accidentally* dropped off the bridge as they walked back to the townhouse. Content everything was as it should be, he took a moment to enjoy the silence. It was only then he realised he'd never answered Alfie's question on whether or not he wanted to be king.

Just as well. He knew now what his answer was going to be. He also knew Alfie would hate it.

CHAPTER 22

The Stockton house was quiet that Sunday. The couple and most of their staff were at church, but the house was not quite so empty that it was safe to take advantage of that fact. So instead of the sounds of Dominick pounding him into the mattress, Alfie had to be content to have the quiet broken only by the light clink of billiard balls knocking together.

Dominick's mood had fluctuated since the funeral the day before. Alfie hailed their time together in the folly for the moments he was content and blamed the rest of this bloody situation for when he wasn't. To Dominick's credit, he hadn't gone storming off without Alfie again when his mood turned dark, so at least there was that.

"Your turn." Alfie stepped back from the billiard table.

"What's the score again?" asked Dominick, licking biscuit crumbs from his fingers. A tray of shortbread had been left for their refreshment and Alfie wasn't playing as well as he usually did, too distracted by having to keep an eye on the tray to make sure none of *his* biscuits were stolen while he played.

"It's ninety-eight to two."

Dominick placed his cue ball on the baize and lined up his shot. "That doesn't sound right."

Alfie shrugged. "Then you should've been paying more

attention to the game."

"Ninety-eight to five." Dominick said as the red ball fell neatly into a corner pocket. "I'll be winning in no time."

As Dominick came around to his side of the table for the next shot, Alfie stepped back to better appreciate the view of him in just his shirtsleeves, bent over in a most suggestive way. Alfie bumped into a small table behind him and had to quickly grab for a teetering vase of flowers to keep it from falling over.

"Now who's not paying attention?" Dominick grinned.

"It's not my fault these bloody things are everywhere," Alfie said, setting the vase at the other end of the room where it would be safe from distracted players. "I certainly appreciate Mrs. Stockton's enthusiasm for her garden, but I'm not sure I'll be able to smell anything that isn't flowers for months."

Dominick hummed as he lined up his next shot. "Do you think they're to hide the smell of the poison?"

If Alfie had still been carrying the vase, he would've dropped it. "What?"

"Poison is supposed to have a smell, isn't it? Like almonds? That could be what she's trying to cover."

The billiard balls clattered against each other, but none went into the pockets.

Dominick hummed. "Or perhaps it's to cover the smell of her other victims. We only know of two poisonings, but that doesn't mean there aren't more."

"You're saying Mrs. Stockton is a multiple murderer and is leaving her victims to rot in the cellars?"

Dominick shrugged. "We've seen similar. And it's your turn."

"In this case, the cook might notice. Are you sure you want to talk about this now?"

"No," Dominick said, a little too brightly. "But this is as good a chance we'll get to talk without being overheard."

"We could always go back to the folly," Alfie argued. He aimed his cue, but didn't have a chance to shoot before there was a warm weight against his back and a hand on his arse.

"Love," Dominick whispered, his lips brushing Alfie's ear. "If we go back to the folly, we're not going to talk at all."

Then he was gone, leaving a slightly dazed Alfie in his wake. He narrowed his eyes at Dominick. "You're cheating."

"You started it. Ninety-eight to two, my arse. And now you're distracting me. Mrs. Stockton is our killer, agree or disagree?"

Dominick's tone was light, but Alfie considered the question seriously. They'd overlooked the murderous abilities of women in the past and it'd nearly gotten him killed, so he wasn't going to make the same mistake twice.

"I'd say she's not the most likely candidate, but we can come back to her. In your mind, who is in our pool of suspects?" Alfie wandered over to grab a piece of shortbread since it looked like Dominick wasn't going to let him focus on billiards for a while.

"Well, there's Mrs. Stockton." Dominick started counting the list off on his fingers. "I'm not leaving her off the list just because she's a woman."

Alfie nodded. "My sentiments exactly. And they do say poison is a woman's weapon. Just look at the Borgias."

"Point them out for me at the next party and I will,"

said Dominick. "The more I think about Miss Lamourette's death, the more I'm certain both she and Lord Boyle were poisoned at dinner. It wasn't the fountain water or anything else at the soiree."

"That would make sense with their deaths being so similar," Alfie admitted. "She died an hour after dessert, would you say? It was probably longer for Batty, but he was easily twice her size, it may have just taken longer to work on him."

"Or he got a smaller dose. Either way, our killer has to be someone who was at both dinners, so our list is: Mrs. Stockton, Stokes, Doctor Mullins, and all three Lamourettes."

Alfie blinked. "All three? Surely you don't believe Miss Lamourette poisoned herself?

"I don't know." Dominick shrugged. "She might have killed Lord Boyle on purpose and then gotten distracted during the dinner party and accidentally poisoned herself."

"I'll agree with one part of that."

The billiard balls were perfectly placed to score a double hazard with a cannon and Alfie quickly earned himself another ten points. He straightened and replaced the balls on the table. "The distraction during the dinner was key. I'm certain you're right, it was when they tried to put that crown on your head."

Dominick scowled. "I'd like to know whose damned idea that was. You think it was part of the plan to poison me or did the killer just take advantage of the moment?"

Alfie didn't like hearing those words said aloud. It made some superstitious part of him worry it was going to tempt someone else into poisoning Dominick again. "If our killer knew it was going to happen, they would've been ready. Or they just saw their chance in the chaos. I was watching you and the rest of the table was watching those fools chase the crown under the table. No one was watching the syllabub."

"Except our killer. All right, we know *when*, but that doesn't help us with *who*. And Alfie," Dominick sounded uncharacteristically hesitant. "I know that the killer was likely trying to kill me because of the whole bit about me being…"

Being the rightful king of France? Being in line to rule an entire nation when the current king of France died, if not before? That bit?

"About me being French," Dominick finished lamely. "So, I know it's the likely motive. But I can't talk about both things at once, so if we're doing murder, let's just stay with that?"

Alfie agreed easily. He'd cheerfully live the rest of his life never talking about Dominick "being French". If only the damned Lily Society felt the same way.

"Murder it is. What if each time one of us says 'France' or 'king' they forfeit their turn?"

"That'll work."

"All right, let's start with Miss Lamourette, since I'd say she's the least likely to be our killer. Let me play my turn and while I do that, you can think up your argument."

Alfie scored another eighteen points before finally missing. He gave Dominick a small bow. "Well?"

"You're damned good at this game," Dominick commented.

Alfie shrugged. "There was a table at university and it's

an easy game to play by yourself. Now, what about Miss Lamourette?"

"She was engaged to Lord Boyle, but didn't shed a single tear over his death."

Alfie held up a hand. "They were engaged? How do you know?"

"Almost engaged. Her brother told me. And Stokes too. I suppose with everything else going on, I forgot to tell you. Their father was arranging it. Lord Boyle needed the money and Miss Lamourette needed the respectability."

"I certainly couldn't believe it was a love match."

"No," Dominick walked around the table, looking for the best shot. Alfie tried for a quick grab at him when he passed, but was batted away.

"Now I think back on it," Dominick continued, ignoring Alfie's second attempt, "Miss Lamourette was already flirting with me at the soiree when Mrs. Stockton introduced us. That was before Lord Boyle died, but if she'd poisoned him at dinner, she would've known it was going to happen. So, say she killed him to get out of a marriage she didn't want and then... I don't know why she'd want me dead."

Alfie snorted. "She certainly seemed interested in having you stay alive. Or just having you."

Dominick had been about to take a shot, but he set the cue down and mumbled something to the table.

Alfie leaned in. Dominick was gripping the edge of the table with both hands. Carefully, Alfie laid a hand on the middle of his back. "What was that?"

"I said she kissed me," Dominick spat out. "I'm so sorry, Alfie."

Alfie blinked, whatever he'd been expecting, it wasn't that. His fingers clenched and Dominick flinched under his hand. How dare she do this to him.

"Why the blazes are you sorry? Nick, it's awful she did that to you!"

Dominick gave him a look like Alfie had just announced he was going to start training dancing bears. "You're not angry?"

"I'm fucking livid, but I can't do anything to her now, someone else got there first."

Dominick shook his head and dropped his voice to a whisper. "No, because I'm only supposed to be kissing you."

Alfie slid his hand down to rest in the small of Dominick's back. "You should be. Right now, and for every foreseeable moment in the future. But that can't happen in this bloody house, so the sooner we get this solved, the sooner we can get back to Balcarres where you can make up for lost time."

"You're… not jealous?"

Alfie sighed. How could Dominick be so kind to others, yet so unkind to himself?

"Nick, I know you didn't want her to kiss you. It's the same as you asking if I'm jealous or mad at you because she ran up and kicked you in the shin."

Dominick stared at him for so long that Alfie was afraid he'd said something wrong.

Finally, Dominick whispered, "I don't deserve you."

"You deserve every good thing in the world. I'm just lucky you think I'm on that list." Alfie said. He ignored the temptation to slide his hand lower and show Dominick exactly how much he cared for him. It was true, but it would only cheapen the moment. Instead, he allowed himself to rest his head against Dominick's for a moment before pulling away. "Now, either take your turn or come up with a good reason for her wanting you dead."

Dominick did both, taking a shot before answering. "It could have been political. Lord Boyle wasn't a member of the Lily Society. If she was as much of a zealot as her brother, that might be reason enough to kill him. And she might have wanted me gone if she secretly disagreed with the plan to make me king."

"Ah! You said 'king'. Forfeit. My turn." Alfie held up a finger. "I do see what you're saying, but if it was Miss Lamourette, poisoning your dessert would've happened bare minutes before she ate it herself. She was flighty, but she wasn't stupid. It occurs to me that if the motivations were political, her brother is the much more likely suspect."

He knocked Dominick gently with his hip to take his spot at the table. "Did you see how quickly Monsieur Henri went from mourning his sister to rallying the rest of society to his cause? Nothing drums up support like a martyr."

Alfie added a few more points to his score, but by now he'd completely forgotten the tally. No matter. If Dominick asked again, he'd just make up a new score.

"I've met as many maniacs who've latched onto politics as those who've latched onto religion or believing they're Napoleon," Dominick admitted. "They're all equally dangerous. But while he's got his martyr now, killing me would've defeated his whole plan. I know there's those who are so mad they work against themselves without knowing it, but surely if he was that far gone, there'd be some other sign. Monsieur Henri doesn't seem the sort to babble to the mirror and if he's heard the voice of God, he's kept it to himself."

Alfie shook his head. "You're right. Unless he's completely mad, he wouldn't want you dead. In fact, I wouldn't be surprised if he started insisting on an armed escort. As horrible as it is to say, I believe he just got lucky with his sister's death. It's done two jobs at once, giving him a tragic figure to put in all his pamphlets and stopping her from getting into another scandal. A big enough one could've jeopardised his entire cause."

The idea of a man profiting from the death of his own flesh and blood, especially his sister, was barbaric. But worse things happened every day. It was certainly possible.

Alfie sighed. "Poor Monsieur Courtanvaux."

That thought settled over them both as Alfie took a few shots. By now, his heart wasn't really in it and his turn ended quickly.

When he finished, Dominick offered him a piece of shortbread, already chewing on his own. "You don't think Monsieur Courtanvaux could've done it?"

Alfie brushed shortbread crumbs off Dominick's shirt. "Any of them *could*, but he's the one with the least reason. He was arranging his daughter's marriage to Batty, so unless he discovered something about him we don't know, I can't see why he would want the man dead. And as for killing you…"

The soul-wrenching howls that had come from Monsieur Courtanvaux when his daughter died would stay with Alfie for the rest of his life. Even in the light of day, the memory of the raw anguish in them was enough to make his hair rise.

"If he did it, he's already paid a worse price than any judge could sentence him to," finished Dominick. "I might almost be able to forgive him. He still could have put the poison in the bowl intending to kill me, but our murderer was there when she ate the poison instead."

Alfie hadn't considered this. "You're right. Even if everyone else was distracted, if you'd put poison in a man's food, you'd watch to make damned sure he ate it. Our killer saw her eat the syllabub instead."

He couldn't repress a shiver at the thought. "Nick, whoever this person is, my God, there's not a word for how monstrous they are. They kept silent and watched an innocent woman eat poison, knowing she would die a horrible death, and did nothing."

"I suppose they had to," Dominick said, his voice dark. "If they'd said, 'Don't eat that! It's poison!' they'd have to explain how they knew. They'd be putting their own neck in a noose."

Alfie imagined sitting across the dinner table from his victim, waiting for his trap to spring, only to watch in horror as someone else wandered into it instead. "I doubt the marquis did it. Even if he has some reason for wanting you dead, he would've stopped her, even if it meant his own death. Monsieur Henri... perhaps not, I don't know. But not Monsieur Courtanvaux."

Dominick nodded. "Not Monsieur Courtanvaux, likely not Miss Lamourette, possibly Monsieur Henri. That leaves three more, do you want to come up with a motive for the Stocktons while I play, or Doctor Mullins?"

"I'll go with Mullins. He's a bit of a dark horse, but I'm sure I can come up with something."

"Don't make up any lies." Dominick grinned. "Just because he had you spewing and shitting all night doesn't mean you can toss him to the gallows."

"If you'd been in my position, you'd disagree," Alfie said haughtily. But he gave the matter due consideration anyway and put most of his prejudice against the man aside. He had allegedly been trying to help.

Dominick cursed as the red ball rolled to the edge of a pocket and hung there. "This is a stupid game. Go ahead then, tell me what you've been cooking up."

"Doctor Mullins. I'll be honest, I wasn't entirely sure I believed him about Batty's death being murder before Miss Lamourette died."

"And that was reason enough to kill again? Just to prove he was right?"

"That almost sounds like we could have two killers then, whoever killed Batty and then Doctor Mullins, to prove he was right about Batty being murdered."

Dominick scrubbed a hand over his face. "Christ, that would be our luck, wouldn't it? Hold on a minute, let me think about it."

Alfie did the same, leaning against the billiard table to take the weight off his leg as he did so.

"No," Dominick said finally. "We just have one killer."

"You're certain?" Alfie couldn't hide the scepticism in his voice. "Because we seem to have a lot of reasons why someone would want one of you dead, but not both. Or are you only saying it so we don't have to add Monsieur Courtanvaux back to the list?"

Dominick hesitated. "Mostly certain. Look at it this way, if there are two killers then either they're working together, in which case, they'd both have motives for wanting Lord Boyle *and* I dead, so our list doesn't really change. They'd also have to trust each other to keep quiet. So, we'll have to be careful to catch both at once, or else the remaining killer might go after us in revenge."

Alfie sighed. "For God's sake, I'd appreciate it if we could go an entire month without someone trying to kill one of us."

Dominick laid a reassuring hand on his shoulder and stroked his thumb over Alfie's collarbone. "If it's a matter of trust, that might be the Stocktons, we haven't discussed them yet. But surely, the point of working together would be so only one of them was present at either death. They were both at both dinners.

"Or, there's two killers, each with one murder to their name. But that doesn't make sense either, because when I died—or rather, when Miss Lamourette died in my place—in the exact same way as the first death, then the first murderer would know someone else knew what they'd done and exactly how they'd done it. Do you follow?"

"I think so," Alfie said. "Two murderers working together is too much trouble, but one murderer copying another is too dangerous for both of them. Besides, why kill the same way? Aside from Doctor Mullins' beliefs, there's no proof Batty was murdered. It might've just been a sudden apoplexy. But by attempting to kill you the same way, the second murderer dooms them both. No one would believe the coincidence. Far better to kill you some other way and hope for the best."

"How reassuring," Dominick said drily. "Also, by killing the same way, the second killer declares war against the first. Either of them might kill the other now, to silence them."

"At least that would solve part of our problem. All right, you've convinced me. Only one killer. I don't like how that makes me feel better."

"It does, doesn't it? Nice to know two people don't want me dead." Dominick laughed. That might just be Alfie's favourite sound in the whole world. And someone had tried to stop it forever. Whoever they were, whatever their reasons, there was no forgiving that. Alfie would ensure they paid for their crimes.

"Oi," Dominick said. "You paying attention?"

Then he wrapped a hand around Alfie's pool cue. The butt of it was resting on the floor, so the tip was about level with their eyes. Still grinning, Dominick ran his hand up and down the shaft, the motion unmistakeable. He tightened his grip on the upstroke and twisted on the way back down in a way that Alfie was intimately familiar with. He swayed forward, barely catching himself. The billiard room was far too warm. If Dominick kept this up, the effect would become unbearable.

Alfie adjusted himself, not even attempting to be subtle. Dominick knew the effect he had on him—there was no room left for shame.

Clearly Dominick agreed, his eyes lighting up. He ran his hand up higher, swirling the pad of his thumb over the tip of the cue. Alfie's hip jerked.

Dominick leaned in, his eyes locked on Alfie's and blew across the tip. "You need to re-chalk that."

He chuckled as Alfie gaped at him.

"You're a cur," Alfie said at last, when he was finally able to speak without begging Dominick to finish what he'd started. He pressed the heel of his palm against his erection, willing it to go down. The pressure against his over-sensitive cock made him hiss. "A goddamn, pox-ridden, flea-bitten, godless, gormless, fucking prick-tease of a cur."

"Now, Alfie, we're in someone else's home. Mind your tongue."

Alfie dropped his voice so he couldn't be overheard, but Dominick would know he meant every word. "If I wasn't worried about scarring the servants, I'd have a suggestion or two for your bloody tongue!"

Instead of cowed, Dominick looked delighted.

"Argh, get away from me." Alfie groaned, knowing his cheeks were red. He tried to think of the most unappealing things imaginable. Frog dissections, algebra equations, Mrs. Hirkins in her nightgown, horrible murder. Ah yes, that did it.

"I doubt Doctor Mullins committed both murders," he said through gritted teeth. "However, it is possible he tried to kill you, either as proof he was right about Batty being murdered or as an experiment to see if he was. That's why he didn't step in when Miss Lamourette took the poison instead. The experiment could still continue."

"Why me specifically?"

Talk of Dominick's death killed the lingering traces of arousal.

"Perhaps just because he didn't know you. It could've just as easily been me. Or because you and Batty are both large men. In different ways, but still. As we saw, the poison killed Miss Lamourette much more quickly than Batty, he may have just been trying to replicate the results as closely as possible."

Dominick sneered. "I don't think I like being an experiment. All right, we'll leave him on the list, even though that means someone else killed Lord Boyle, and you know my thoughts on that. Oh fuck, one more thing. I gave Doctor Mullins a snuffbox I took off Lord Boyle. I thought there was only tobacco in it, but…"

Alfie straightened up, "When did this happen?"

Dominick closed his eyes, clearly trying to remember. "The first society meeting? Yes, then. He was talking about studying Lord Boyle's organs and I gave him that to study instead. He was very excited, but I never got a chance to ask him if he'd found anything. Do you think he went straight from testing on stray dogs to testing on me?"

"It's certainly a possibility," agreed Alfie. "He seems more of a scientific sort than to jump straight to that, but it's definitely enough to keep him on the list. Now, let me take my turn, you menace, while you think up our next set of motives. Only two left."

"I'll go with Mrs. Stockton. You know Stokes better, so you should have the honour."

Alfie did a few test shots. He'd abandoned the game several rounds ago, so he didn't even bother pretending to play for points, just trying different angles while Dominick stalked around the table, deep in thought. On one of his passes, he picked up one of the shortbread biscuits.

"That one's mine," Alfie said. "You've had all yours."

Dominick stuck two fingers up at him. "What's yours is

mine," he said and continued pacing.

Something about that nettled Alfie. Not Dominick being rude and helping himself to Alfie's things; if that bothered him, he'd have smothered Dominick with one of those paper-thin workhouse pillows when they were children. There was something else about it, but he didn't know what.

"Mrs. Stockton," Dominick said, breaking his concentration and sending the slivers of thought spinning out of reach. "She wanted Lord Boyle dead because he and her husband were lovers."

Alfie let out a surprised laugh. "You can't be serious."

"Why not? You said they were close."

"There's close and then there's *close*." Alfie glanced at the door. "Besides, surely we'd be able to tell? Like knows like, doesn't it?"

Dominick pursed his lips in a tiny smile that was knowing, amused, and completely infuriating. "You'd be surprised. I admit, that wasn't the impression I got, but I suppose you never know."

Alfie shook his head. "From their behaviour in some of the more sordid hells they dragged me to, I'd be willing to swear they'd never so much as look at a man if there was anything vaguely female in the vicinity. And that includes most female livestock. I would wager Batty remained a vocal proponent of the ancient sport of wenching up until the day he died. And unlike most married men, Stokes actually appears to love his wife. But even *if* they were lovers, then what would be Mrs. Stockton's reason for killing you?"

Dominick's smile bloomed into a full grin. He gestured

at himself with both hands. "How could he resist me? I'm clearly a threat to any marriage."

"You're a threat to me keeping my breakfast down. Besides, you've had, what? One full conversation with the man? I pity her, if her marriage is so weak that one conversation is all it takes. Jarrett's been offering himself to you on a platter for months and I'm still not worried about you succumbing to his charms."

"What if Jarrett just isn't my type?" said Dominick with faux outrage. "Lord Stockton might be."

Alfie levelled him with a flat look. "You're telling me your type isn't admittedly attractive but occasionally peevish men younger than you?"

Dominick opened his mouth to respond, then shut it with a click. "I can't answer that safely."

Alfie rolled his eyes. "Smart man. Now, do you have any actual reasons to suspect Mrs. Stockton of being our killer, aside from an imagined affair and her filling the house with flowers to cover the smell of her victims?"

"I'd forgotten about that. But yes, from what we've heard, Lord Boyle had a title but only Stokes had funds. She may have just been tired of him leeching off her husband. That might be why she didn't let us into Stokes' study either. If there were bills with Lord Boyle's name scattered all over the place, she wouldn't have wanted us to see that.

"Then later, she tried to kill me because she realised that with me involved, the Lily Society was about to shift from being a social salon to a political movement and she hadn't signed on for that. It would take too much time away from her gardening."

"So, she killed you to spend more time pulling weeds?"

Dominick raised a hand in a "Who knows?" gesture. "Could be. I've never had a garden. Perhaps it's immensely satisfying."

Alfie wrinkled his nose at that. "I'd prefer if Stokes and Batty had been lovers. But I see your point. She didn't want to get embroiled in the whole mess."

Dominick let out a heavy sigh. "I don't blame her. If only… Never mind. If I say anything else I'll forfeit again. Come up with your reasons why Stokes is our killer. Christ, have we crossed anyone off the list?"

"Monsieur Courtanvaux probably. Doctor Mullins and Miss Lamourette possibly."

"Probably and possibly. Wonderful."

It didn't take long for Alfie to come up with a list of suspicions against Stokes. The man had always irritated him, especially his repeated insistence of calling Alfie "Freddie" no matter how many times he told him to stop. As such, it did take some time to remove the petty reasons from his list, leaving only the substantial ones.

"Stokes wanted Batty dead for the same reason we believe Mrs. Stockton did. Not your cock-and-bull lovers theory, but because he'd been funding Batty for years and had enough of it. As proof, he was the one who handed Batty the glass of fountain water at the Pump Room. Yes, I know that wasn't what held the poison, but it shows Batty was used to taking food and drink from Stokes without question. He wouldn't have hesitated at dinner that night if Stokes had handed him a tainted glass of wine.

"Not only that, but when Batty collapsed, Stokes first said he was drunk and then later started crying about it being his heart. I daresay if Doctor Mullins hadn't said otherwise, we would've all agreed and Stokes would've gotten away with murder."

"That seems reasonable. And what about me?"

Alfie hesitated. What about Dominick would make someone want to kill him? His snoring, obviously, but Stokes wouldn't know about that.

"I'm not entirely sure. It might have been political. It might have just been that he's sick of us taking up space in his house. Oh! The dinner was held at his house, so it's likely he either helped plan your mock coronation or at least knew it was going to happen. They'd have needed a place to hide the crown until the opportune moment, after all."

Dominick was nodding along. "You may be onto something, only… Did you see Stokes that night? He was so tightly laced he could barely get up from the table. Would he have been fast enough to poison my food without anyone noticing?"

That was a fair point. "He could have poisoned it before it came out of the kitchens?" But no, they'd already eliminated that as all the bowls of syllabub were served more or less at random.

"There's still the chance both Stocktons are in on it together," Dominick offered. "He distracts, she poisons. It doesn't answer all our questions, but—"

"But none of them do!" Alfie snapped, the frustration of it all hitting him. They'd spent all morning wandering in circles around the billiard table trying to work out this damned problem and were no further ahead than they were before. Two murders had been committed right in front of them. If they couldn't solve that, then what hope did they have of finding Dominick a way out of this whole royal mess?

He growled, the sound a mixture of fear and agitation.

Warm hands cupped the sides of his face. "Enough of that. It's all right, love. Relax, you'll give yourself wrinkles."

Dominick's thumbs stroked the gentle skin at the corner of Alfie's eyes. He let himself bask in the soothing touch.

This was the part about being in public with Dominick that was the hardest, not being able to touch him freely. To not be able to offer strength and reassurance and love whenever it was needed, or accept the same in return. Having to go long periods without making love was frustrating in more ways than one, but having to limit when and how they could show even the slightest affection was excruciating.

"There you are," Dominick said. "You said this to me and now it's my turn to say it to you. It'll all work out. Even if it means denouncing the lot of them to the magistrate to sort out as we catch that mail coach to the coast, we'll find a way. Together."

"I said that?" Alfie smiled. "I sound very wise."

"You are," Dominick agreed. Then he cocked his head to the side. "Unless it was one of my other lovers who said it. Jarrett perhaps. Or Stokes."

Alfie laughed despite himself and swatted Dominick on the arse, pleased with the satisfying hiss Dominick made as his hand connected. Good. That would give him something to think about the next time he decided to tease Alfie.

"Now who's the cocktease?" Dominick whispered.

"Right, well this may have been a waste of time, but at least we can say we tried. Now let's do a quick game so when they ask how we spent the morning, we don't have to lie about a winner. First to twenty? Then we can go to the baths. If I can't have my way with you, I want to at least be able to look at you in silly outfits."

"All right," Alfie said, pushing himself up and resetting the billiard table. "But I get to go first. I'll wager I can get to twenty without you even having a turn."

"I'll take that bet. I'll even let you start with my ball on the table too, to make it easier for you."

Alfie sized up the table. The problem with going first was that the most valuable ball, the red one, was at the opposite end of the table from his and Dominick's less valuable cue balls. He held his cue out to measure the angles, then took aim. His ball flew across the table, striking the red ball with a satisfying clack. Both bounced off the far rail and started rolling back towards him. The red ball rolled to a stop, but Alfie's continued, connecting with Dominick's ball and sending it straight into the pocket.

"Christ, that was a good shot!" Dominick exclaimed. "That'll teach me to bet against you!"

"Thank you," said Alfie, as he weighed his options for the next shot. "But I wasn't aiming for you."

They both froze. The silence was so sudden all Alfie could hear was the rushing in his ears.

I wasn't aiming for you.

He looked back down at the billiard table. He missed the shot he'd been trying to take, but one of the balls had still been removed from the table. Not only that, but he was still lined up to take another shot at his first target.

"Oh *Christ*, Alfie."

Alfie spun to look at him. Their eyes locked and he saw the same realisation there.

"Oh Christ," Dominick said again. "It's like the shortbread, I—"

"You always—"

"Do you think?"

Alfie swallowed. It was the only thing that made sense. "Yes."

Dominick let out a rush of air, like an athlete finishing a race. "Is it enough for an arrest?"

"No, but perhaps if—"

"Right."

Alfie hesitated. "If he'd be willing to, of course. We'd have to be discreet in asking."

Dominick was nodding. "I'm sure he will. That sort love to show off."

Excitement bubbled up in Alfie, making him giddy. "We'll still need a confession to be sure. With witnesses."

"Fuck, not another dinner party."

"No." Of this one part, Alfie was certain. Not a dinner party. Back to where it all began. "One final soiree."

CHAPTER 23

Stepping into the Pump Room was like stepping into the past. The first time they'd walked into the grand space, Alfie had only been an earl staying in accommodations below his station, sent an invitation as a rote politeness and dragging Dominick along behind him as his uninvited companion.

At the time he'd only been Dominick Trent, everything to Alfie, but nothing to the world. Just another forgotten workhouse orphan, but one who'd been lucky enough to escape. He'd been here looking for information about his family, hoping to find a cobbler and a maid perhaps, or a fishmonger and a fishwife. They could never return to that time before they'd known the truth, but at least they could make this one thing right.

Dominick almost expected to see Lord Boyle and Stokes walking towards them, together as always, and hear delicate laughter tinkling over the sounds of the crowd, knowing that Miss Lamourette was out there somewhere in the crush. But none of that happened. Instead, the only laughter he heard came from strangers, and as the Stocktons greeted each of their guests as they arrived, the space next to Stokes remained woefully empty.

There was a brush of fingers against his own and when Dominick turned, Alfie was standing beside him, looking out over the room. It wasn't as full as it had been the night of the first soiree, only members of the Lily Society were invited this time, but from the look of things, every single member had cancelled their other engagements to attend. It'd only taken Alfie mentioning to the Stocktons that Dominick wanted an appropriate venue to make an announcement to the society and everything had been arranged.

In other circumstances, Dominick would feel guilty for deceiving them, but now all he hoped was that they would get through the night without another senseless death.

"So you know for the future," Alfie said. "This is more what a soiree should actually look like."

"I hope the entertainment's usually better."

Alfie hummed. "Everything's in place. Do you want to wait for any stragglers to arrive?"

Dominick shook his head. "Everyone who matters is here. Let's get it over with."

Hidden from the others by the angle of their bodies, Alfie's fingers brushed his once more. If anyone did see, they might think it an accident, instead of the only safe contact they could have in a room full of watching eyes.

"I'll be ready to step in at any point if you want me to," Alfie said. "And Nick, I checked. A mail coach should be rolling through Bath in just over an hour. If things go too awry, I'll meet you there."

Despite the situation, Dominick couldn't help but smile. "Let's hope it doesn't come to that."

Then with a deep sigh, Dominick climbed the few steps onto the platform that had been erected for the occasion. The stage didn't put him that much higher than the rest of the room, but it was enough to allow him to see out over the sea of lily-bedecked hats and lapels. It'd been years since he'd done any pickpocketing, but there was enough floral-themed jewellery in the room to make his fingers twitch.

As he reached the centre of the stage, all heads turned towards him and a smattering of applause broke out. He raised his hands to stop them, but that only caused Monsieur Henri and a few other of the more passionate members to clap harder.

Dominick looked towards the sound. Monsieur Henri was standing at the foot of the stage to his left, with the Stocktons, as the actual hosts of the soiree, dead centre in front of him. Stokes was outlandishly fashionable as always and Mrs. Stockton looked radiant in a pale blue dress with matching flowers, no doubt from her own garden, woven into her hair. He searched for Monsieur Courtanvaux and eventually found him seated on a chair at the side of the room, his pale face powder looking more ghoulish than ever. With his wig and dated clothes, he was a living reminder of the lost grandeur of the courts he'd once seen, and the horrors he'd endured in the years since. Doctor Mullins was standing near the marquis, casting him concerned looks. All Dominick could hope was that what was about to happen wouldn't be too much for the old man.

With one last glance at Alfie standing by the base of the stairs, Dominick cleared his throat.

"Ladies and Gentlemen. I know why you think you're here. You think I've got something important to say. I do, but it's probably not what you think it is."

Christ, he was rambling. He'd never had to speak in front of people like this before. The opinions of Dominick Trent, boxer and prostitute, weren't anything anyone wanted to hear. Apparently the same wasn't true for Dominick Trent, heir to the throne of France.

Alfie was smiling at him encouragingly though, and that gave him enough courage to go on.

"There have been two murders since I came to Bath, one in this very room and another… in my arms. To me, finding out who killed these two people is more important than any talk of politics, and I hope you'll agree. Even worse, one of those people wasn't supposed to die. The wrong person was murdered."

"My sister!" Monsieur Henri cried, as if everyone in the room hadn't also been at the ill-fated dinner party. "She intercepted poison meant for the true king of France and died in his stead, a martyr to the cause!"

"No." It was all Dominick could do to get the single word out. He took a deep breath. "I was never the target. She was the one the killer wanted all along."

This caused an uproar. The entire society began talking at once, some gossiping, others accusing. Dominick raised his hands again to stop them, but it did nothing until a series of sharp raps cut through the air. Dominick looked towards the source of the sound and saw Alfie striking his cane hard against the stage again and again until the crowd quieted down.

"In billiards," Dominick continued, "if you pocket your opponent's ball, even accidentally, you get a handful of points, but it stays off the table for the rest of your turn. However, this still leaves the more valuable red ball on the table, and may even clear the path to it, so your second shot can't miss. That's what happened here."

He pointed at the fountain. "Moments after Lord Boyle, Lord Crawford, and Mr. Stockton took a drink of the famous Bath waters, Lord Boyle collapsed, never to rise again. We thought at first all three of them had been poisoned."

He had to stop here, memories rushing over him of that night, sitting by Alfie's bed, terrified each breath would be his last and praying he'd see the dawn. Out of the corner of his eye, he saw Alfie come up the first few steps of the stage, ready to take over, but Dominick waved him away. He'd held the bodies of both Lord Boyle and Miss Lamourette. For them, he could do this.

"Fortunately, that wasn't what happened. When we found out only Lord Boyle had been poisoned, we assumed he was the only target and the poison had been somehow administered to his glass moments before drinking it. But that wasn't true. He didn't know it at the time, but he was already dying and his killer was nowhere near him. I don't know if they didn't want to see it happen or if they were trying to create an alibi, but either way, it was a vile, cowardly act."

Here he paused, "Monsieur Courtanvaux, you don't want to hear what I have to say next. I'll wait if you wish to leave."

Monsieur Courtanvaux raised his head and looked directly at him. Even across the room, Dominick could see the steel hidden under his faded silks and powder. For the first time he got a glimpse of the strength that had allowed the marquis to survive losing his home, his country, all his friends, and now his daughter.

"I will stay." The marquis' whisper reverberated like a thunderclap.

"Then know I'm sorry, but someone hated your daughter so much that even after they killed an innocent man, they wouldn't stop until she was dead."

"That's ridiculous." Stokes' nasal whine cut through the hushed whispers. "We all saw what happened. It was your poisoned syllabub she ate, not her own."

"Yes, she did. You all saw her sitting in my lap and eating my dessert with… clear intent. She even mentioned it being bitter, but none of us realised what was happening right in front of our eyes. Well, except one person.

"Miss Lamourette was a woman who, having lost her reputation, rather than hide in shame, went after what she wanted. After all, she was already being gossiped about and it wasn't as if she could lose her reputation twice. And, forgive my bluntness, what she wanted was a man with real prospects."

He couldn't look at either of the surviving Lamourettes as he spoke. "She only went after me once she found out about me being royalty. Before that, it was Lord Crawford. And I'll wager it was any number of men before that, both married and unmarried."

"That's nonsense," said Stokes. "She was going to marry Batty."

Dominick noticed neither of the Lamourettes was defending her name. There would be no point—everyone in the room had seen her at work.

"She referred to you as 'Charles' more than once," interrupted Alfie. "Tell me, Stokes, you're a married man.

Do you often let unmarried women call you by your given name?"

Stokes puffed up as much as his tailoring would allow. "How dare you make such implications!"

Alfie made a rude noise and Dominick was reminded once again that underneath all his fancy trappings, Alfie was still the filthy little blackguard boy from the workhouse he'd always been.

Alfie shouted to be heard over Stokes' indignation. "Her fiancé, Batty, was a Baron, but he was penniless! Do you honestly believe she wanted to marry him? You, Stokes, don't have a title, but even just as your mistress she would've been able to retain the lifestyle she'd enjoyed all her life."

"I am a happily married man, sir! Miss Lamourette was an old family friend and if she chose to be overly familiar —"

"So, you're saying she never ate off your plate the way she did with Mr. Trent?"

That knocked Stokes off his stride. "Well, I won't say... that is, I never encouraged her behaviour, nor was I responsible for her actions. Her family should have been the ones to rein her in, not me."

Monsieur Henri swore in French. "Speak of her that way again, you laced up sausage, and it'll be the last thing you say!"

Before a row could break out, Dominick continued. The truth had started tumbling into the light and it couldn't be stopped until it reached its bitter, bloody end. "I imagine Miss Lamourette ate off the dessert plates of many men. It was a practised flirtation, and one our killer was relying on. The night she died, all it took was a moment of distraction to dust the deadly poison not over Miss Lamourette's syllabub, but my own, knowing that she wasn't going to pass up such a suggestive treat.

"I don't know if I would have died if I'd allowed her to feed me a bite, but after what happened to Lord Boyle, I doubt the killer cared about another innocent's death. You see, Lord Boyle had the same bad habit of eating off others' plates. Not out of flirtation, but out of friendship, because he was so close to that person that he knew it was all right.

"I have the same bad habit," Dominick admitted. He couldn't help but glance at Alfie. "I have a dear friend, one I'd do anything for and I know, without question, that he'd do anything for me. But with that kind of closeness, edges soften. The other day, I took a piece of shortbread, knowing it was rightfully his, and in return I frequently have bits of my breakfast disappear off my plate. Stokes, you told me Lord Boyle used to do the same thing to you."

Stokes' face, always pale, was now whiter than Monsieur Courtanvaux's powdered one. Dominick worried he was going to faint.

"Plum cake," Stokes whispered. "He used to steal my plum cake at breakfast and… Oh God. The night he died…"

As gently as possible, Dominick asked, "Whose dessert plate did he eat off of that night?"

Stokes faltered and began to sway dangerously. Immediately, his wife was there to catch his arm, propping him up. His voice cracked with emotion as he said, "Mine."

"Yours." They'd known it had to be true, but to hear Stokes confirm it made the whole thing more terribly real. "A fashionably trim figure is important to you. I doubt you ever eat dessert, but at dinner parties, everyone is served every course, whether they're going to eat it or not. Which was why our killer both knew you would be served dessert and that you wouldn't eat it. They counted on Miss Lamourette eating it instead, but hadn't considered Batty, his appetite, or that your friendship meant he'd help himself to your dish without even asking. Worse, once the mistake was made, the killer watched him do this, knowing what would then happen, and said nothing."

"*Mon Dieu!*" Monsieur Henri exclaimed. "You mean to tell us he wasn't poisoned at the soiree, but dinner that night? A dinner Batty ate at our house?"

"Yes," replied Dominick. "A dinner attended by you, your father, Lord Boyle, Mr. and Mrs. Stockton, and Doctor Mullins. And of course, your sister, Miss Lamourette. One of the people at that table wanted your sister to die. And all of you, all of you still alive at least, are here tonight."

Morbid excitement rippled through the crowd.

"The killer took advantage of some distraction, perhaps a spilled glass of wine, and sprinkled the deadly poison on Stokes' dessert. But Lord Boyle got to it before Miss Lamourette did, and several hours later, when the poison had worked its way through him, he died a terrible and terrifying death. Then, since the trick had worked right up to the point an innocent man died instead of the intended target, the killer tried the exact same thing again. This time, their aim was true. The poison found its mark."

Dominick watched the crowd and saw the moment excitement turned to real fear. Good. An unrepentant killer was in their midst, with nothing to stop them from killing again. Nothing, except for Dominick and Alfie, and perhaps the help of one other person.

"I admit," Dominick said, "that I don't know much about poisons. I certainly don't have the expertise our killer does, so someone who was at that dinner and does know could tell us more. Doctor Mullins?"

"I really don't know if I should," Doctor Mullins said weakly.

Dominick glanced over at Alfie. His lover had been so certain that the doctor would be tripping over his own feet for a chance to show off his knowledge, but these quiet sorts needed a bit of prodding.

He shrugged. "As a doctor, you know about poisons and you were at two dinners where people died. Because of these two things, right now everyone in this room suspects you're a murderer. If nothing else, that's going to be bad for business."

"Well, in that case!" The doctor scrambled up the stairs, nearly bowling Alfie over in his haste to get on the stage. Dominick stepped back to give him room.

Meanwhile, Alfie was working his way through the crowd until he was standing by their killer, ready to act when the moment came.

"Ah, yes, well, hello," Doctor Mullins stammered at first, but the more he spoke the more confident he became. "When Lord Crawford and Mr. Trent first approached me with their suspicions about Lord Boyle being poisoned at dinner instead of the soiree, I was certain they were accusing me of the crime. But I assure you as I assured them that I take my vows as a physician seriously and would never do harm to any of my patients."

If he hadn't been watching Alfie so closely, Dominick

might have missed him rolling his eyes at that. Clearly, he still hadn't forgiven the doctor for the bleeding.

"Nor would I harm anyone not under my care, either!" Doctor Mullins continued, taking a moment to nervously wipe his spectacles. "But then they clarified that they wanted my advice as a medical professional and well, that I was happy to give. Mr. Trent had even been kind enough to give me a snuff box belonging to Lord Boyle to test its contents, but as far as it was possible to tell, it only contained a very fine tobacco.

"However, while it is relatively easy to say if something is poisoned or not by whether the subject ingesting it dies, there are very few poisons that our current science allows us to detect once they have entered the body. So, to identify *which* poison was used, we are left to rely on the observation of symptoms alone.

"Now, poisons. Unlike what many believe, they are not all alike. Some can only be derived in a laboratory; others exist in nature. Many rocks for example, contain poisons, arsenic being the most well-known example, although even then it needs refining to be truly deadly. If you tried to kill yourself just by eating rocks you wouldn't die of arsenic poisoning, just of eating rocks."

The society was growing restless.

"That said, most poisons are derived from elsewhere in nature. Cyanide, for example, is found in apple seeds and cherry pits. But apples and cherries themselves are not dangerous. However, in some cases, the entire plant itself is poisonous and of these, the most deadly are those that look like other, entirely innocuous, common species. Even then, the exact symptoms caused by the deadly imitator may vary by subtype, so unless you know precisely what you're looking for, you won't find it.

"However, there having been witnesses to both deaths, we knew the symptoms: slurred speech and increased salivation, which might be mistaken for signs of intoxication, as well as pupil dilation and uncontrolled shivering. These were then followed by a paralysis of the muscles beginning in the legs and slowly making its way through the body until the heart stopped.

"We also knew that the poison was bitter, perhaps tasting like aniseed. That is why, while you were all gathering here this evening, Lord Crawford and I, knowing the symptoms and suspecting their source, went in search of the poison."

Doctor Mullins fumbled for something in his coat pocket. The society watched with rapt attention, which was the only reason Dominick was able to hear the click of Alfie releasing his sword cane from its sheath. He stepped closer to the edge of the stage, ready to leap down if it looked like Alfie was in trouble. But the killer was watching Doctor Mullins with fascinated horror along with everyone else and was totally unaware of the trap Alfie was about to spring.

Doctor Mullins pulled a handkerchief from his pocket and carefully unwrapped it. As one, the entire crowd stepped closer to view its contents. He angled his palms towards the crowd for a better view. Lying side by side in the handkerchief were two thick white roots attached to stalks of fernlike leaves.

"Here is an excellent example," said Doctor Mullins. "You see, one of these plants is a harmless parsnip, while the other is deadly hemlock. To the untrained eye, they appear completely identical.

Alfie laid a restraining hand on the killer's shoulder. "But you can tell the difference. Can't you, Mrs. Stockton?"

CHAPTER 24

Mrs. Stockton tried to pull away, but Alfie held firm. After all that she'd done, he wasn't going to allow her to slip from his grasp.

Gasps and cries of alarm came from the society members closest to them. Stokes blinked up at Alfie from where he was still clinging to his wife for support.

"Freddie?"

"Step back, Stokes," Alfie said as gently as he could. "I don't want you to get hurt."

"This is ridiculous," Mrs. Stockton cried. "Charles, you can't actually believe I did these dreadful things?"

Stokes, never a man to make a decision when one could be made for him, looked from his wife to Alfie and then to Doctor Mullins.

"Of course not," he said, but it was clear his heart wasn't in it.

"Then why are you growing hemlock in your garden?" Dominick's tone was soft, but the question made Mrs. Stockton tense under Alfie's hand.

"I—I did no such thing. Or if I did, it's only because I didn't know what it was. You said it looks like parsnip, doctor. I had no idea!"

"We've had parsnips for dinner several times since we came to stay at your home, Mrs. Stockton," Alfie said calmly. "Including the night of the dinner when Miss Lamourette died. If you had truly mistaken the two, it's remarkable that she was the only one poisoned. And unless you happened to have brought parsnips to the Lamourettes' home for dinner the night Batty was poisoned, then I'm afraid that defence will not hold up in court."

"And you told me yourself that no one is allowed to pull plants from the garden except for you." Dominick added. "That's because only you know which ones were safe. And those *are* from her garden, aren't they, Doctor Mullins?"

The doctor blinked. "What? Oh, er, yes. That's where we found them. There were some by the fountain and others mixed in with the parsnips themselves. A tragedy waiting to occur, really."

"It did occur," Dominick said. "Twice."

His voice was fierce. Remembering the way he'd looked so completely broken holding Miss Lamourette's body, Alfie had to fight to keep from shaking the damned woman like a terrier. How dare she cause so much suffering to so many innocent people! Not just her victims, but their families as well. He couldn't see Monsieur Courtanvaux from where he stood, but he could see Monsieur Henri. His expression made Alfie glad he had his sword cane, not to protect the rest of the Lily Society from Mrs. Stockton, but to ensure she stayed alive long enough to stand trial.

"Dellie?" Stokes asked. Despite Alfie's advice, he was still gripping her arm. "Why?"

"Because that damned French whore was going to steal you away from me!" Mrs. Stockton snapped. "She didn't even have the decency to be coy about it either! After all I did for her, trying to make her into a respectable woman, and she threw it back in my face. Every time we saw the Lamourettes she was fawning all over you and you never told her 'no', not even once! I tried so hard to help her and in thanks I was going to lose my husband and everything we'd built together. I wasn't going to go back to being a farmer's daughter. Not when I could do something about it."

Alfie had never felt more sorry for Stokes than he did at this moment. His haughty veneer, his fashionable affect, they all flaked away, leaving behind a man who'd just had his world torn apart.

"I'd known her since she was a girl," Stokes said. "I never looked at her that way. Since we married, I never looked at anyone that way but you."

Mrs. Stockton snorted. "You say that now. But it was only a matter of time. I did what I had to do to save our marriage."

"But..." Stokes sounded like a hurt child. "But you killed Batty."

It was only then that he stepped away from his wife, a small, lurching half-step of a man whose world wasn't quite steady anymore and might never be again. She tried to go to him, but Alfie held firm.

"I didn't mean to," she said. "I was horrified, but there was nothing I could do. Then when we got to the soiree, I took the first excuse to get away from him. I couldn't bear to see it happen."

She started to cry. "And then when it did, when I came and saw you in that room with Batty all laid out like that and Doctor Mullins leaning over you, I was terrified

I'd done something wrong and you'd eaten some of the dessert as well. I didn't know what to do. I was trying to save us and I couldn't bear the thought that I might have killed you too."

"You were trying to protect him." Alfie prompted. "That's why you didn't let us in his study. You knew what we'd see."

Mrs. Stockton laughed wetly. "You'd have seen my husband had every reason to want Lord Boyle dead. Promissory note after promissory note. Letters from tailors asking for payment on suits three times my husband's size. Unpaid bills from restaurants, hotels, entire lines of credit opened up in my husband's name, all from that parasite he called a friend."

Stokes looked as if he'd been struck. "He was going through a hard time. We'd been friends for so long, my money was as good as his when he needed it."

"Your money was *ours*, not his. And who would have believed that nonsense after he died? If anyone knew the truth about how he was bleeding us dry, they'd say you killed him to stop him. I didn't realise myself until I went to lock up your study while you were ill. My God, Charles, had I known how bad it was, I would have killed him on purpose."

Alfie thought they'd all heard quite enough. He raised his cane in the air. At his signal, the doors to the Pump Room were opened and a magistrate was led in followed by several constables who all seemed more awed by the majesty of the room than the duties of their office.

Mrs. Stockton craned her head to see what was causing the commotion and when she saw the magistrate, started desperately trying to open her reticule and retrieve something from within.

"I think not, darling," Dominick said. He'd made his way down the stairs while everyone was distracted, and took the small bag off her. "I'm sure there's things in here the magistrate will want to examine for himself, perhaps with the help of Doctor Mullin's scientist."

She let out a cry like a trapped fox. For just a moment, Alfie's grip loosened in surprise, but it was all she needed. She tore herself away from him and flung herself on the stage, clawing desperately at Doctor Mullins. He skittered back, his arms windmilling comically before he fell.

The two roots flew into the air. One landed beside Mrs. Stockton and she grabbed it. Before anyone could stop her, she viciously shoved it into her mouth, eating the entire thing, leaves and all.

"Fuck!" yelled Alfie. He and Dominick surged forward, dragging her back off the stage. Dominick held her, his hands pinning her arms to her sides.

"Which one was it?" Dominick shouted. The answer would determine whether another woman died in his arms. "For Christ's sake, man! Which one was it?"

Doctor Mullins was crawling on all fours, chasing after the surviving root as it rolled across the stage. He finally caught it and held it up, turning it in the light and inspecting it closely.

"Hemlock!"

Alfie's heart sank. There was no chance she'd survive, killed by her own poison. And it was all his fault for wanting to stage this grand spectacle to get her to confess rather than just telling the magistrate and hoping for the best. Stokes let out a sob but Mrs. Stockton said nothing, her eyes blazing with fearless determination as she faced her coming death.

"Hemlock!" Doctor Mullins shouted again. "This one's the hemlock! She ate the parsnip."

Alfie doubled over, his body limp with relief. If it wasn't for his cane, he would've sunk straight to the floor.

"Magistrate, we've all had quite enough," he said weakly. "I believe I instructed you to have your constables bring their wives. Please have them make sure Mrs. Stockton isn't carrying any more deadly secrets. Her victims deserve for her to live long enough to face her punishment."

The magistrate came forward and took possession of Mrs. Stockton from Dominick, directing one of the constables to take her reticule from him as well.

Stokes reached out towards her, but she shook his hand off.

As quiet as it was, Alfie could still make out the hurt in Stokes' voice as he asked, "Dellie, how could you do this?"

She shrugged, looking straight ahead. "I was going to lose you. I loved you too much to let that happen."

Stokes' face twisted in confusion. "You were never going to lose me. I love you. I've never loved anyone but you. But you killed my best friend and an innocent girl!"

"Innocent." Mrs. Stockton muttered, the word soaked in bitterness.

Then the magistrate led her away. Monsieur Henri spat as she went by, but she said nothing more.

The saddest part was, Alfie believed Stokes when he said he loved her. And that she loved him just as much in return. They could have lived the rest of their lives happily, him arriving at each party in a new outfit with his beautiful wife at his side, her tending to her garden, surrounded by loveliness that matched her own. Batty could still be living life to the fullest and Miss Lamourette laughing gaily. They might have even been good for each other if they'd been willing to try. Now they'd never know.

That was the real tragedy of it all, how completely senseless it was. None of it needed to happen and two—soon three—lives were lost because of nothing.

The members of the Lily Society glanced from one to the other, clearly having no more idea what to say than Alfie did himself. He looked over at Dominick, but he was looking down at his hands that had kept Mrs. Stockton from escaping, slowly clenching and unclenching them.

"*Merde!*" Monsieur Henri spat again. He was sneering, but Alfie could all but see the swirling clouds of rage and sorrow circling around him. "You should have let her eat the damned poison! Let that *salope* suffer as my sister suffered!"

He turned slowly, taking in the entire society. "My sister suffered. She suffered for years. She suffered and she died because of petty British people who made her life hell. I hate this place. She made one girlish mistake and none of you ever let her forget it. You ridiculed her, you ostracised her, and one of you," he pointed at the doors closing behind Mrs. Stockton and the magistrate, "believed she didn't deserve to live."

His speech knocked Stokes from his stupor. "Dellie only did it because she was afraid of losing everything."

"And now we have both lost all." Monsieur Henri's voice

was like ice. He shook his head in disgust. "You believe you are all so civilised, but you are barbarians. You claim to want to build a better world, a better France, but none of you believe in the principles, you just want a cause to care for, like a pet. All while you smile as you laugh behind your hands and carry hatred in your heart. This is a barbaric country. I will not remain here a minute longer than I have to."

Monsieur Henri straightened like a general about to lead his men into battle. "Monsieur Trent, if we leave now, we can catch a ship for France in the morning and never see this blighted country again."

His words were so close to Alfie's own plan for their escape, yet so terribly different. Monsieur Henri wanted to take Dominick to France where he could be a king, but no matter what hopeful lies Alfie had told Dominick, he knew in his heart that doing so would mean he'd lose him forever.

For a single, dark second, he understood why Mrs. Stockton would do such terrible things to keep the man she loved. But Alfie wasn't her. He loved Dominick, loved him more than he thought possible. And because of that love, Alfie wouldn't stand in his way. He wanted Dominick to have every happiness. He deserved that. He deserved more than that. By birth, he deserved a crown and if having that would make him happy, then Alfie would continue loving him for the rest of his life, even if it was from afar.

"Monsieur Trent, enough time has been lost already. *Lives* have been lost already. Tell me now, will you stand up for your family and for the people of France? You are a king. Will you take your throne?"

Dominick looked at Alfie, a miserable expression on his face. Alfie didn't know what that meant. Was he anguished because he was going to claim the crown and lose the life they had or because he wasn't and felt guilty for his selfishness? His heart pounded in his chest. Dominick was right there next to him, but he'd never seemed further away.

He gave Alfie a wistful smile, then opened his mouth to answer.

The scraping sound of a chair being pushed back cut through the tense silence of the room. At the edge of the crowd, Monsieur Courtanvaux slowly got to his feet. Alfie had forgotten he was in the room. He'd heard the woman who murdered his daughter confess and said nothing, but he spoke now.

"There is nothing for Monsieur Trent in France. He's not a king."

CHAPTER 25

Dominick couldn't believe what he was hearing. The bird rings, the little chest of pewter trinkets, the book with its story of Marie Antoinette's smuggled baby, Monsieur Courtanvaux had confirmed himself that Dominick was that child, whether he wanted to be or not. If there was even the slightest chance it wasn't true…

His heart beat wildly at the thought. He wouldn't be forced to leave Alfie, leave their home, their love.

Or did the marquis mean something else? Had he found out something about Dominick's past and meant he wasn't *fit* to be king? That was certainly true, but if he revealed the kind of man Lord Crawford kept with him, Alfie would be ruined.

Monsieur Courtanvaux pulled a small book from his coat. He removed several pieces of paper that were tucked between its pages, then with a rueful smile, tapped the cover of the book and returned it to his pocket. He held up the pages.

"I have here proof that Monsieur Trent is no king at all. His mother was not Marie Antoinette, but a chambermaid who served her named Colette."

Colette. My mother's name is Colette.

Dominick's chest was tight. He'd gone a lifetime knowing nothing about his mother, then was told a grand fairy tale about her being a queen. Now he knew something true, her name. *Colette*.

The marquis continued. "This is a letter she left to me when she died."

A hope Dominick hadn't known he still carried crumbled to ash. His mother's name was Colette and she was dead. He would never get to meet her.

He hadn't noticed the shoulder pressed against his until Alfie tapped his cane against Dominick's shoe. He leaned against Alfie gratefully, borrowing his strength for whatever came next.

Monsieur Courtanvaux shuffled through the papers. "In this letter, she details leaving France with the blessing of her mistress, Marie Antoinette. It was Colette, not the queen, who gave birth during those early months of the royal family's confinement, and it was she and the child she bore who were smuggled out of France. She says Marie Antoinette gave her what few trinkets she still had, but the cost of reaching safety was high and by the time she reached England all she had left was a pewter ring bearing the image of a bird in flight.

"Penniless in a strange land, she was unable to find work as an unmarried woman with a child. So, she was forced to entrust her baby to the workhouse, leaving with him the ring as her promise she would return to claim him as soon as she could afford to do so. Alas, that day never arrived."

Dominick swallowed, trying to hold back a heat behind his eyes that felt suspiciously like tears. He wasn't going to cry in front of these people. He'd already given them more than enough to gossip about.

"What proof have we that any of this is true?" yelled a voice from the crowd.

"I have with the letter a document from the workhouse, verifying the receipt of a child, bearing the description of the token left with him—the ring—so that Colette, or any who came to claim the child on her behalf, only had to bring this paper or describe the ring and the child would be returned to her."

"That doesn't prove she was the baby's mother," Monsieur Henri said. He had a wildness about him, a man who was watching his dreams being torn away and was clinging to them however he could. "It could have still been Marie Antoinette's child that she was smuggling to safety. She would hardly have told the workhouse she was leaving them with a French prince, after all."

Some of the society members began to murmur in agreement.

The marquis smiled sadly at his son. "This letter was written many years later when everyone, queen, king, the France she knew, all were dead. Colette herself was dying. She knew she would never see her child again and…"

He had to stop there for some moments to collect himself. "And I now know that feeling. It is a pain that cannot be fabricated to maintain a lie. That pain is in every line of this letter. The child Colette left behind was hers. She went to her grave regretting never coming back for him."

"Then why did you say it was him!" Monsieur Henri exploded. "All this time you knew he was nothing more than a maid's bastard and you said nothing!"

"For that I am sorry, Henri. I had forgotten many of the

details from the letter and when you told the story of the smuggled child from your book, I remembered it all. When I said to Monsieur Trent, 'It's you' I meant the child spoken of in the letter, and seeing the ring only confirmed this. I did not realise until you bowed that you thought I meant he was some phantasm of a prince. I should have said something then, but I expected you would come to your senses soon enough. But then others started to believe your madness and before I realised it, wheels had begun to turn that I did not know how to stop. I'm truly sorry, to you both."

Monsieur Henri glared at his father. "I cannot believe this. He is the rightful heir of France! Why are you lying?"

"Henri," Monsieur Courtanvaux said softly. "You are my son. My only living child. I would not do anything to cause you pain. But even for you, I cannot lie about this."

Even in the midst of the crowd, it was as if there were only the two Lamourettes as the father and son held each other's gazes, the silent communication passing between them unintelligible to any who weren't family. Or perhaps it was that there were no words in either French or English that could capture what they needed to say.

For the first time, Dominick could truly see the resemblance between the two men, both proud, determined, and resolved to do what they thought was right, even if it meant the destruction of the world around them.

He could never have been that brave.

It was Monsieur Henri who looked away first. "You have ruined me, father. I will be a laughingstock. My word will be meaningless. *The man who mistook a maid's son for a king.* My goals, dreams, plans, all will come to naught when word of my humiliation spreads. For this I can never forgive you."

Then Monsieur Henri turned his back on the marquis. His slow, measured steps echoed as exited the hall, his head held high and his reputation in tatters.

Monsieur Courtanvaux sank back into his chair and said no more. The society milled about, unsure of what to do.

"Nick," Alfie whispered. When Dominick turned to him, his expression must have been truly dreadful, because Alfie risked not just brushing their fingers together, but squeezing Dominick's hand. "The magistrate will want to question all the witnesses to Mrs. Stockton's confession. Why don't we take Monsieur Courtanvaux to a side room to recover while they do that in here."

Dominick shook his head. "You went with Doctor Mullins to get the hemlock. They'll want your story."

"That can fucking wait," Alfie hissed. "You think I'm abandoning you now?"

No. Dominick knew to the depth of his soul that Alfie never would. He risked squeezing his hand back.

"You stay here and organise the interviews. I'd like to talk to the marquis by myself."

Alfie studied his face. "You're certain?"

Not anymore. Not about anything. Nothing except that this man, his Alfie, was more important than any crown. He'd been a fool to think, even for a moment, that the right choice could ever have been one that forced them apart.

In the grand history of the world, kingdoms were a penny a piece. But a love like theirs was a rare and valuable thing.

Besides, even if he'd tried to get on a ship to France without Alfie, Dominick probably would've made them turn back halfway across the channel. And that was assuming Alfie hadn't attached himself to the side of the ship like a bloody barnacle.

The image made him smile. "I'll be all right. You handle this mess and I'll talk to the marquis."

Alfie looked back at the Lily Society. "I'm not sure which of us I envy least."

❋ ❋ ❋

Dominick hadn't been in this room since Lord Boyle's death. He slowly led the marquis to the chair where Alfie had sat that night, the old man gripping his elbow tightly as he settled himself. Then Dominick looked uneasily at the lounge where Lord Boyle had died before dragging over Stokes' chair for himself. He hadn't noticed before that this room also had a wall of windows looking down onto the baths. It'd been night then, so he wouldn't have been able to see anything anyway, but the sun was still setting now and the warm light glinting off the water turned the rising steam into ghostly dancing figures.

"I suppose you have more questions," Monsieur Courtanvaux said at last.

"A few," Dominick admitted.

"Let me start by saying again how sorry I am I let things go this far without telling you. Perhaps if I had..." His throat clicked. "But no, that woman would have found some other chance to murder my daughter. The Stocktons were our friends. We dined with them almost every week. No, I do not blame you, although for some time I did. Perhaps that is why I did not speak up afterwards."

"You spoke up now," Dominick said. "But if you knew about all this, why didn't you get me from the workhouse yourself?"

He was afraid of the answer, but needed to know.

Monsieur Courtanvaux smiled sadly. "I tried. Your mother, Colette, found work for many years with a family in London, but she had little English and was paid a pittance. She didn't know the family was moving to Bath until she was trundled up in a coach with the rest of the servants. She thought it was just for the season, but they never went back and she didn't have the money to make her own way.

"Some years later, I made the acquaintance of the family and by chance met Colette, who had since risen to the rank of housekeeper. I did not know her well, but we both enjoyed the chance to speak our own language again with someone who truly understood. I believe this is why she left me this letter when she died. She recognised my bird ring, just as you did, and knew what it meant, but she never told me she had been one of the maids I'd seen laughing with Marie Antoinette. I understand why. The revolution turned friends and family against one another. She was right not to trust me. I didn't even know she'd died until I happened to dine with the family some months later and they said she'd left something for me.

"In the letter, she begged me to find her son and make sure he was all right. I went myself to the workhouse, but it had been so many years, you had already grown and left.

There was no record of where you'd gone."

The marquis hadn't said how long ago. How much time had they missed each other by? A decade? A year? A week? Dominick didn't want to know.

"London's a big city," he said. "I see why you didn't find me."

"Yes, a big city and a foreign one. I did not know London, but I do know one thing, *les Français*. I spread word amongst every French man and woman I could find, telling them of the ring and that if they ever saw it, to tell the man wearing it where to find me."

Dominick couldn't help but laugh. "It worked. A maid in one of the hotels sent me. I thought she was mad at first, telling me to look in the bath."

The marquis smiled. "I suppose she could have been clearer. But you made it."

"I made it." It'd taken years, but in the end, Dominick had. "So, the maid in London, she wasn't…"

Monsieur Courtanvaux shook his head. "No relation to you. It has not just been the aristocrats who have fled France in the last few decades."

Dominick nodded. That answered one lingering question at least. He still had dozens more. "What was she like, my mother?"

"As I said, I did not know her well and it has been some years. Give me a moment."

The marquis closed his eyes. "She was very strong for a woman; I see you take after her there. I once saw her carry a trunk filled with a week's worth of clothing up a stairwell like it was nothing. She enjoyed jokes and detested beetles. Her hair was a little darker than yours and on her half-day she liked to walk by the river and feed the birds."

Dominick had to look away so the marquis wouldn't see the tears in his eyes. Staring down at the baths, for a moment a swirl of steam appeared to be a woman looking back up at him, but then he blinked and she was gone.

He cleared his throat. "What about the rest of my family? Do you know anything about them?"

Monsieur Courtanvaux shook his head. "There is no father's name on the document from the workhouse. If she knew it, she did not say in her letter. A letter which is yours now, as is this."

He took from his pocket the small book from which he had removed the papers earlier and handed them all to Dominick.

He took them reverently. The letter was in French so he couldn't understand it, but he ran his fingers over the writing anyway. His mother's writing.

"The book is in French too, I'm afraid," said Monsieur Courtanvaux. "It is a book of poetry. You may be able to find a copy in English. You also have the workhouse papers, although there is nothing on there you do not already know. They recorded frustratingly little. However, she wrote a dedication to you in the book. The first words mean, 'To my son'."

Dominick opened the book with trembling hands. Inscribed on the first page were the words "*A mon fils...*" and then the longest collection of letters Dominick had ever seen in one place, some with dashes over them or curlicues underneath.

"Christ, what does that bit mean?"

The marquis laughed. "That's your name. The one she

gave you."

Dominick blinked hard. He read the letters again and winced.

"I can help you with the pronunciation," Monsieur Courtanvaux offered, clearly amused.

Dominick looked at it a little longer, then slowly closed the book.

"Thank you, but I think I prefer 'Dominick'."

"As you will. If you ever change your mind, you found me once. I'm sure you can again."

"I'd like that," Dominick said. The marquis looked tired, as if telling Dominick the truth had taken what little strength he had left. With another thanks, Dominick rose but at the door he hesitated, not sure if the marquis would want to hear what he had to say. But the bird ring was heavy against his chest, and his mother's letter was reminder enough of the pain that came with regrets.

"Monsieur Courtanvaux, when I first saw your ring, I thought it meant you were my father. I want you to know that if you were, I'd have been honoured."

The marquis let out a heavy breath, suspiciously close to a sob. Not knowing what else to do, Dominick gave him a quick bow and opened the door.

"Monsieur Trent?"

Dominick turned. The marquis was watching him with a small smile.

"There is no mention of your father in that letter. From my days in Versailles, you should know that Louis XVI was a tall man with blue eyes and a penchant for dallying with his wife's maids. You might not be a *legitimate* heir, but men have been made kings for less."

Dominick hesitated, his hand still on the doorknob. "Thank you, but I still prefer 'Dominick'."

He left Monsieur Courtanvaux looking out over the healing waters. One day, he hoped the marquis would heal as well.

EPILOGUE

Petals floated down from the trees and landed in the river with barely a ripple. As they crossed the bridge out of Bath, Alfie watched the gentle current pull them along and wondered how far they had to travel to reach the sea.

The weather had warmed even further. As they strolled up the hills surrounding the city, he and Dominick stopped to remove their overcoats, carrying them over their arms as they walked. They didn't speak as they climbed, but this was not the fraught, miserable silence that had punctuated their last few weeks, but the quiet contentment of two men who knew each other so well that they didn't have to talk to enjoy each other's company.

As they came over a small rise, another walker came into view, heading their direction. Alfie didn't recognise the man, but from his lily cravat pin, he was obviously one of the members of the Lily Society. As they came closer, he looked directly at them, then very pointedly looked away, ignoring them until he'd passed.

Dominick let out a low whistle. "I suppose I don't need to worry about sitting through another fancy dinner before we leave. That's the toff equivalent of spitting on my boots, isn't it?"

Alfie laughed. "More or less."

He should probably take offence at such an obvious

cut, but it was far too beautiful a day to be worried by such things. "We're the least of their worries right now. I overheard one of the maids saying this morning that Monsieur Henri had vanished in the night. He took all the valuables in the Lamourettes' house that weren't nailed down and left a note saying he was headed for France."

Dominick raised an eyebrow. "Did he really? Well, better him than me."

"Now that I heartily agree with," Alfie said. "Still, I do feel sorry for his father, having lost first one child and now the other."

They walked a little further before Dominick responded. "At least Monsieur Henri isn't lost to him forever. I hope he comes to his senses before it's too late."

"As they say, 'Where there's life, there's hope.'"

Dominick nodded. "I wish both Lamourettes a great deal of each. They'll need them."

The days since the arrest of Mrs. Stockton had been tense. How could they not be, when Stokes was dealing not only with learning his wife was a murderess, but also housing the two men responsible for her imprisonment.

He'd generously said they were welcome to stay as long as they wished, but in a tone that meant he wanted them gone as soon as possible. Alfie was happy to oblige. They'd done their best to avoid Stokes for the days that it took the magistrates to sort everything out and for them to make appropriate travel arrangembents—*not* the mail coach —back to Scotland.

And now the promised day had arrived, giving them just enough time to stretch their legs before the long journey. Within a few hours they'd be on their way home.

They'd had to promise to return if necessary for the trial, but with the testimony of Doctor Mullins and the Lily Society members, not to mention Mrs. Stockton's own confession, he doubted that would be necessary.

"It's peculiar, isn't it?" Alfie mused as he navigated over some tree roots. "We all got so tied up in this grand world stage, seeing assassins and revolutionaries in every corner, when really the murders were the result of a small domestic matter. Strange how one woman's insecurities can have such disastrous results."

The path turned steeper here, and it was a few minutes before he had enough breath to finish the thought. Dominick slowed to match his pace to Alfie's, a tiny gesture in the scheme of things, but such a meaningful one. And wasn't that just the point? It was the little things that had the most importance in the end.

"Of course," Alfie panted as they crested the hill, "I suppose I should be sorry you didn't turn out to be royalty, but I'm actually quite relieved that assassins aren't something we have to worry about now. I don't like the idea of a target on your back. No crown is worth that."

Dominick hummed and pointed ahead. Alfie had a good idea of where they were heading but laughed anyway. He took a quick glance around to ensure they were alone.

"Really, Nick? The folly? Our bags are being packed as we speak and I intend to buy out an entire coaching inn if that's what it takes to get us some privacy tonight and a real bed to enjoy it in. No offence meant to your old overcoat."

"It was a good coat," Dominick replied, his eyes glinting with mischief.

Alfie patted his shoulder. "And it made a worthy sacrifice. But now you've only got the one, so you'd better save it for the coach ride. It might be warm now, but I imagine it's still quite wintry at Balcarres."

Dominick looked pointedly at Alfie's overcoat. "You've got a spare."

Alfie narrowed his eyes at him. "It's not a matter of whose coat, you daft sod. If you believe for a moment that I'm letting you fuck me in some dirty little room right before I have to spend hours in a bumpy carriage, you can find your own way back to Scotland. As I recall, I'm still owed several forfeits and I intend on making certain they are paid in full. I'm going to require a full night's rest after the things I intend to have you do to me."

Dominick's grin went wolfish and Alfie was almost tempted to say "bugger it" and let Dominick do whatever the hell he wanted, wherever the hell he wanted.

Fortunately, at least one of them had some self-control. It was just surprising that it turned out to be Dominick.

Dominick shook his head. "We never climbed to the top last time. We should take in the view before we go."

He hadn't expected the view from the top of the folly to be that much better than at its base, but when they got up there, Alfie had to admit it was. From the top of the tower, the river that separated the countryside from the city could just barely be seen under the curve of the hill. Beyond it the city of Bath sprawled, its townhouses of yellow stone all lined up like soldiers in their uniforms. He could pick out a few landmarks they'd visited, the graceful arc of the Royal Crescent, the circle of houses that made up the Circus—their chimney pots like the crenellations on an enormous crown. He shied away from that part of town.

Further south, the great glittering windows of Bath Abbey caught the light, the glass twinkling in a thousand different colours. From where they stood, the abbey shielded the Roman baths and the Pump Room from view, and Alfie thought the scenery was all the better for it. They could see far beyond the city too, nestled in the river valley as it was. Beyond it lay farmers' fields and forested hills, a low haze blurring the line where the sky met the land. It was absolutely beautiful.

He turned his head and took in an even lovelier view. Dominick was leaning against one of the battlements with his arms crossed, the breeze tousling his golden hair. A fine sheen of sweat clung to his skin from their climb, darkening the hair at his temples and grounding his beauty, making him all the more desirable. There was a pensiveness about his eyes that Alfie recognised as him being deep in thought, but from the small smile that played about his lips, it wasn't the terrors of the last few weeks that so consumed him, but something far more pleasurable.

"Penny for your thoughts?"

Dominick smiled at him and Alfie wondered if they had time to make use of the room below after all.

"Do you ever want to travel?" Dominick asked. "The papers from the workhouse didn't have much of use, not even my birthdate, just the day I was left there. But it did have the name of the town my mother came from in France. I suppose she could've been lying, but it might be nice to visit, if only to learn French so I can read her letter for myself. I'd like that."

The request was so sincere that Alfie couldn't have said no even if he wanted to. Although damn waiting until they went to France, there had to be someone in Scotland who could teach Dominick French. He envisioned Dominick walking through vineyards and lavender fields, charming with the locals in their own language. The two of them sharing a bottle of wine every night as the sun set, before retiring to the little house they'd rented for their visit.

He licked his lips. "Why stop at France? We can take a whole grand tour if we want. We're a bit old for it, but just think, France, Italy, Greece… any country we want. Well, any that aren't currently at war with England. That may limit us somewhat. Still, it would be a wonderful adventure."

He hesitated, realising he might have gotten a little carried away. "But I read far too many adventure novels. Just visiting your family home sounds lovely too."

"My family home…" Dominick tapped his chest in thought. Then he nodded to himself, some decision made. "I've already found it."

He started pulling at his collar, and Alfie stepped forward to help with whatever it was he was trying to do. Before he could, Dominick had slipped the chain from around his neck and unclasped it. His pewter ring tumbled into his palm.

"I spent so long wondering about my family," Dominick said, rolling the ring around until they could both see the worn outline of the bird. "Wondering who they were, why they'd left me, if-if they'd love me. I spent so much time thinking about them that I forgot my real family was right beside me all along."

Alfie couldn't restrain his gasp when Dominick reached out and took Alfie's hand in his.

"You're my family." Dominick smiled. "You have been since the first time I saw a drowned little creature covered in mud looking up at me with those big eyes of yours. Yes, just like that. I never stood a chance."

Alfie's heart was racing. He knew how Dominick felt about him, knew it because he showed Alfie in a hundred different ways each day. But to say it, to lay bare what Alfie was to him—what they were to each other—was almost too much to bear.

Dominick slid the ring onto Alfie's ring finger, turning it gently so the little bird faced up.

"Of course it's a bloody perfect fit," Dominick muttered.

Alfie couldn't help but laugh. Dominick grinned at him, before bringing Alfie's hand to his lips to kiss his knuckles. The feeling of his lips and the ring together was so perfect that Alfie had to steady himself. He wasn't going to ruin the moment by swooning. Dominick would never let him hear the end of it if he did.

"You know," Dominick said with another kiss, "that ring fit me right up until the day we met again. That boxing match. I haven't been able to wear it since."

"That sounds like fate."

"It does a bit, doesn't it?"

When Alfie looked at Dominick now, he didn't just see the man before him, but all the other versions of Dominick he'd known, the frightened child, the cocky boxer, the fierce protector, the fine gentleman. He loved every single one of them, and if they were lucky, he had years to learn all the other versions of Dominick too, the ones he hadn't yet become. Trusting the high tower walls to shield them, he stepped closer to Dominick and kissed him there under the open sky with the entire countryside unspooling around them.

He lost all track of time, only noticing it'd passed at all when Dominick pulled away enough to rest their foreheads against each other while they caught their breaths.

Their hands had been crushed between them this whole time but Dominick didn't let him go, instead running his thumb over his ring on Alfie's hand again and again.

"I had more of a speech planned out," he said, and Alfie felt the words as gusts of breath against his lips. "You interrupted me."

"Go on then," whispered Alfie. "I won't say anything until you tell me you've finished."

Dominick flicked Alfie's nose with his own. This close, he was nothing more than a blur of gold hair and blue eyes, but a blur so familiar that Alfie would know it anywhere.

"It wasn't that good a speech," Dominick admitted. "I was going to say something about how I know we can't get married, but we already are a bit married in a way, and I just wanted you to have my ring as a symbol of that. Of what we are to each other. I want to be with you for the rest of my life, Alfie. A piece of jewellery won't change that, but I want you to have it all the same."

He stopped, then after a few moments let out a huff. "All right, I'm finished now."

There were a thousand things Alfie could say to that: "I've always been yours", "Good luck trying to get rid of me", "I love you. I love you. I love you." He couldn't choose just one, so he said them all, punctuating each one with a kiss to make sure it stuck.

Finally, he had to push Dominick away or else he'd never stop. "Our carriage will be waiting."

As their hands parted, he had a split second of fear that it would somehow break their connection. But instead, the weight of the ring only made it all the more real, a piece of Dominick that was always with him, even when it wasn't safe for them to touch.

He took one last look at Bath, then followed as Dominick led the way back down the stairs.

"You know," Alfie said, as he tested a suspicious looking step with his cane. "These follies are a grand idea. Perhaps we should build one back home."

"Including the little room?"

"Obviously," Alfie sniffed. "What would be the point otherwise? We can have it built while we're on our grand tour as well, so we don't have to deal with all the dust and noise."

Dominick laughed, the sound carrying clear and full over the countryside. "Well, let's get back to Balcarres first before we start haring off across the world. It might not be as busy as London, or as pretty as Bath, but dreary old Scotland is growing on me. It'll be nice to be home. Besides, I've learned that with you around, there's always plenty of adventure!"

He stopped halfway down the stairs, forcing Alfie to stop as well. "But we don't have to go back just yet. We spent all this time trying to hunt down my family. Do you want to spend some time looking for yours? Your original ones, I mean, not the earl and his wife. It's only fair."

Alfie didn't even have to think about it before shaking his head. "I remember a little of my mother—the swish of her skirts, bits of song, that sort of thing. But she died, and what I remember of the rest of them is vague but... unpleasant.

"I don't need to know who they are to know I'm better off with my family now. Besides, after this mess, with our luck we'd hunt them down only to find out I'm the son of the King of Siam and Catherine the Great! Thank you, but I'm happier as I am."

He gave Dominick a tap on the shoulder with his cane to encourage him on his way. Their carriage really would be waiting.

"By the way," Alfie continued as they descended. "Have I told you yet how glad I am that you didn't turn out to be the secret child of Marie Antoinette? I doubt there was a way that was going to end with either of us happy. Thank goodness you turned out to be a maid's son in the end."

To anyone else, his words might have sounded callous, but he knew Dominick would know what he meant. He was proved correct when Dominick gave him a hand down the final step, one that was just a bit higher than the rest, with a grin.

"That's me, regular old Spitalfields workhouse Dominick. Son of a maid. Poor as dirt and common as mud."

"If you're poor as dirt after getting half an earldom, you need to stop letting Gil handle your money; he's bleeding you dry." Alfie sniffed. "And you've never been common. I'd rather the Nick I love in my bed than in a crown. It's a good thing Monsieur Courtanvaux spoke up when he did and made it clear to everyone that you have no claim to the throne."

Dominick chuckled. "Well…"

Then he started down the path towards the city, leaving Alfie gaping behind him.

"*Well*? What do you mean, 'Well'? Nick, come back here! Damn it, Nick! What the blazes does that mean? '*Well*'?"

Dominick turned back towards him. The afternoon sun lit him from behind, crowning him with golden light. Then he extended a hand towards him. Alfie reached out, taking his hand with the one that carried their ring.

"Come along." Dominick grinned. "Let's go home."

The End

Alfie And Dominick Will Return

AUTHOR'S NOTE

I always like to include a little historical context in my author's notes, but I think this time all I can really say is, "No, I swear, I didn't make that up!" At least, right up until the point I did.

The story of the Lost Dauphin is real—or at least, a real legend, much like Anastasia. However, the story of the prince born in captivity isn't. The faux castle on the hill overlooking Bath is real too, but as far as I'm aware, it doesn't contain a secret sex room. By the way, a similar folly was built on the crag overlooking Balcarres Manor in the early 1820s. I think we can say Alfie and Dominick were appropriately inspired!

Funnily enough, billiards was such a new sport that there weren't any standardized rules at the time, so by sticking with proper scoring (except for Alfie's blatant cheating) I was actually a bit too accurate! In addition, hemlock is exactly as dangerous and innocent-looking as described, although each variety of the plant produces different symptoms. The variety described here is spotted hemlock—be glad I didn't use some of the others as the murder weapon as their effects are even nastier.

When necessary, I did simplify a few things for the sake of readership. Both French politics and proper forms of address for French nobility of the era were so incredibly complicated, I had to distill them a bit or there wouldn't have been room in the book for any murders! Also a quick thank you to my brother and father for their history expertise. I doubt this is how they expected their knowledge to be used, but they deserve the thanks anyway!

I want to again thank Veruska for giving this her keen eye and I have to apologize to Emily; her notes made this book a thousand times better, but once again I rewarded her dedication by making her discuss the sex scenes in great detail to make sure they worked.

Finally, a thank you to all the friends, readers, newsletter subscribers, and fellow authors who offered their encouragement during the writing of this book. I literally couldn't have done it without you.

BY SAMANTHA SORELLE

His Lordship's Mysteries:

His Lordship's Secret
His Lordship's Master
His Lordship's Return
His Lordship's Blood
Lord Alfie of the Mud (Short Story)
His Lordship's Gift (Short Story)

Other Works:

Cairo Malachi and the Adventure of the Silver Whistle
Suspiciously Sweet
The Pantomime Prince

ABOUT THE AUTHOR

Samantha SoRelle

Samantha SoRelle grew up all over the world and finally settled in Georgia, USA where the humidity does all sorts of things to her hair.

When she's not writing, she's doing everything possible to keep from writing. This has led to some unusual pastimes including perfecting fake blood recipes, designing her own cross-stitch patterns, and wrapping presents for tigers.

She also enjoys collecting paintings of tall ships and has one pest of a cat who would love to sharpen his claws on them.

Join her newsletter at www.SamanthaSoRelle.com and receive a FREE short story in your inbox. Also be the first to know about new books, sales, freebies, and other goodies!

CAIRO MALACHI AND THE ADVENTURE OF THE SILVER WHISTLE

The first time I met the love of my life, he died in my arms.

Cairo Malachi, Conduit to the Spirits, is a liar, a thief, and a fraud. He may be building a reputation as one of the most fashionable mediums in London, but he doesn't even believe in ghosts and has certainly never conjured one. Which is why, after he witnesses the brutal slaying of a handsome young constable, he's shocked when the man's spirit appears in his home, begging for his help.

Constable Noah Bell is everything Mal can never be—honest, funny, and kind. But it's ridiculous to be attracted to a man he can't even touch, especially when every step they take towards solving Noah's murder is one step closer to bringing him the justice he needs to move on—and out of Mal's life forever.

As their investigation brings unexpected enemies to light, the secrets they're keeping from each other may prove even more dangerous. Mal and Noah will have to work together... or risk a fate worse than death.

Available Now